**"Must you always o...
Society?"**

"I don't understand."

"You are always polite to the point it can become aggravating."

Her eyes widened. "Would you have me be otherwise?"

"At times, yes! The ton did not collapse when the children began to address me as Arthur. It feels absurd when you continue to call me 'my lord.' Why don't you do as they do?"

"They are children. They are excused from making such a faux pas."

"How can it be a faux pas if I ask you to address me so?"

Maris had no quick answer to give him. To let his name form on her lips… If other servants or members of his family heard, would they be as accepting as they were with the children?

As if she had aired her thoughts aloud, he said, "It would be only when we're with the children or when we are having a conversation like tonight. Could we at least try tonight?"

"Yes."

He raised a single brow.

"Yes, Arthur," she said with a faint smile. How sweet his name tasted on her lips!

Jo Ann Brown has always loved stories with happy-ever-after endings. A former military officer, she is thrilled to have the chance to write stories about people falling in love. She is also a photographer, and she travels with her husband of more than thirty years to places where she can snap pictures. They live in Nevada with three children and a spoiled cat. Drop her a note at joannbrownbooks.com.

Books by Jo Ann Brown

Love Inspired Historical

Matchmaking Babies

Promise of a Family
Family in the Making

Sanctuary Bay

The Dutiful Daughter
A Hero for Christmas
A Bride for the Baron

Visit the Author Profile page at Harlequin.com for more titles.

JO ANN BROWN

Family in the Making

HARLEQUIN® LOVE INSPIRED® HISTORICAL

Recycling programs
for this product may
not exist in your area.

 LOVE INSPIRED BOOKS

ISBN-13: 978-0-373-28333-0

Family in the Making

Copyright © 2015 by Jo Ann Ferguson

www.Harlequin.com

Printed in U.S.A.

For there is no man that doeth any thing in secret,
and he himself seeketh to be known openly.
If thou do these things, show thyself to the world.
—*John* 7:4

For my dear son Peter and his beautiful bride, Meghan

You are beginning your lives together as a family

May you always be as filled with joy and love
as you are on the day you say "I do."

Chapter One

Porthlowen, Cornwall
October 1812

Another inch. One little inch, and she would have it.

Maris Oliver stood on tiptoe on the chair and stretched her arm across the top shelf, groping for the box she had seen from the floor. When she had asked the cook about a box of small cups, Mrs. Ford told her to look in the stillroom. She wanted to retrieve the cups that were decorated with nursery rhyme characters to use in the nursery.

"Just another inch," she muttered to herself as the stool wobbled under her toes.

She could have waited and asked a footman to help her, but she wanted the cups for the children's next meal. She had read the rhymes to them, and they would be excited to see the characters. Making the youngsters smile always was a delight.

The four tots and tiny baby in the nursery, as well as the little boy who lived with the parson and his wife, had been discovered floating in a jolly boat in the harbor. Brought to Cothaire, the great house on the hill overlooking the cove, they were taken in by the Trelawney family. Its patriarch, the Earl of Launceston, had given his children carte blanche to provide for the youngsters until it could be discovered who had put them into that boat and set them afloat and why.

Shortly after their arrival, Maris was offered the position of nurse to oversee the children and the nursery. The position would end once the search for their real families proved fruitful. She should worry about where she would go next, but she spent her time focused on the children, guiding them, teaching them manners, playing games with them in the nursery.

She doted on the adorable urchins. When she was with them, she could forget why she had run away to West Cornwall in the first place. She had found a haven in Porthlowen, and the children had found a way into her heart.

A perfect solution…at least for now.

Her fingers brushed the edge of the box she sought. It rocked.

"C'mon," she murmured. "An inch more."

Could she stand higher on her toes? She tried and managed to push aside the box beside the one she wanted. It bumped into others, and one toppled onto another. She held her breath, but nothing fell to the floor.

One more try.

Extending her arm and hand as far as she could, she hooked one finger over the side of the box. She drew it back carefully. It moved an inch, then stopped.

"Bother!"

She was not going to give up. She gave another tug, then a harder one.

Too hard. Her finger popped off the side of the box. The motion propelled her backward. She windmilled her arms before grasping the edge of the shelf. The stool stopped rocking beneath her. She let out her breath in a soft sigh. That had been close.

Suddenly, an arm wrapped around her waist, yanking her off her feet. A shriek burst from her throat. The moment her toes touched the stone floor, she was shoved against the lower shelves. As she was held there by a firm chest, terror took control of her. No! She would not let this happen. Not again! She tried to pull away, but broad hands tightened on her.

Exactly as hands had at her dear friend's house that evening when Lord Litchfield refused to let her escape him as he squeezed her to the shelves behind her. The brash, flirtatious young lord had proved he was no gentlemen when he had chanced upon her in the book room. The echo of her own screams burst from her memories, his breath hot against her face, the screech of ripping fabric…the laughter of his friends.

Not again! She would not let it happen again.

She drew back her arm and drove her fist into her captor's gut. Air whooshed out of him, but he did not release her. She aimed her fist at him again. She froze when boxes cascaded down beyond her captor. They struck the stone floor and broke apart. Wood splinters flew in every direction. He pushed her head to his chest. His face hid in her hair. Glass shattered, and metal clanged.

Silence except for her uneven breathing…and her captor's. No, not her captor. Her rescuer!

Voices rang through the room. She started to raise her head, but the man pushed it against him again. She opened her mouth to protest. Anything she might have said vanished as another storm of boxes fell from overhead, crashing and splintering.

The man holding her recoiled toward her. Had he been struck? She did not move until he lifted his head off hers as silence returned.

"Are you hurt?" called Mrs. Ford from the direction of the kitchen.

Maris opened her eyes and closed them as a cloud of dust and debris swirled around her. How many boxes had fallen? There had been more than a score on the topmost shelf and many others on the lower ones.

Mrs. Ford's voice grew more frantic. "Are you hurt? Miss Oliver? Lord Trelawney?"

Lord Trelawney?

In horror mixed with dismay, she looked up at the man who still held her close to the shelves. She was accustomed to looking down when she spent time with the children, so it felt strange to raise her eyes to his. Arthur Trelawney, the earl's heir, was strikingly handsome with his ebony hair that curled across his forehead. She had seen him on occasion in Cothaire's hallways, but never this close. His face was tanned, for he often rode across the estate on the family's business. Because his features were sharply drawn, when he moved changes of light and shadow played along them intriguingly. His dark navy coat, which accented his broad shoulders, was cut to his specifications by a skilled tailor. His crystal blue eyes were bright as his gaze moved up and down her.

She tensed, too conscious of how close they stood, for she was aware of each breath he drew in. She must look a complete rump. Her apron was stained with food from the children's luncheon, and her hair was escaping from its sedate chignon to wisp around her face as if she were a hoyden racing across the garden.

"Are you hurt?" the viscount asked.

"No." She hastily looked away. Why was she gawking like a foolish chit when she should be apologizing? "My lord…"

He waved her to silence, stirring the cloud of dust, then called, "Mrs. Ford, we are unharmed."

"I will send Baricoat for footmen to clean up the mess," the cook said, then ordered one of her kitchen maids to take her message to the butler. "I am relieved to hear you are not injured, Lord Trelawney."

His name was an awful reminder that Maris had struck the earl's heir when he was trying to keep her from being hurt. She must hope that he would not give her the bag for such outrageous behavior. Where could she find another safe place to hide?

Again she began, "My lord, I am sorry—"

"One moment." He vanished into the brown cloud, and she heard china crack under his boots.

A burst of damp autumn air swept into the room, and the dust was flushed out through the stillroom's garden door. Blinking, Maris coughed as she breathed in fresh air to cleanse her lungs.

When a handkerchief was held out to her, she took it with a whispered, "Thank you." She dabbed her watery eyes, then faltered. Blowing her nose on Lord Trelawney's handkerchief did not seem right, especially if he expected her to return it to him.

As if she had spoken her uncertainty aloud, he said, "You may leave it in the laundry, Miss Oliver."

"I shall." She took a steadying breath, then looked at him again. There was something about his cool blue eyes that sent a pulse of warmth through her, even though his terse answers suggested he wished to put an end to this conversation immediately. So did she before she said the wrong thing and jeopardized her position at Cothaire. "Thank you, my lord, for saving me. Please forgive me for striking you."

"I…I shall survive." A faint smile tugged at his lips, but was gone so quickly that she was unsure she had seen it. Again his pale eyes examined her without hesitation. "You?"

"I am fine, my lord." Her voice was unsteady, and she was shocked how a wisp of a smile could send another beat of a sweet sensation through her.

"Good."

She waited for him to say more, but he was silent. Was he waiting for her to speak or move away? Uncertain, she blurted out the first thing that came into her mind. "Next time I need something on a high shelf, I will ask for help."

"Good."

She wished she could be as calm as he was. Her knees trembled with the residue of her fear. The memories that usually only haunted her in her nightmares had surged forward the moment he had touched her.

Or was it something other than serenity that kept his answers short? The household maids had warned her that the viscount seldom spoke to anyone other than his family or the upper servants. Some believed he was arrogant; others more graciously suggested he might be so busy with his many tasks that he was lost in his thoughts and did not notice anyone around him. A few whispered that he simply was shy.

When Lord Trelawney strode over broken crates

and crockery toward the kitchen door, Maris remained where she was. She was not sure which opinion was correct. He had spoken to her. However, he said only as much as necessary. He had come to her rescue, but Lord Litchfield had acted caring, too, before he had forced himself on her. She once had prided herself on being a good judge of character. She had been a fool when she let herself trust Lord Litchfield instead of making sure she was never alone with him. She was no longer that naive girl, and she would not be want-witted with another man, whether he be a gentleman of the *ton* or a lowly laborer. Before coming to Cornwall, she had chosen the most unflattering clothes and hairstyle. No man in Porthlowen had given her a second look, just as she wished.

But Lord Trelawney had given her a second look…as Lord Litchfield had. She did not want to think of what could happen, but she must be careful. Unlike with Lord Litchfield, warmth had bubbled within her when the earl's heir smiled at her. Letting her thoughts wander in that direction could ruin her as surely as Lord Litchfield had vowed to do.

She knew better than to trust any man. She must make sure she could always trust herself.

"And I assume you will be prepared to announce your plans to marry her before Christmas."

Arthur Trelawney, heir to the Earl of Launceston, fisted his hands behind his back as he listened to his father. He wondered if the whole world had gone mad. What other explanation was there for his father's plan for his older son's future? Maybe one of those boxes had fallen on Arthur's skull in the stillroom. He had thought his only wound was a small cut on his nape where a china shard had struck him while he tried to protect Miss Oliver. He should have moved out of the way, but had kept his face pressed to her golden hair, which was laced with the faint scent of jasmine.

By all that's blue! He should not be letting his mind wander to the pretty nurse. And she was a delight for the eyes, something he had not noticed until they stood close. The few times their paths had crossed before, she had hurried in the opposite direction as if hounds were at her heels. His impression had been of her gray gown and tightly bound hair.

No, he had no time to think of that. Instead, he concentrated on his father. All his life, he had admired the Earl of Launceston, who handled the most dire emergency with a cool head. Even when Father's health began to trouble him, condemning him to pain-filled days and sleepless nights, he had accepted God's will without railing or rancor.

But now...

"Pardon me," Arthur said, struggling to keep his voice even. He needed to emulate his father and deal with this unexpected situation with aplomb and solicitude.

As Father had always done, until this outrageous conversation.

"Yes, son? Do you have a question?"

He had a thousand questions, but the foremost one was why his father was acting bizarrely. Instead of blurting that out, Arthur said, "Forgive me, but this is abrupt. When you asked me to come here, I did not expect you to make such a request."

His father leaned back in his favorite chair in his favorite room. The smoking room's windows provided a view of the garden and the moors beyond it. Paintings of horses, some life-size, and hunt scenes were interspersed on the walls along with swords and antiquated pistols. It was a man's room where women were seldom welcome.

"You are my heir," Father said, "and it is high time you have an heir of your own."

"But—"

He did not let Arthur finish. Or even begin. "Lady Gwendolyn Cranford is the daughter of my oldest friend."

"Gwendolyn?" That was not a name he had thought to hear during this conversation. Perhaps there was more to his father's request than he had guessed. Or his father truly knew. He must proceed with care. He decided the best course would be to act as if his late best friend's wife's name had not set him on alert. "Yes, of course I realize her father is Lord Monkstone, your friend since you were in school together. That does not explain your request."

"Since his daughter was widowed by that heinous attack on her husband by a low highwayman, and left with two young children, Monkstone has fretted about her future. As I have about your future, son, and the future of our family's line. How better to ease our disquiet than solving both with a single offer of marriage?"

It took all of Arthur's willpower not to retort that he believed Louis Cranford's murder had not been a bungled robbery. Someone must have made it appear so, because Cranny, as Arthur thought of him, could have easily fought off a highwayman. His death was murder, and Arthur had futilely sought that cur for more than a year.

"I have not spoken with Lady Gwendolyn since the funeral." *Lord, help me keep from lying. Guide me in choosing words that are truth-filled, but allow me to conceal the truth that could endanger my family.*

Arthur had also spent the past year fulfilling Cranny's duties as a secret courier for the government. No one but Cranny's wife knew of his work passing along information from the Continent and the war against Napoleon. She had asked Arthur at her husband's funeral to take over the task of conveying coded messages across Cornwall. He had agreed, and so far his family was none the wiser. He explained his absences by saying he was checking the tenant farms on the estate. And he did so, because he refused to lie, but those visits were the perfect cover for his other activities.

He had hated lying and liars since Diana Mayfield made a chucklehead of him by feeding him such a banquet of falsehoods that he had fallen deeply in love with her. He was ready to ask her to be his wife when he had learned how she was making a fool of him. She had left without looking back and found herself another gullible sap, who did not care that she had a bevy of lovers. After that, he could not help seeing how many aspects of the courting rituals were based on half-truths. He had withdrawn from such games and gained a reputation of being either shy or arrogant because he kept to himself.

"Lady Gwendolyn is lovely," the earl went on, drawing Arthur back to the conversation, "and she has a placid disposition."

"I am aware of that."

"Yes, I thought you might be." Father held up a folded page sealed with dark blue wax. "This arrived for you today. You and Lady Gwendolyn have been writing to each other often. I suspect Monkstone has taken note, and he contacted me about a match between his daughter and you."

Arthur reached out to take the note, wincing as the simple motion stung his nape where he was cut. He refrained from snatching the page, tearing it open and reading its contents, which would be in the code Gwendolyn used when communicating with him. She was his primary contact, and he always received his orders through her. Instead, he thanked his father, as if the page were of the least importance.

"Monkstone assures me," Father said, "that his daughter is an accomplished hostess and her needlework is exquisite."

Arthur might have laughed if the situation were different. He doubted many men chose their wives because of their skill with a needle.

"I know she is a paragon," he replied, eager to put an end to the conversation so he could read Gwendolyn's message. "But, Father, it is October, and I doubt I will have time to call on the lady before—"

"No need to worry about that." Father pyramided his fingers in front of his face and smiled through them, his silver-gray eyes bright. "Miller is planning a hunt gathering early next month. He sent us an invitation along with his hopes that you would take time to be there."

"A hunt gathering?" Arthur frowned. "I have never heard of a justice of the peace hosting such a costly event."

"Mr. Miller is, as you must have seen, determined to elevate his status from country squire to nobility."

"By hosting a hunt?"

"If he impresses members of the *ton*, who knows

what might happen? But that isn't important. What is important is that Monkstone and his daughter will be attending. I cannot imagine a better place for you to prepare an announcement of your impending nuptials." Father chuckled. "If God grants me another year on His good, green earth, I may be bouncing *your* heir on my knee by next Christmas."

His father had every detail set, so Arthur knew this decision was not a spur-of-the-moment one. Father and Monkstone must have been discussing this for some time.

However, Arthur was intrigued by the idea of a hunt. Miller, the justice of the peace, was an encroaching mushroom, and he would invite every member of the *ton* in southwest England. Among the guests might be the person who had murdered Cranny or ordered his death. Only a member of Society could have arranged for the number of horses and riders seen fleeing from the site of the attack. Even the most successful highwayman seldom had more than a few men accompanying him.

Father must have taken Arthur's silence for acquiescence, because he continued, "You will be able to court Gwendolyn during that hunt. After all, she is a widow and you are past your thirtieth birthday, and you have known each other for a long time. So it is not as if you have to woo her with rides in Hyde Park and act as her escort to assemblies in Town. You need do little other than ask her to wed you."

Arthur nodded. In the past year, he had pushed the idea of finding a wife to the back of his mind, focusing rather on his duties as a courier and overseeing the estate on his father's behalf. Apparently, during that time, his father had given up on Arthur finding a bride on his own.

As if privy to his thoughts, Father asked, "Well? Don't you see this is a good solution?"

"I think the plan has merit." That was a safe answer, because he would make no promises until he had a chance to speak with Gwendolyn. Was she even aware of the plans to provide her with a husband? It was true that Arthur needed a wife and an heir, and maybe Gwendolyn was being pressured by her father. If so, such a union would not be the worst in history, though it would be no love match.

"I am glad you see it that way." Father became abruptly serious. "If my health was not failing, I would not insist on such an arrangement."

"You will be here for many more years," Arthur replied.

"I will be here as long as God wishes me." Father scowled as he shifted his ankle, which was swollen with gout. "Mr. Hockbridge tells me that the chest pains I have been suffering can be deadly."

Arthur had noticed his father's pallor, but had not realized he had conferred with the village doctor. Up until recently, his father had worn the dignity of his age with ease. His hair, once as black as Arthur's, was turning gray. His gout symptoms returned more frequently. In addition, life had become far more frantic in the house and Porthlowen Cove since six small children were discovered floating in a rickety boat in the harbor. The situation had grown quieter in recent weeks on the estate. The stable had been set afire by the French sailors who tried to overrun Porthlowen last month. Now those pirates were in prison. Arthur's younger sister, Susanna, was away on her honeymoon, and the harvest was almost in on the tenant farms. All messages he had been given were on their way toward London. Everything was going as it should…

Except he had not unmasked the person who had murdered Cranny.

"Thank you, son, for agreeing to such an outlandish request," Father said.

"Not outlandish," came a light voice from near to the doorway, "for daughters have been asked to do much the same throughout time."

Arthur glanced over his shoulder as his older sister, Carrie, came into the room. She was teasing, but her blue eyes, the same deep shade as his own, snapped with strong emotions. He wondered why. Had something been discovered about the baby in her arms? His sister called the youngest waif Joy. Since the children were rescued in Porthlowen Harbor, the baby had seldom been out of his sister's arms. She was happier than she had been since her husband's death at sea five years ago.

His siblings were, in his opinion, baby-mad. Carrie with baby Joy. His brother, Raymond, and his new wife, Elisabeth, had one of the older boys, who was close to four years old, living with them at the parsonage. His younger sister had become attached to a set of twin girls, who were a year younger.

His family had, it would appear, lost their collective minds. These children came from somewhere. They belonged to someone. Eventually they would have to be returned to those people. And the rest of his family would be lost in grief, as they had when Mama died around the same time as his brother-in-law. Arthur hated the idea of that. They had mourned enough for the past five years.

"Caroline, come and join us," Father said with a smile.

The rest of the family used her full name, but Arthur continued to think of his older sister as Carrie, the nickname he had given her when he was young and could not pronounce her full name. She was a lovely woman who carried a bit more flesh than the *ton* considered acceptable. He used to tease her about being well-rounded, but he had set aside such jests years ago.

She gave Father a kiss on the cheek, then straightened. "Arthur, I had hoped to find you," she said in that same carefree tone. "May I speak with you?" She gave the slightest nod toward the hallway.

He swallowed his sigh at another delay before he could read Gwendolyn's message, but looked at Father. "If you will excuse me…"

"Go, go. I am sure you have many matters to consider." His father's smile returned.

Arthur nodded. He did have many matters he should be thinking about. On the family's vast estate set on the sea and across the Cornish moors, there were repairs to the faulty barn roof on Pellow's farm and the new well that must be dug before winter for the Dinases' farm. The old one had suddenly gone dry last week. It might be because of a new tin mine being dug south along the moor, or it could be another cause completely. First, they must get a new source of water; then they could investigate why the well had dried up.

How could he think of any of that when he was curious about what Gwendolyn had written?

Carrie said nothing as they walked to the small drawing room they used *en famille*. French windows opened onto a terrace with a vista of the sea and the garden. The Aubusson rug with its great white roses was set in the middle of the room, and furniture was spread atop it to allow for easy conversation.

His sister sat in a chair not far from the hearth. Not that he blamed her. The fire burning there chased away the autumn afternoon's chill. When she motioned for him to sit, he shook his head.

"I would prefer to stand…unless this conversation is going to be a long one."

"That is up to you." The lightness vanished from her voice, and her eyes narrowed.

"Me? You asked me to speak with you."

"Because I am sure you have many things to say about Father's plan that you would not in front of him."

Arthur was not surprised that Father had discussed with Carrie the matter of a match between him and Gwendolyn. Since their mother's death, his older sister had become Father's sounding post.

"I never expected Father to ask *this* of me, Carrie." He leaned forward and put his hands on the settee.

"It is your duty to marry." Her voice gentled. "Father expected an announcement by the time you celebrated your thirtieth birthday."

"I have been busy with other duties." That was his usual excuse.

She gave him a sympathetic smile. "I know that you have been avoiding the *ton* since that incident with Miss Mayfield, which is why when Father told me about this arrangement he has made with Lord Monkstone, I did not say that I believed the whole of it was addled." She looked at him directly. "Tell me, Arthur. Are you truly agreeable with this match?"

"As you said, daughters have come to terms with

such arrangements for millennia." He ran his hand through his hair, grateful that he did not have to lie.

"I know. Will you be able to ask her?"

Her question startled him. Then he reminded himself that his sister believed, as most of the world did, that he was too shy to say boo to a goose. He had never corrected the mistaken assumptions. "I would hope so. There must be some way."

"You are resourceful, Arthur."

"I suppose I could write a flowery poem that ends with 'Will you marry me?'"

"Writing love missives is all well and good, but you have not made her an offer of marriage." A smile tipped Carrie's lips. "Don't look surprised, Arthur. You should know that nothing stays a secret for long here, especially when you receive letters from her week after week."

He hoped his sister was wrong, because no one else must learn how he had assumed Cranny's secret duties. As long as everybody believed the notes were focused on avowals of love, his secret should be safe.

"I know you probably find it simpler to put words on paper than to speak them," Carrie said, "but even if you propose via a love poem, you still must say 'I do' at the front of the church." She reached out and patted his hand. "But let us take one step at a time. There must be some way to make it easy for you to propose to Lady Gwendolyn." She rose and began to pace in front of the French windows. When the baby began to fuss, she paused. "I must take Joy to be fed. Oh!"

"Oh?" he asked.

"It is simple. Why didn't I see that before?" She crossed the room and placed the baby in his arms.

He tensed, because he had never held such a tiny

infant. His nose wrinkled at the odor of a dirty, wet napkin. "Carrie, I am not accustomed to little babies."

"I know. The practice will do you good, especially because Lady Gwendolyn's younger child isn't much older than Joy." Carrie's eyes filled with tears. "How sad to have a child born after the death of its father." She squared her shoulders, all business once again. "The other is about three or four years old. My advice to you is to get those children to like you, so she will see you are sincere even if you are hesitant when you ask her."

"Why?"

"The quickest way to a woman's heart is to win the hearts of her children."

He did not say that hearts had nothing to do with the arrangement he and his father had discussed. Something twinged in his chest. Regret? He disliked the idea of a loveless match.

The baby grumbled and wiggled. He shifted her so he would not drop her. As he looked down at her tiny rosebud mouth, he asked, "And how do you suggest I win over her children?"

"Play with them. Talk to them."

"I honestly don't know much about children."

"Then learn."

"You make it sound easy."

Carrie grinned. "Isn't it? There are five small children living under our roof and another staying with Raymond and Elisabeth at the parsonage. Why not practice with them?"

"I would not know where to begin." *Or when I would have the time. If Gwendolyn's message requires me to travel, I must take my leave immediately.* He yearned to tell Carrie the truth, but bit back the words.

She stepped behind him and put her hands against his back. Giving him a slight push, she said, "Start with the expert. Ask Miss Oliver. She will be glad to help, especially after you gallantly rescued her this afternoon."

Glancing over his shoulder, he chuckled. "You heard of that."

"Even if the sound of crates falling had not resonated through Cothaire, do I need to remind you that nothing stays secret here?" Not giving him a chance to reply, she said, "Will you ask for her help?"

"Yes." He would have to find a way to balance his sister's request with his other tasks.

"Off with you then. Joy needs to be fed, and taking her to the nursery gives you the perfect opportunity to speak with Miss Oliver."

He walked to the door. Another delay before he could read the note after he deciphered it, but the visit to the nursery could be done quickly. He would go through the motions of spending time with the children so Carrie did not become suspicious. Once he had a chance to read Gwendolyn's message, he would know what he needed to do next. Going to the nursery would not take much time.

And he could see Miss Oliver again to assure himself that she had recovered from the fright of the boxes falling on them. He would give her the baby, ask for her help to convince his family he was making an effort to be a good suitor for Gwendolyn, and then retreat to his private rooms to read Gwendolyn's message. What could be simpler than that?

Chapter Two

"Look! Look! Look!"

Maris smiled at the children as she selected one of the storybooks on the shelf in the Cothaire day nursery. It was their favorite book. She wanted to read it to them before their tea was brought up, along with four of the child-size cups that had survived falling off the shelf. Eight were usable, and two more were being glued together. The rest had smashed into too many pieces to try to repair.

Putting the book under her arm, she went to where Gil and Bertie pointed out the window overlooking the harbor. She knelt on the padded bench there and shaded her eyes as she scanned the waves, which glittered like dozens of fabulous diamond necklaces.

"I see it," she said, when she realized the little boys were gesturing toward the sails of a ship far out near the horizon. Bertie was, by her estimation, at least four years old, while Gil probably had his third birthday not too long ago.

"Cap's?"

Before she could answer Bertie, the three-year-old

twin girls who had been playing with dolls by a large dollhouse repeated, "Cap?" They jumped to their feet and ran to the window. "Cap's boat?"

"No," Maris said, shifting to give Lulu and Molly, the twins, room to get on the bench. She hated dashing the children's hopes. They missed Captain Nesbitt, who had rescued them from Porthlowen Harbor, but he was not due back for at least another fortnight.

"No Cap's boat. No Cap for Wuwu." Lulu's lisp mixed with her mournful tone.

"But it is a pretty ship." Maris stood to give the girls more room.

The four youngsters plus baby Joy kept her busy. On occasion, Toby, the sixth child from the jolly boat that had drifted into Porthlowen Harbor, came to play with the others. He was close to Bertie's age. Parson Trelawney and his wife had offered to take the little boy the first night, when Toby and Bertie would not stop annoying each other. That temporary solution had become permanent…or permanent until the truth about the children could be uncovered.

Maris watched the children, who chatted excitedly about the ship and what might be on it and where it might be bound.

"Ship go bye-bye." Lulu's voice was sad.

"Bye-bye, ship," echoed her twin.

Maris sat beside them and held out her arms. The children nestled next to her, and she drew them closer. Talking to them about the day they had toured Captain Nesbitt's ship while it was being repaired in the harbor, she was glad to see their sweet smiles return.

Who had abandoned these children in a jolly boat that was ready to sink? If Captain Nesbitt and his first mate had failed to see them and come to their rescue, the children could have been dashed upon the rocks in the cove. Whose heart was so unfeeling? As she stroked the silken hair on their tiny heads, Maris wondered why someone had put them in that boat. The children were too young to explain, and every clue had led to a dead end.

"Shall we sing a song about a ship?" she asked, grateful that, no matter how they had come to Cothaire, they were safe.

The two boys began singing. The tune did not resemble the one she had taught them and half the words were wrong, but their enthusiasm was undeniable.

They broke off as footsteps came toward the nursery. Strong, assertive footsteps. The servants were quiet when they walked through the house. Maybe the parson was bringing Toby to play with the children.

Hushing them, Maris disentangled herself and eased out from among them. She brushed her hair toward her unflattering bun as she stood. She opened her mouth, but then realized the silhouette in the doorway was taller than the parson or his wife.

"Miss Oliver?" asked the Earl of Launceston's older son. He stood as stiff as a soldier on parade.

"Lord Trelawney," she squeaked, sounding as young as her charges.

What was *he* doing here, so soon after the mishap in the stillroom? In the weeks since her arrival at Cothaire, the viscount had never come to the nursery. Not that she had expected him to, because his duties lay elsewhere. Still, it had seemed odd, when everyone else in the family, including the earl, had stopped in once or twice to ask how the children fared.

Uneasiness tightened Maris's stomach. Had the viscount come to dismiss her? She could have misread his concern for her well-being. She had been wrong about men before, terribly wrong.

Could it be almost a year ago when she had made her final visit to her friend Belinda, the daughter of an earl? Because Maris's father was a country squire whose tiny estate bordered Lord Bellemore's vast one in Somerset, the two girls had spent many hours together as children. As they grew older, they had less in common, but after Maris's parents died, Belinda had invited her to stay. Her widowed father often needed another female to even the numbers at the table. Dear Belinda was oblivious to the disapproving glances in Maris's direction, but Maris had been aware of each one from the earl's other guests.

If she had not offered to get a familiar title from the earl's book room to read her friend to sleep that evening...

Maris wrapped her arms around herself, holding herself together. It would be easy to fall apart whenever she thought of Lord Litchfield and what he had done. No! She was safe at Cothaire.

Or was she? The nursery was on the upper floor where few adults came. Lord Trelawney would know that she was alone.

Stop it! If you offend him by accusing him falsely, he will dismiss you without a recommendation to help you get another position. Not that she had been unable to solve that problem in getting her current position, but she might not find another household with such a need for a nurse that they gave the fake recommendation she had penned herself such a cursory examination. Familiar guilt at her lie pinched her, but she had been desperate.

"Some help, please," Lord Trelawney said in his rich, baritone voice.

Astounded, she realized he carried Joy— awkwardly, as if he feared he might drop the infant at any moment. "I will take her. Thank you."

Little Gil raced after her, crying with excitement, "My baby! My baby!" No one knew if Gil and Joy were actually brother and sister, but the little boy had laid claim to the baby after being rescued.

Maris calmed him and the other children, who clustered around her and the viscount. She held out her arms and repeated, "I will take her, my lord."

"May I…?" He glanced at the children and cleared his throat. "May I come in?"

Every instinct urged her to say no, but she really had no choice. She put space between them, herding the children away from the doorway. They wanted to greet Lord Trelawney with the same enthusiasm they showed everyone, but she doubted the cool, composed man would welcome their curious questions or their fingerprints on his pristine black coat. As he came into the room, she stepped around the small table where the children ate. It was not much of a shield, but it was all she had.

You are being silly, that soft voice whispered in her mind. *Lord Trelawney is not Lord Litchfield. He has never been anything but polite when he passed you in an empty hallway. And he did save you from injury earlier.*

Maybe so, but she would not take the chance of being hurt by another man and then abandoned by those she thought she could depend on.

"Will you…?" He motioned with his head toward the baby.

"Certainly." She left her scanty sanctuary and scooped Joy into her arms, then wrinkled her nose. "She is rather pungent, isn't she?"

He glanced down at his sleeve where a damp spot warned that the napkin had leaked. "Yes."

"I shall see that she is changed and fed, my lord. Thank you." The nursery seemed oddly cramped with him in it. Or maybe it was because the children gripped her skirt, making it impossible for her to edge away again. "I assumed Lady Caroline would bring Joy to the nursery."

"Yes, my sister seldom is parted from this baby. I hope…" He did not finish.

He did not need to, because Maris understood. Lady Caroline would be bereft when the baby's parents were found.

"You look well, Miss Oliver," he added.

She was startled, then realized he must be referring to what had occurred in the stillroom. "Thanks to you." She lowered her eyes. "I hope your injury was minor."

"How did you know?"

"We *were* standing close, and I felt you flinch as the debris flew about."

He smiled. "'Tis a scratch." He paused for so long that she thought he was done; then he said, "I appreciate you asking."

Laying the baby on the higher table, where a stack of fresh napkins waited, Maris began to change Joy. She was aware of Lord Trelawney behind her, even though he was silent. After sending the children to play, she looked at him.

"Is there something else you need me to do, my lord?" she asked.

"'Tis my sister. She thought it was time that I visited the nursery and learned more about the children living here."

"She did?" What a peculiar suggestion! In an upperclass home such as Cothaire, the children's lives seldom intersected with their elders'. "Of course, you are always welcome."

"She suggested that… That is, she thought you might guide me in getting to know the children better." He glanced at where the twins were chasing the boys. "Next month, I will be spending time with a widowed acquaintance who has two children of her own, and Carrie thought if I learned about these children, I would have an easier time with meeting Gwendolyn's."

Maris put a clean napkin on the baby and pinned it in place. It would seem that Lord Trelawney had made his choice of a bride. She had heard the household staff discussing whom he might choose and how his new wife might change Cothaire. No doubt the widow's name was being discussed in whispers in the servants' hall.

Lifting little Joy from the table, Maris cradled her close to her heart. The baby's mouth tasted the air, a sign that she wanted to nurse. Maris watched Lord Trelawney gaze down at the child. He lightly touched her soft hair, his expression unguarded for a moment.

Biting her lower lip, Maris said nothing. If she expressed how endearing it was to see the oh-so-correct viscount reveal a tender vulnerability, she might embarrass him. She did not move as he looked from the baby to the other children, his thoughts bare on his face. He was perplexed by them, but fascinated, too. Few strong men would reveal that, nor would they be concerned about the well-being of a servant who had caused an accident in the stillroom.

As he gently brushed the baby's head, he looked up. His gaze caught Maris's, no longer cool, but filled with emotions she could not interpret. Standing with the baby between them, she noticed, as she had not before, that darker navy rings encircled the pale blue of his eyes. She never had seen any like them. Her fingers tingled, and she had to fight to keep them from rising to curve along his cheek as she told him how sweet she found him to be with the baby. Being so bold might suggest she was the easy type of woman Lord Litchfield considered her.

That thought compelled Maris back a half step. "Lord Trelawney, we can discuss how you can get to know the children better once I take Joy to the wet nurse. She is waiting in the kitchen."

His hand hung in the air now that Joy's head was no longer beneath it. He lowered it. "I should go. I need to—"

The other children shrieked as they raced from one side of the room to the other, giggling.

"I will be but a moment." Maris pointed to each child and spoke his or her name, before adding, "Children, this is Lord Trelawney. He is Lady Susanna's older brother. Just like Parson Raymond."

They smiled at him, but uneasily, then looked at her. Had they sensed, as she did, that he wished he were somewhere else? With a sigh, she suggested they go to the window to see what else they might spot outside. They clambered onto the window bench. She hoped they would remain distracted and well behaved until she returned.

She lowered her voice as she turned to the viscount. "Watch so they don't get hurt. I shall be right back." She hurried to the stairs leading down to the kitchen, before she laughed out loud at Lord Trelawney's expression.

He had looked unnerved at her suggestion that he stay alone with the children. Could he truly have no experience with little ones? Lady Susanna was more than a decade younger than he was, so he must remember her as an infant and toddler. Then Maris remembered that Belinda's brother had been sent away to school by the time he was ten. Most likely, Lord Trelawney had been attending boarding school when Lady Susanna was born.

In the kitchen, Maris handed Joy to the young woman who came from the village several times each day to nurse the baby.

Mrs. Ford looked up from stirring a bowl. "Miss Oliver, I cannot believe you left those young ones on their own upstairs. That is not like you."

"I didn't leave them alone," she said.

"Lady Caroline has more important—"

"I did not leave them with Lady Caroline."

She had the attention of everyone in the kitchen, and one of the maids blurted, "Then who?"

"Lord Trelawney."

Gasps rushed around the kitchen, quieting when Mrs. Ford gave her staff a frown. Putting down the bowl, the cook wiped her hands on her apron as she walked over to where Maris stood with her foot on the first step of the nursery stairs.

Too low for anyone else to hear, the cook asked, "Is this a jest?"

"No." Maris could trust Mrs. Ford, who had begun

her service at Cothaire before Maris was born. "Lady Caroline suggested he get to know these children better before he meets the children of a lady named Gwendolyn next month."

"Ah." The cook smiled. "Thank God! Lord Trelawney is going courting."

Maris put her finger to her lips. "Shhh!"

"You don't need to shush me. I know how to keep my mouth shut about the family's business, but this is good news, it is." Sudden tears bloomed in the cook's eyes. "It is high time for Lord Trelawney to take a bride and spend less time riding around the estate. He needs to be here for his father. The earl is not well, and it is important for him to see his heir's heir."

Maris nodded. She deeply missed her own parents, who had died when she was sixteen. Her one comfort was that she had had many wonderful days with them. Lord Trelawney had his duties, but those should include treasuring every moment he could with the earl.

"Do your best to help him, Miss Oliver, and you will have done this household a great service." The cook returned to her task without waiting for an answer.

Maris went up the stairs, then paused on the landing near the day nursery door. If his intentions were to marry the lady named Gwendolyn, why had he gazed intently at Maris with those incredible eyes? Or had she read more into the moment than he intended? She was a poor judge of men; that much was for sure. She should not accuse Lord Trelawney of a misdeed when he might not be guilty. His attention might have been on Joy rather than on her. After all, she was the nurse, and he saw her as a useful tool to help him learn more about children.

Perhaps he might even be grateful and let her stay on at Cothaire. Even after the children's pasts were uncovered, a nurse would be needed for Lord Trelawney's children. That would mean Maris would be assured of a roof over her head and plenty of food for years to come. She had learned about the fear of hunger after her parents died, and the debts they had amassed in order to live at the edges of the *ton* had consumed the money from the estate's sale. Only the generosity of her friend had enabled Maris to survive.

Equally as important, she would be invisible in the nursery, so she could avoid lecherous men like Lord Litchfield. While she did her best to assist Lord Trelawney, she would wisely make sure they were never alone. So far, he had been kind to her, but she would not be duped again.

A cry came from the nursery. Maris threw the door open and rushed in.

Lord Trelawney had not moved, but heaps of toys surrounded him. The poor man looked as lost as an explorer on an untouched shore. The children danced around him, singing of ships.

He glanced toward her as she came into the nursery. With relief, she noted.

"I am back, Moses," she said with a laugh she could not silence.

"Moses?"

"Your expression reminded me of when Moses said, 'I have been a stranger in a strange land.'"

The viscount's brows arched, and the corner of his lips curved.

She looked away, shocked by her own words. To speak brazenly to him was unthinkable. As unthinkable as her quoting a passage from the Bible. Even though she had attended church since her arrival in Porthlowen, she had not prayed since she fled from her friend's house after the attack. God had not heard her in the midst of the attack and sent someone to save her. Afterward, when Lord Litchfield threatened her with ruin and her friend's family turned her out because they believed his lies that *she* had tried to seduce him, she wondered if He had ever listened to her.

She was saved from her own thoughts when the children ran to her, greeting her as if she had been gone for five days rather than five minutes. She hugged each one, but spoke to Lord Trelawney. "I assure you, my lord, that they do not bite, except each other occasionally, but we are working on that."

"No bite," Bertie said, as serious as a judge pronouncing a sentence.

She fluffed his hair, which was fairer than her own. "That is right."

The viscount glanced toward the door, clearly eager to make his escape.

"My lord," she continued, when he did not answer, "may I suggest you join the children and me on our walk tomorrow?"

"Tomorrow? Where?"

She hesitated. The obvious place was a section of the cove's sandy shore. Many of the buildings in the village, including the parsonage, overlooked it. The nearby harbor always bustled with activity. There, she would never be alone with Lord Trelawney.

"Down to the water," she said. "With their short legs, that journey is enough to tire them out long enough to sit still. While we are there, you can talk to them."

"About what?" His full attention was on her.

"Whatever you or they have on their minds."

"That should be interesting." He bid her a good day and strode toward the hallway door.

Beside her, Lulu asked, "Is the big man coming back?"

"Yes." And she must be prepared. She could not make another horrible mistake as she had with Lord Litchfield.

Arthur had half hoped that Miss Oliver would send him a note that neither she nor the children were going to visit the harbor. He could have used the time instead to encode a message to Gwendolyn and ask what was in the message she had sent to Cothaire. Either she had changed the code without alerting him, or she had made mistakes in writing the note. It made no sense other than a few random words.

Or had he made the mistakes? He had checked the message a second time and still it made no sense, but he admittedly was distracted. Miss Oliver kept popping into his mind. The shapeless apron she wore over her gray dress failed to hide her pleasing curves, and her smile lit her pretty face. He wondered why she made such an effort to appear drab.

As he walked across Cothaire's entry hall, he warned himself to keep his mind on the task of getting to know the children, not their nurse. He had agreed to Carrie's request, and he must do as he promised. And, he reminded himself, the outing would keep him from wondering about Gwendolyn's odd message.

The breeze was brisk when Arthur emerged from the house. Lighthearted voices came from the left where the children surrounded Miss Oliver. They bounced in every direction like a handful of dropped coins, but

Miss Oliver radiated calm. She answered their questions with an unwavering smile while she kept them from wandering away.

She wore a simple gray spencer and a bonnet of the same color that did not flatter her complexion. Her cheeks were brushed with a charming pink, and he could not keep from thinking of how his fingertips vibrated when they had curved around her slender waist as he pulled her out of the way of toppling boxes. The exotic jasmine scent from her hair clung to his senses, and he was curious if she wore it again today. Her deep green eyes twinkled as she reached behind her and pulled out a bag. The four children clamored to see what was in it.

When Arthur walked toward them, the younger boy noticed and raced toward him. The child stopped right in front of him. "Look! Ship!" He held up a tiny wooden ship for Arthur to see.

"Very nice," he said.

"Go now!"

Miss Oliver took the little boy's hand and drew him closer. "Forgive Gil, my lord. He is excited to sail his ship in the harbor."

Arthur noticed that she did not meet his eyes, even when she spoke to him. Was she having second thoughts about helping him?

Bertie let out a shriek. The older boy's tiny ship lay broken on the ground. It must have fallen out of his hand.

Arthur bent to collect the pieces and bumped into Miss Oliver when she did the same. A quiver, as if the earth beneath his feet trembled, rushed outward from where their hands touched. He jerked his back at the same time she did. Beneath her bonnet, her face flushed nearly to the shade of a soldier's scarlet coat.

He was relieved when she turned away, because he did not want her to discover he was unsettled by the peculiar, fascinating sensation when his fingers grazed hers. Picking up the broken toy, he examined it. The children quieted while they waited to see what he would do or say. Balancing the tiny ship on his broad palm, he realigned the two cracked masts, then held it out to Bertie.

The little boy looked from him to the ship and back.

"I am no shipwright," Miss Oliver said, "but I suspect it will float well, Bertie. Thank Lord Trelawney."

Bertie mumbled something as he wiped his eyes and nose on his sleeve, then reached to take the boat.

Miss Oliver put a hand on the boy's shoulder and asked, "Shall we go, my lord?"

He nodded. The sooner they went, the sooner he could return to write out his coded note.

As they walked down the hill toward the village, the children prattled with excitement. Miss Oliver seemed to understand everything they said, but to Arthur much of it sounded like the chatter of Indian monkeys as they all talked at once.

Miss Oliver glanced at him several times and arched her brows. He comprehended her silent question, but he had no idea how to jump into the babble. Perhaps he would do better if he spoke with one child at a time. There surely would be an opportunity when they reached the beach.

He glanced at the village as they passed its single street. It was quiet in the morning sunshine. One woman was hanging clothes near a stone cottage, and another was dumping out a bucket. Water ran between the cobbles on the steeper section that led down toward the harbor. A single word of caution from Miss Oliver kept the children from sticking fingers in the water as it rushed by.

At low tide, Porthlowen's sandy beach was a few yards wide. It offered enough space for fishermen to pull their boats up onto the sand to work on them. Flat stretches of stone were visible where the water had pulled back. They would be invisible again once the tide came surging around the curved edges of the cove, where two sets of cliffs challenged even skilled navigators.

Arthur helped Miss Oliver take off the children's shoes and socks. She piled them on the grass beyond the sand. Next, she tied a string connected to each tiny ship around a child's wrist, so the toys would not be lost. As they ran to put their ships in the water, he was impressed how easily Miss Oliver managed to keep an eye on all her charges seemingly at the same time.

He walked to where the glistening blue water lapped against the shore. He should have been so cautious the year he turned sixteen. He had brought Susanna to the cove. She had been no older than the twins, and he old enough to know better than to turn his back even for a second. Yet he had, and his baby sister had almost drowned. When he realized she was gone, he had found her floating facedown in the water, and he thought she was dead. Desperate to get her breathing, he had put her over his shoulder like a baby being burped. A couple quick slaps to the back had made her vomit water, but she had begun breathing again and, in a few minutes, was fine.

But he had not been. His parents had trusted him to watch over Susanna. That was the last promise he had ever broken. He had learned his lesson that day about responsibility and God's grace on young men who thought they knew everything.

A small hand tugged on his coat. In astonishment, he saw one of the twins had come over to him. He was not sure which one it was, because he could not tell them apart. She raised her dripping ship toward him.

"You boat?" she asked.

"No," he answered, his throat tight as he forced the words out. "Yours."

"Wuwu."

"What?"

"She said her name is Lulu." Miss Oliver joined them. "Her real name is Lucie, but we call her Lulu. She wants to know if you want to sail her ship."

"Me?" He glanced from the child to the nurse, realizing that their eyes were almost the same color. Lulu's were bright with innocence. Shadows clung to Miss Oliver's, even when she smiled.

Sadness or some other emotion? He wanted to ask, but that was too personal a question.

"If you wish, my lord…" Miss Oliver's gaze led his to the little girl, who patiently held up the boat.

He reached down. When the child grasped his hand as he took the wooden ship from hers, he was startled how small her fingers were. The last tiny hand he had held was Susanna's…right on this shore that horrible day.

"In water," Lulu said when he hesitated.

He motioned for her to lead the way, then asked Miss Oliver, "Are they always so bossy?"

"Always." She smiled.

His lungs compressed, but he could not release his breath when her face shone as if she had swallowed sunlight. Her curls emphasized her high cheekbones, which were burnished by the breeze to a deeper pink. He was tempted to tell her to stop attempting to make herself look plain, because those efforts were futile and a waste of time.

"I had no idea that you were at the mercy of miniature despots," he said, knowing he must not keep staring at her in silence.

"Fortunately, they are benevolent despots." She laughed. "As long as they are fed on time, have plenty of toys to play with and can negotiate a few extra minutes before bed." She stepped aside as he went with Lulu to the water's edge. "Hold on to the string before you place the ship in the water. As you know, the currents are tricky here."

Lulu confidently squatted and looked up, gesturing toward the sea. She could not understand why he was hesitating. The sight of a little girl at the water's edge, unaware of the danger awaiting her if she went in too deeply, sliced into him like a fiery sword.

Maybe the whole of this outing was a mistake. He should excuse himself and return to Cothaire. Yet he had given Carrie his word that he would make an effort to get to know the children. These experiences would prove worthwhile if Gwendolyn really wanted him to marry her. He wished he could ask her, but doing so in a coded note was not the way.

Miss Oliver came to his rescue when she took the ship and placed it in the water. The toy bobbed on the waves. Rising, she glanced at him, then nodded toward Lulu before she went to check on the other three. She gently herded the children closer so they were within arm's reach.

He looked down at the little girl in front of him. What should he say to her?

"Ask her the name of her ship," Miss Oliver whispered.

He nodded, then paused so long that she repeated her instructions. He was tempted to fire back that he had heard her the first time. Instead, he asked, "What do you call your ship, Lulu?"

"Pony."

"Why?"

"Pony pwances." She smiled.

He took a moment to figure out the word her lisp distorted. "Ah, I see. A pony prances like your ship does."

She did not answer as she drew the toy closer to her before letting it drift on the current again.

Miss Oliver edged closer, but kept watching her charges. "See? It isn't hard to talk with children." Suddenly she gasped and sped past him.

He turned to see Bertie chasing his boat's string, which had come loose from his wrist. The child tried to grab the end, but the waves pulled it across the flat rocks toward deep water.

Arthur did not hesitate. He ran across the slick stones. His boots slid, but he kept going. Passing Miss Oliver, whose dreary bonnet bounced on her back, he heard her shout the child's name.

So did the little boy. He turned and teetered on the edge of a rock.

She screamed.

Arthur threw himself toward the child, grabbing his arm. His right foot skidded as he pulled Bertie to him. A hot spear pierced his knee as he fell with the boy on top of him. Arthur's breath burst out painfully.

Miss Oliver scooped the little boy off him and hugged him. "Bertie, you must not leave the shore."

"Boat go."

"We have others. Let it go. Maybe it will reach Cap's ship." She carried him to shore where the other children were watching, wide-eyed.

Arthur winced as he pushed himself up to sit. Every bone had jarred when he had twisted to keep from falling on the boy.

Miss Oliver rushed back to him. "Are you hurt, Lord Trelawney?" She ran her hands along one of his arms, then the other. When she started to do the same to his right leg, he grasped her arms and edged her away.

"I am fine." He was struggling to think and did not need the distraction of her jasmine-scented curls caressing his cheek when she bent toward him.

His words must have been too sharp, because she rose and wiped her hands as if wanting to clean them of any contact with him. "I am pleased to hear that, my lord. Thank you for saving Bertie."

By all that's blue! He was making a muddle of everything, and he could not blame his rudeness on the pain blistering his leg. As she walked away, he pushed himself to his feet.

Or tried to.

Agony clamped around his right ankle and sent a new streak of fiery pain up to his knee. He collapsed with a choked gasp as he prayed, *Lord, don't let anything be broken. I need to continue the work I promised I would do in Cranny's stead.*

Miss Oliver whirled and ran to him. "You are hurt, my lord! Shall I go for help?"

"No. If I can…" He groaned as he tried to move his right leg.

"At least let me help you up."

"You are too slight."

She squatted beside him. "I am going to help you, whether you wish it or not. I do hope you will cooperate."

She put her shoulder beneath his arm and levered him to his feet. He kept his right foot off the ground and balanced on his left. As he drew in a deep breath, it was flavored with the fragrance of jasmine, the perfect scent for her.

"Thank you, Miss Oliver. If you will release me—"

"Do you intend to hop to Cothaire?"

"No, the parsonage." Once he reached there, his brother would help him return to the great house.

"You cannot hop that far, either."

Pain honed his voice. "Miss Oliver, has anyone ever told you that you can be vexing?"

"Many times." She motioned with her free arm toward the shore where the children waited. "Shall we go?"

He nodded, but groaned as he took a single step.

On the beach, Bertie cried, "Is—is—is he a bear?"

The children stared at him, scared. He must persuade the youngsters that he was no danger to them. What a mull he had made of the outing! He tried another step, then halted, realizing he had an even bigger problem. How would he be able to do his work as a courier if he could not walk?

Chapter Three

Arthur had never been more relieved to see his younger brother than when Raymond rushed out of the parsonage. Raising Arthur's free arm over his shoulders, his brother nodded to Miss Oliver.

She stepped back with a soft sigh. No doubt she must be glad to hand over the burden of supporting him to someone else. The walk from the beach had been slow. The only pauses were when she asked the children to collect their footwear and when she had sent two of the village boys to inform his family of his injury, one to the parsonage and the other to Cothaire. She had talked to Arthur at first, urging him forward with each step, but his silence had put an end to that. After that, she spoke only to the children.

For him, any conversation was hopeless because his teeth were clenched to keep his groans from leaking out. The children were scared of him, and he did not want to frighten them more.

Raymond turned him toward the front door. His red-haired wife, Elisabeth, held it open. Dismay lengthened her face as she stepped aside to let them enter.

Arthur propped one hand against the doorjamb, but did not enter when he heard a loud rattle and the pounding of hooves. He saw Miss Oliver pulling the children onto the grass as an open cart slowed in front of the parsonage. The driver jumped down and handed out Carrie, who, for once, was not holding the baby.

That did not halt the littlest boy from running to her as he called, "My baby!"

She bent and said something to him before taking his hand. As fast as the child's legs could move, she rushed toward the door.

"How badly are you hurt, Arthur?" she asked.

"Not bad," he replied.

Miss Oliver quickly contradicted him. "He cannot stand on his right leg. He twisted his knee or his ankle or both."

Carrie shot him a frown before turning to the nurse. "Twisted? Not broken?"

"I cannot say for sure, my lady. Without removing his boot, it is impossible to tell, and he wisely has kept it on."

"Raymond, help me get him into the cart. I have alerted Mr. Hockbridge. He should be at Cothaire by the time we arrive."

Arthur was not given a chance to protest that if he had a chance to sit quietly, he would be fine. His brother led him to the cart and, with the driver's help, lifted him in the rear. Everything went black, and his head spun. He would not faint like a simpering girl! He fought until he could see again, and discovered he was lying on his back. He almost cried out when the cart bounced. Had someone climbed in?

"Fine. I am fine," he muttered when Carrie asked how he fared.

"So I see! If you had any less color, you would be dead."

He opened his eyes and then closed them when he saw the alarm on his sister's face as she leaned over the side of the cart. She might tease him, but she could not hide how worried she was. He wanted to reassure her that he would be as good as new in no time, but she would not believe him. He was unsure if he believed it himself. He had not felt such pain since he fell off a stone wall when he was seven and broke his arm.

"Thank you," he heard Carrie say, a moment before something damp and warm covered his brow. "Keep it there."

Keep it there? To whom was she talking? A breeze brushed across his face, bringing a hint of jasmine. Miss Oliver! He wanted to ask why she was with him instead of Carrie. Where were the children? He tried to open his eyes, but it was worthless. The damp cloth covered them.

"We will be leaving as soon as the driver assists your sister up," Miss Oliver whispered.

Many words rushed through his head. Apologies for ruining her outing with the children, gratitude for how she had helped him to the parsonage, questions about how he could repair the damage he had caused by scaring the children. None of them formed on his tongue.

He sank into the darkness as the cart began moving. When he opened his eyes again, light struck them. The cloth had been removed.

"Stay still." Miss Oliver's voice was so soft he could barely hear her.

She must have guessed how much his head ached. Had he struck it when he fell?

"Can you sit up, my lord?" He recognized that voice, as well. It belonged to his valet, Goodwin. The young man knelt beside him in the cart. When had Miss Oliver left? Time seemed to be jumping about like a frightened rabbit.

"Yes." Not needing his valet's help, Arthur sat. His head spun, and the pain swelled, but he was able to climb down on his own. His valet assisted him through the curious crowd gathered by the front door. Goodwin guided him to the small drawing room where he had talked to Carrie… Could it have been just yesterday afternoon?

Mr. Hockbridge was waiting. His hair was almost white, but the doctor was close to Arthur's age. He had a placid aura about him as he pointed to the settee. "Place him there."

Biting back a moan, Arthur lowered himself to the cushions. He was relieved the gawkers had not followed him into the drawing room. His sister stood near the door, her arms folded in front of her and that same worried look in her eyes.

"What happened?" the doctor asked.

"I fell," Arthur replied. Even those two words rang through his skull as if someone struck it with a sledgehammer. He put his hand to his brow and leaned his head against the settee.

The doctor sighed, then added, "You were with him?"

Arthur raised his head, astounded to see Miss Oliver beside his sister. She looked as uncomfortable as a kitten in a kennel.

She stepped into the room, holding her bonnet in front of her. "Yes, sir, I was with him."

"What happened?"

With quiet dignity, she explained what had taken place in the cove. He appreciated that she did not embellish the tale in any way. Yes, he had saved the little boy, but he felt more like a clumsy oaf than a hero.

"Thank you, Miss Oliver," the doctor said when she finished.

She curtsied gracefully and took her leave.

Arthur almost told his sister to call Miss Oliver back, but how could he explain such a request? He did not understand himself why having Miss Oliver near helped. Something about her kind smile offered him comfort, but he could not say how or why. Perhaps it was as simple a thing as when he thought about her, he was not worrying about how an injury would complicate his work as a courier.

Thoughts of the nurse vanished when the doctor ran his hands along Arthur's right leg. The pain was excruciating by his knee, and he could not silence his yelp when the doctor's fingers touched his ankle.

With a sigh, Hockbridge straightened. "There is no choice but to cut away the boot, my lord."

"Do what you must." His jaw worked as he surrendered himself to the doctor's ministrations, determined he would not allow pain to halt him from his duties. Too many depended on him, and he refused to let them down.

Maris opened a cupboard door and peered inside. It was empty. Where was Bertie? It was not like him to sneak away. When the children first arrived, they often had slipped out of the nursery to sleep in Lady Susanna's room. But it was not the middle of the night.

So where was the little boy?

She glanced at the other children, glad the baby was with Lady Caroline. If Maris asked Lulu and Molly and Gil, she might upset them further. They were on edge after what they had witnessed on the shore. Even Lulu, who usually was the leader in any mischief, was clingy and too quiet.

Bertie had been crying earlier about the loss of his little ship and the scratch he had on his left hand, his sole injury from when Lord Trelawney saved him. He had fallen asleep in a corner about a half hour ago.

Where was the little boy now?

While she searched the day nursery, Maris had sent a maid to do the same upstairs in the night nursery where the children slept. The maid had returned minutes ago without finding the missing child.

"Rachel," she said to the maid, who usually worked in the kitchen, "I need you to stay here with the children."

"Yes, Miss Oliver."

"Do not let them out of your sight."

"Yes, Miss Oliver."

"If I am not back before their tea arrives, pour their milk and make sure they eat their meat and cheese before any cakes."

"Yes, Miss Oliver." Rachel waved her hands toward the door. "Go. I raised five younger sisters and brothers. I can take care of these three."

Maris ran out of the nursery. She glanced in both directions along the upper hallway. The day's last sunshine poured along it, highlighting everything. Even a little boy could not hide there.

She recruited each servant she passed to help in her search. If the Trelawneys learned that Bertie was missing, she might be dismissed, but she could not worry about that. Not when Bertie had vanished.

Horrible thoughts filled her mind. What if the person who had set the children adrift had come to Cothaire and snatched Bertie? She could not imagine a reason why someone would do that, but she also could not guess why anyone had abandoned them in an unstable boat.

She faltered when she reached the wing where the family's private rooms were. She hesitated, not sure she should venture in that direction. But Bertie could be anywhere. If the family saw her, she would be honest about what she was doing there. However, she would rather not have them learn about Bertie's disappearance until he was safely in the nursery.

Even so, Maris tiptoed along the corridor, barely noticing the plaster friezes and the portraits on the light yellow walls that seemed to glow in the day's last light. Most of the doors were closed, and she would have to obtain permission from the butler to knock on them. She needed to find Baricoat straightaway, because she was wasting time wandering the hallways.

A faint click came from farther along the corridor. A door opening? A shadow shifted. A *short* shadow! Was that Bertie slipping into a room? If so, she must collect him before he could disrupt anyone in it.

She ran down the hallway to the door where the shadow had been. It was slightly ajar. She raised her hand to knock, then halted. If she startled Bertie and he was examining the possessions inside, something could get broken, and he could be hurt.

Slowly she edged the door back, holding her breath when the latch made that soft sound again. She expected a demand for her to explain why she was entering the room without announcing herself or to have Bertie run into her as he rushed out.

Neither happened.

She swung the door wider. Beyond it, a large room was draped in shadows. Furniture was arranged in front of an ornately carved hearth and near a window that rose almost fifteen feet to the coffered ceiling. No light but the fading sunshine challenged the shadows concealing the subjects of the paintings hanging in neat precision.

Scanning the room, she saw no one. Perhaps she had picked the wrong door, or her ears had misled her. She began to draw the door closed, then froze, her hand clasped over her mouth to halt her gasp.

Bertie!

The little boy was on the far side of the room next to a chair beside the window. And he was not alone. Lord Trelawney sat in the chair, his right foot propped on a low stool. A blanket over his lap hid any bandages Mr. Hockbridge might have used. His head tilted to one side, and she wondered if he was asleep.

Bertie poked Lord Trelawney's arm. "Are you really a bear?"

The viscount's head snapped up. When he shifted, he moaned.

The little boy jumped. "No eat Bertie, bear!"

Maris rushed forward and grabbed Bertie's hand. She kept her eyes averted as she said, "I am sorry he disturbed you, my lord. Bertie, we need to let Lord Trelawney rest."

"Is he a bear?" the little boy asked, planting his feet firmly against the floor. He looked at the viscount, then at her. "Is he really a bear?"

"Bertie—"

She was shocked when Lord Trelawney laughed and said, "The boy deserves an answer. Yes, Bertie, I am a bear."

"Oh!" His eyes nearly popped from his face as he scurried to hide behind her.

Maris tried to suppress her exasperation. How could the viscount say such a thing? Didn't he know how terrified the children had been…how terrified they still were after seeing him and Bertie fall on the rocks?

"Miss Oliver," the viscount said, "stop looking daggers at me and let me explain." He added to the little boy who pressed his face to her skirt, "Bertie, did you know my name is Arthur?"

Bertie shook his head, but did not look up.

"Arthur is my name, like Bertie is yours. Every name has a meaning, and Arthur comes from a very old word that means bear."

Maris said nothing as Bertie raised his head. He did not release her skirt.

"You are a bear!" With a cry, he hid his face again.

Kneeling beside the little boy, she put her hands on either side of his face and tipped it up so she could smile at him. "But Lord Trelawney is not the kind of bear who is dangerous to you. Remember? He kept you from tumbling into the water. He is the kind of bear who protects others."

"A good bear?"

She looked over Bertie's head to the viscount. His eyes were bright. Had Mr. Hockbridge prescribed laudanum to ease his pain? A dose of that might account for his prattling like a chatterbox.

"Yes," Maris answered. "He is a good bear, and good bears need to rest, as good boys do." Standing, she held out her hand. "We must let Lord Trelawney rest."

"Arthur," insisted the boy. "His name is Arthur."

"That is so." Lord Trelawney chuckled again. "Do you know how I know that Arthur means bear, Bertie?"

The little boy shook his head, his eyes focused on the viscount's face. "How?"

"Because a long, long, *long* time ago, there was a brave king." Lord Trelawney leaned his elbow on the chair's arm and slanted toward Bertie. "Maybe the bravest king who ever ruled our country, and he was called King Arthur because his name meant bear."

"King bear!" Bertie clapped his hands with glee.

The viscount nodded. "Exactly."

"What does my name mean?"

Lord Trelawney faltered, his eyes seeking Maris's. She knew he wanted her help, but what could she say? She had no idea what Bertie's real name might be. It could be Albert or Robert or Herbert or even Athelbert…or simply Bert. Or his real name might not be any of those. Even if she was sure of his name, she had no idea what its original meaning was.

The viscount continued to hold her gaze with his powerful one as he said, "It means friend of the bear."

Bertie clapped his hands again and danced around. When she saw Lord Trelawney wince, she groped for the little boy's hand. She caught it and drew him to her, unable to look away from the viscount. She should, because for once he wore his emotions openly, except for the places in his eyes that were as shadowed as the chamber where he sat. Secrets? About what? He was not hiding his worry and pain and sorrow and regret. She searched for happiness and found an iota when he smiled at Bertie's reaction to his answer.

Why was he sad? From what she had heard from the other servants, he happily served as his father's eyes and ears on the estate. The Trelawneys were a close and loving family. He was courting the woman named Gwendolyn. He should be joy-filled, but he was not.

And Maris found that sad.

She looked away, cutting the connection between them, which was growing too intimate. What might he have seen revealed on her face? That she was a liar because she had falsified a recommendation to get her position here? That she had been a fool to trust an un-principled young lord? That she had believed—quite wrongly—that her friends would defend her against that young lord, even though she was not part of the *ton*? That she was lonely after her parents died, and she would be again when the children were no longer a part of her life?

She would not share those secrets with anyone.

Keeping her eyes focused on the floor, she said, "If you will excuse us, my lord, I need to get Bertie to the nursery and let the others know that he has been found." She dipped in a curtsy and turned to lead the little boy out of the room.

"Wait…" Lord Trelawney's voice snapped like a riding crop against the high ceiling.

She stopped, her heart thudding against her breastbone. She faced him because it would be rude to look over her shoulder. "Yes, my lord?"

"Wait, Miss Oliver." This time, his voice was less sharp.

Though every instinct told her to run, she said, "Of course, my lord."

"Ouch!" Bertie chirped. "Don't squeeze my hand so hard. Ouch!"

She lessened her grip as the viscount's eyes narrowed before he looked to his right.

"Goodwin!" he shouted.

The short, muscular valet came through a door beside the fireplace. His hair was almost as dark as Lord Trelawney's, but his eyes were a common brown. When she had seen him in the corridors, he always had offered her a friendly—but not too friendly—smile and a kind word. He did not even glance in her direction as he spoke to the viscount.

"Do you need something, my lord? Another pillow, perhaps? Some of the liquid Mr. Hockbridge left for the pain?" His voice was a warm tenor, surprising in a man of his solid build. "I wish you would take at least a single dose. He said it would help you sleep."

Maris clamped her lips closed before she could reveal her astonishment. She had assumed Lord Trelawney was talking so much because he had taken laudanum. If that was not the cause, what was?

"Will you light some lamps?" the viscount asked. "It is getting dark in here." Humor laced through his words as he added, "Unless I am about to swoon again."

"I think not. Mr. Hockbridge says there is nothing more wrong with your head than usual."

Maris was further amazed when Lord Trelawney guffawed as his valet lit a lamp on either side of the viscount's chair. Goodwin had made a jest, a rather insulting jest, at the viscount's expense, and Lord Trelawney found it amusing. Was the stern, almost silent man different in the privacy of his own rooms? She had seen his sadness and regret, but what other aspects of himself had he kept hidden from her…and the rest of the world?

"Goodwin," the viscount continued, "Miss Oliver needs young Bertie returned to the nursery and the word to go out that he has been found none the worse for his adventures. Take the lad to the nursery and hand him over to…?"

"Rachel," Maris supplied.

"Yes, hand him over to Rachel and let her know that Miss Oliver will be returning shortly."

"Certainly, my lord. I will spread the word that Master Bertie is safe."

"Yes, thank you, Goodwin."

The valet bobbed his head, then crossed the room to where she stood with the child. He held out his hand.

Bertie stared at it, but did not move.

"Go with Goodwin, Bertie," she urged. "You heard Lord Trelawney ask him to take you to the nursery."

"Want you."

"I will be there soon, but you need to hurry, or the cakes for tea will be gone."

As she had guessed, the mention of sweets changed Bertie's mind. He placed his hand in Goodwin's and went toward the door. "Goodbye, Arthur," he called over his shoulder.

The valet exchanged a startled glance with Maris.

"Goodbye, Bertie," the viscount said.

When the door closed behind the servant and child, Maris clasped her hands in front of her. Her feet again urged her to flee, but she could not leave without being dismissed. She had no idea if anyone else was in the viscount's rooms or even nearby.

"Miss Oliver, would you mind sitting where I can see you without craning my neck?" Lord Trelawney asked.

Meekly, feeling like a lamb bound for slaughter, she walked toward where he sat. When she hesitated, he gestured at a chair to his left.

She sat on the edge, her shoes pressed against the floor. She was being silly. Lord Trelawney had never been anything but polite and respectful, even when he was in pain.

Shame flooded her. She had not asked what the extent of his injuries were, but she quickly rectified that.

"A strained knee and a twisted ankle," he said, leaning back in his chair. "Hockbridge told me to rest my leg today and to use the laudanum if I needed it to sleep tonight. In spite of Goodwin's nagging, the pain is tolerable. Tomorrow, the doctor wants me to walk around a bit, using a cane, and to increase the distance I walk each day after that. He tells me in a few days I will experience no more than some twinges."

"That is good to hear."

"Very good to hear. How are the children?"

"At the moment, they are subdued, but I am sure that by the morrow they will return to their normal selves. From what your sisters have told me, after they were rescued, they recovered swiftly, save for a few nightmares. Those nightmares may have nothing to do with what happened to them. Maybe normal childhood fears of the dark and big animals."

"Like bears?"

"Yes. Thank you for your kindness to Bertie."

"He is a fine lad."

"When he is not being a naughty one."

The viscount chuckled again. "I saw your face when I admitted to being a bear. I want to assure you that I had no intention of scaring the boy. Not again, at any rate."

Her face heated, and she wondered if she was blushing again. "I should have known that, my lord."

"Why? You don't know me well enough to guess beforehand how I might act." He did not pause as he said, "Do me a favor, and do not chastise Bertie for calling me Arthur. I would prefer that he do so with a smile than cower away from me as he did before."

She rubbed her hands together on her lap and stared at them. "I must warn you that when one of the children takes on a bad habit, they all seem to latch on to it quickly."

"That is fine. As my goal is to get to know the children better, anything I can do to make them more comfortable with me is a step in the right direction. But you know them better than I. Would you agree with that opinion?"

"Yes," she answered without looking up.

"Good. And now, Miss Oliver…"

He added nothing more, and she waited and waited. As one minute, then another, then a third passed, she wondered if she should excuse herself. Maybe he had fallen asleep. She raised her eyes.

Her breath caught as her gaze met and was held by his. He leaned forward and folded one of her hands between both of his. She stiffened, knowing how alone they were, but he made no further move toward her as he held her hands as gently as she would the children's.

"Miss Oliver, if you do not look at me, I doubt the children will, either. They take their clues from you."

"I am sorry. I did not mean to—"

"There is no need for an apology. I would rather speak of our next outing with the children."

"Next?"

"As I told you, I have not given up on the idea of getting to know them. My sister has encouraged me to do so, and I learned as a child myself that doing as my sisters wish often makes my life easier." He smiled.

Maris did, too. There was something so honest and earnest about his grin that she could not help responding. She wanted to ask why he hid behind his arrogant mask. She bit back the words, telling herself to be grateful that he was willing to speak more than a handful of words to her.

Instead, she asked, "When do you think you will feel well enough to spend time with the children again?"

"Is tomorrow possible?"

"But Mr. Hockbridge said—"

"I will not be running about with them. Rather, I thought you might bring them to the garden. They could play for a while, and then we can take a light tea together. That way, they will become accustomed to me."

"If you are certain…"

"I am." He released her hand as he covered his mouth to hide a yawn. "In the meantime, I shall make sure I am prepared." He did not give her a chance to ask the obvious question before he said, "Now that Bertie believes he knows the meaning of his name, I am sure the others will wish to know theirs. If you would tell me more about them, I will devise something for each of them."

Something softened inside Maris at his thoughtfulness. As she began to share stories about the children, she slowly sat back when he did. She could not recall the last time she had spoken easily with anyone. A part of her mind stayed on alert, but she focused on coming up with the perfect stories to describe each child.

She watched Lord Trelawney's eyelids grow heavier. Yet he was listening closely, because he chuckled over some of the youngsters' more mischievous antics. She kept talking until Goodwin returned. A single glance from him told her that Lord Trelawney's valet believed it was time for the viscount to rest, as the doctor had ordered.

She stood, asking the viscount to excuse her to return to her duties. Lord Trelawney caught her hand as she walked past his chair. When she looked down into his ice-blue eyes, that sweet warmth glided through her anew.

"Thank you, Miss Oliver," he said, trying to fight his obvious exhaustion. "I appreciate you telling me about your charges. Please bring them to the garden an hour or so before tea tomorrow afternoon."

"Of course, my lord." She drew her fingers away from his, her skin aquiver where his had touched it. "I know the children will be eager to race about after being inside this afternoon."

"Good."

It took every bit of Maris's will for her to tear her gaze from his and walk toward the door. As she passed Goodwin, he gave her a silent nod. He opened the door so she could leave. She was glad he did, because her fingers trembled, and she was not sure she could have managed the latch.

She rushed toward the stairs leading up to the nursery floor. Tonight, the children needed to rest after their eventful day. But in the morning, once they finished breakfast and were clean and dressed, she would let them know about the outing with Lord Trelawney. They would be excited to have their tea al fresco. While they played, she would sit with the viscount for what she hoped would be another comfortable coze.

She halted in the middle of the staircase and clutched the banister. Oh, sweet heavens! Was she looking forward to seeing Lord Trelawney again on the morrow? She had no idea which version of him would be there: the quiet, almost forbidding man who had gone with them to the cove or the genial man whom she had spoken with minutes ago.

But it should not matter. The abrupt change should be alarming rather than appealing, a signal to remind her that becoming involved even a tiny bit in the viscount's life could lead her into a desperate situation. As when Lord Litchfield had chanced upon her alone in the book room. Had she completely lost every bit of her good sense? It would seem so, and she must recover it fast.

Very fast, before she ruined everything again, including herself.

Chapter Four

Though clouds gathered on the western horizon, sunlight shone through the changing leaves as if the whole world was bedecked in stained glass. Arthur inhaled deeply as he sat on the terrace overlooking the garden and the sea spread out to the horizon. Some autumn days could be unforgivingly windy, and today seemed like a special gift, before winter took Cornwall in its unforgiving grip.

He savored sitting in the sunshine while a breeze carried the pungent aromas of salt, drying fish and tar from the harbor. Even though he had been confined to the house less than a day, it seemed longer to a man accustomed to a life outdoors.

The rhythm of hammers came from where the stable was being rebuilt. It had burned two months ago, but the new one was rising. He had overseen the plans for it, and the building would be well suited for their use.

"You look satisfied with yourself," said his older sister as she stepped onto the terrace. Carrie shifted into the shade so the baby she carried would not be bothered by the sunshine.

He started to rise, then thought better of it when pain slashed up his leg. Sinking into the chair, he said, "I was thinking of how those French pirates who tried to invade Porthlowen did us a favor by giving us an excuse to build a new stable."

Carrie shivered and sat facing him. "You have an odd way of seeing good in something terrible."

"As Shakespeare wrote, 'Ill blows the wind that profits nobody.'" Arthur chuckled. "My tutor despaired of me ever retaining his lessons, but for some reason that quote stayed with me."

She slapped his arm playfully. "Do not pretend with me, Arthur. You always loved learning. While Raymond, Susanna and I were eager to play, you clung to the schoolroom. The dutiful son, learning his lessons and staying out of trouble."

"Sometimes." Again, the image burst into his head of his baby sister lying facedown in the water. "When I was younger, I was not as responsible."

"None of us were." She gazed out at the sea. "How could we spend our time in books when we had a vast wonderland to explore in Porthlowen?"

They sat in companionable silence, enjoying the sunshine. He kept his leg motionless, not wanting more of the jagged pains that sliced up from his ankle when he walked. He had refused to allow Goodwin to call for a couple of burly footmen to carry him from his bedchamber through the house. Being toted about like a helpless fool would be humiliating. Perhaps he had been foolish to give chase after the child instead of allowing Miss Oliver to retrieve him, but Arthur would not hesitate to do the same again.

You have the heart of a hero. Cranny's words echoed

in his memory. *Always ready to go to someone's rescue, no matter the cost.*

At the time, Arthur had taken the words as a compliment. Now he was less certain his friend had intended them that way. Of course, Arthur would never be the great man that his friend was, giving his life in service to his country.

His hands fisted on the arms of his chair. His attempts to find out the truth about Cranny's murder had led him to dead ends. The people present at his friend's death had gone to earth and taken the truth with them.

"How are you getting along with the children?" Carrie's voice intruded on his thoughts.

He pushed them aside gratefully. Until he had a new lead, losing himself in his frustration was a useless exercise. He pasted a smile on and faced her. "I seem to have made a friend of young Bertie."

"I am glad to hear that." She laughed. "They will be arriving soon, I am sure."

"Who?"

"The children." She dimpled as she laughed again. "Oh, Arthur, you are transparent at times. You have been glancing at the door every few seconds. Each time you do and no one is there, your disappointment is all over your face."

Had he been eyeing the door that frequently? He had not been aware of that, though he was eager to see the children again.

And Miss Oliver.

He ignored that unsettling thought as he had others. It would be easier if the mention of her name, even in his mind, did not bring forth the image of her gentle smile and her bright green eyes. Though she kept her blond hair pulled back, the wisps about her face looked like spun sugar, soft and teasing his fingers to brush them aside.

"You seem to have taken to the children," Carrie said, serious once again, "with an alacrity I did not expect. Perhaps I was mistaken in thinking you had no real motivation for getting to know them. I assumed, after she married, your affection for Gwendolyn had cooled."

"I have always considered her a dear friend."

"I do hope you did not present your proposal to her in that letter you sent off to her this morning."

He wagged a finger at his sister. "I listened to *all* your advice, Carrie."

"Good, because I would not wish you to make a muddle of this before it even begins."

He chuckled, and he saw her surprise. Had she thought he would be so burdened with pain he would be dreary company? No, he realized with astonishment. His sister did not expect to hear merriment coming from him because he had laughed seldom since the news of Cranny's death reached Porthlowen.

As the months passed, his plans to avenge his friend consumed him. He tried to heed his brother's counsel to accept the words in Romans 12:19. Raymond had even written out the passage on a page Arthur had tossed atop his desk: *Dearly beloved, avenge not yourselves, but rather give place unto wrath: for it is written, Vengeance is mine; I will repay, sayeth the Lord.*

It was impossible to forget Gwendolyn's face lined with pain and sorrow as she had stood by Cranny's grave. If there was any way Arthur could help God in this matter, he must.

Footsteps sounded inside the house, and he sat straighter. He watched the door, wondering which youngster would run out first.

Two white-haired women emerged. The Winwood twins lived in a simple cottage close to the harbor. They were the eldest residents of Porthlowen, but as spry as people half their age. Neither had ever married, because they had cared for their parents until the twins were deemed long past marriageable age. Whether that determination was made by the bachelors and widowers of Porthlowen, or the Winwoods had made that decision, the two women seemed happy.

They had identical straight noses and full lips. The only way to tell the two apart was that Miss Hyacinth Winwood always wore a feather or a bit of lace in the same light purple shade as her name. Miss Ivy Winwood never was seen unless she had something dark green with her.

They smiled broadly as they walked to where Arthur was pushing himself to his feet. He hid his grimace at the pain.

"Good afternoon, ladies," he said as Carrie signaled to a footman to bring two more chairs.

"For you, my lord," said Miss Hyacinth, the older of the sisters by what was reported to be ten minutes.

Miss Ivy held out the plate topped by a pile of sugary treats. "You have always been partial to our almond macaroons."

He took one, knowing she would not move the plate until he did. Everyone in Porthlowen was aware of how kind the twin sisters were and how stubborn.

"It is the least we could do for a man who risked himself to save a dear little boy," Miss Hyacinth said.

"Such a brave and noble act." Miss Ivy refused to let her sister have the last word on any topic.

"Do sit," he said, motioning toward the chairs.

"We will," Miss Hyacinth replied, "so you will do the same and rest your injured leg."

"And you must not come to your feet when we leave." Miss Ivy gave him a look that could have halted a charging bull.

Arthur nodded and wondered if the tales he had heard were true. It was whispered in the village that, when the French pirates had tried to break into the Winwood cottage, they were met with cast-iron pans and brooms. Though he doubted the truth of the tale, for his family had learned firsthand how vicious the pirates were, he also knew no damage had been done to the women's home.

Miss Hyacinth was not satisfied. "Promise us that you will set your always gracious manners aside this once."

"You must promise us."

"I promise you, ladies," he said.

"Excellent."

"Most excellent."

Arthur resisted the yearning to shake his head. Listening to the sisters was like watching a game of battledore and shuttlecock, back and forth the words went. Always quick, always insightful. Or so Carrie assured him. He found the two women amusing in their eccentric ways, though no one could question the warmth of their generous hearts.

He ate the macaroon and listened to Carrie talk with them. The confection was delicious, and he reached for a second one, which set off another round of comments about how nice it was to see a man enjoy sweets as he did.

The elderly twins paused when childish shouts came from past the far edge of the terrace. The youngsters came bouncing around the corner. Toby, who lived at the parsonage, was among them. He and Bertie were shoving each other playfully as they chased the other children. Giggles and shouts of excitement rose in the afternoon air.

"Oh, there are the dear babes," Miss Hyacinth said, jumping to her feet.

"Aren't they adorable?" Miss Ivy added.

"Utterly adorable."

"Utterly."

Arthur guessed they could go on and on forever without a break, but his ears could use a respite. Hoping they did not consider him rude, he called out, "Miss Oliver, we are over here." He could not see her around the corner of the terrace; yet he had no doubt she was nearby. She seldom allowed the children out of her sight.

As if on cue, she ran into the clump of youngsters. She picked up Gil and swung him around. The moment she set him on the ground, little arms reached up as each child begged for a turn.

She must not have been aware of the group gathered on the terrace, because she laughed, sounding as young and carefree as her charges. Arthur was unable to pull his gaze from her. He watched how the sun glinted off the golden strands peeking from beneath her sedate bonnet. A smile lit her face even more brightly while her simple gown swirled about her ankles. She enjoyed the children's exhilaration as much as they did.

"When were you last that untroubled?" asked Carrie softly.

He discovered his sister's steady gaze focused on him. "I don't know."

"I thought so. A good father needs to find time with his children."

"I know." He noted the high spirits Miss Oliver evoked in the children and recalled how his own father had played games with his children.

Knowing what he did now, he was astonished that Father could have carved out the hour or two he spent with each of his children every week. Those hours were among Arthur's most precious memories. He had forgotten in the midst of his duties, especially in the past year. Until this moment, he had not guessed what his search for the truth was costing him.

"There is more to that young woman than meets the eye," Miss Ivy pronounced.

Miss Hyacinth gawked at her twin, then, recovering herself, nodded.

Arthur hid his amusement at the older sister's reaction to her twin speaking first. Miss Ivy usually joined a conversation after she did. Miss Hyacinth acted a bit perturbed at her sister altering the pattern.

Gil abruptly shouted, "My baby!" He ran toward the terrace.

Miss Oliver glanced over her shoulder, and color rose on her cheeks, tinting them a pale rose. Her gaze met Arthur's before she lowered her eyes. She did not look in his direction as she herded the children after Gil. The little boy rushed to stand beside Carrie and gently caressed the baby's blanket.

"Good afternoon." Miss Oliver's precise, proper tone

belied the high spirits she had revealed with the children. "I hope our play did not disturb your conversation."

"Not at all," he assured her.

"Miss Oliver, you are such a good nurse for these waifs," Miss Hyacinth said with a broad smile.

"A very good nurse." Miss Ivy's smile was even wider than her sister's.

"Thank you." Miss Oliver seemed unduly interested in the stones of the terrace.

Bertie was not circumspect. He wrapped one arm around Arthur's and said, "Arthur, tell Lulu about her name."

What had he and Miss Oliver decided to tell the children? He could not recall. Not when thoughts of everything but the pretty nurse had vanished from his mind.

"Patience, Bertie." Miss Oliver put her hands on the little boy's shoulders and said, "Children, please greet Lord Trelawney, Lady Caroline, Miss Winwood and Miss Winwood."

The children complied, astounding Arthur. He smiled when Bertie called him by his given name rather than his title, but replied by asking if they were ready for their tea. That brought excited chatter.

As two benches were brought for the children, Gil pointed to the Winwood twins and giggled. "Boat!"

"Excuse me?" asked Miss Hyacinth, her eyes narrowing.

Before her sister could say anything, Miss Oliver answered, "The children sailed their little ships yesterday. It was an exciting day for everyone."

"So we heard," Miss Hyacinth murmured.

"So we heard," echoed Miss Ivy.

Arthur was surprised when the two spinsters rose.

He started to set himself on his feet, but paused when he recalled his promise to remain sitting as they took their departure.

"Thank you for the macaroons," he said as the sisters excused themselves. "That was kind of you."

"Our pleasure," Miss Hyacinth said.

"Yes, our pleasure." With a pat on each child's head, Miss Ivy followed her sister into the house.

A hearty tea was served under Baricoat's watchful eye. The butler checked that there were enough plates and cups and saucers as the footmen carried the trays to the low table set in front of the children. A taller one was brought for the adults.

Arthur seated his sister where she could manage both eating and holding the baby. He recalled a small wagon his mother had used after his younger sister was born. It could be wheeled anywhere, indoors and out. He wondered if it still was stored in the attic and was usable.

He leaned on his chair as he waited while Miss Oliver made sure each of the toddlers had food. For once, the youngsters wore serious expressions as they watched her spoon out vegetables and fruit before she set small sandwiches in front of them. He was impressed when the children sat quietly while Miss Oliver said a quick prayer. As soon as she finished, they reached for their plates.

Miss Oliver's eyes widened when he gestured for her to join him and Carrie. Her hesitation before she accepted was so slight he doubted he would have noticed if he had not been watching closely. Why was she acting as skittish as a lamb when the wolf was nigh?

He could not ask that question, so he sat gratefully when she did. Carrie began talking to Miss Oliver about the baby. Maybe he had been imagining the nurse's hesitation.

As Arthur served himself some of Mrs. Ford's fish pie, Bertie's voice rose above others. "Arthur is really a bear, you know."

When Carrie chuckled, the little boy looked discomposed.

"Bertie is right," Arthur said. "We talked about it yesterday after we returned from the shore."

Miss Oliver leaned forward and whispered into his sister's ear. An odd sensation, a feeling he could not name, gripped him. It was far too easy to imagine the pretty blonde's breath soft and fragrant while she whispered in his ear.

He took a cup of tea from his sister. He needed to curb his imagination and remember that Miss Oliver was helping him prepare for marriage to Gwendolyn. Nothing more. He had promised to offer for his friend's widow, and he would not let his words become a lie.

After wiping up the pool of milk from the children's table, Maris wrung the cloth out over the grass. Lady Caroline had retired to the house for Joy's afternoon nap. The baby was fussier today than usual, and Maris would not be surprised to feel the hard nub of a tooth beneath Joy's gums.

Lord Trelawney remained at the tea table. The children chased each other across the grass and beneath the branches of fruit trees in the orchard beyond the garden.

"No farther!" she called to the youngsters. "Stay where you can see us."

"I am keeping a close eye on them," the viscount said. "You must not allow them to set the boundaries, my lord." She finished cleaning up the milk and laid the cloth on top of the low table. Straightening, she wiped her hands on her apron. "Children must know and accept the rules established by their elders."

He bowed his head toward her. "I leave such issues in your capable hands, Miss Oliver."

"Most parents use their own parents' ways to guide them." Sitting where she could watch the children, she added, "We learn by example, whether from a book or from life."

"You must have given this much thought before you decided on becoming a nurse."

"I have learned from the children." She did not want to speak untruths, so she chose her words with care. "Every child is unique."

"So I have seen."

"Tomorrow we plan to have an outing along the cove. Would you like to join us?" Realizing how bold she was to ask such a question, she continued, "Of course, you may have other obligations. I wanted to let you know in case you wished to come." She was babbling, but she could not halt herself. "The children seem more comfortable in your company each time they see you."

"Do you think Bertie believes I am truly a bear?"

"I have discovered children's imaginations are wondrous and boundless." She smiled, glad he had not chided her for the unseemly invitation. "And I have no idea what goes on in their little heads, though I try to watch for signs of mischief brewing."

"Maris!" Molly's shriek rang across the garden.

Jumping to her feet, Maris hurried to where the little girl ran toward them, tears streaming down her face. "Are you hurt?"

"Not me. Gil."

"Has he fallen down?"

"No. He up. No down. Up."

Puzzled, Maris saw the other children waving frantically from the orchard. She gasped when she saw Gil high in a fruit tree, holding on to the trunk.

She ran to the orchard, pushing aside low branches to reach the tree. Gil was perched too high for her to grasp him. "Can you climb down a bit? Then I can get you."

"No!" Gil shook his head, then wrapped both arms around the narrow trunk.

"Let me." Lord Trelawney appeared at her elbow.

She stepped back gratefully while he reached for the child. Looking down, she asked, "Why is he up in the tree?"

"I told Bertie to go," Toby said, glowering at the other boy. "He was too afraid."

"I told Toby to go. He was too scared." Admiration slipped into Bertie's voice. "Gil went."

She took both boys by the hands and drew them away from the tree so Lord Trelawney could get closer. Their explanations told her everything she needed to know. The bigger boys had dared each other to climb the tree. When neither of them did, Gil had had to prove he was as big and brave as they were.

Her relief disappeared when she realized Gil was too high up in the tree for the viscount to pluck him down, even when Lord Trelawney stood on his toes. When he dropped to his heels, he winced and rubbed his injured knee.

"Move the children farther away," he ordered, "in case a branch breaks while I climb up to the boy."

"You cannot climb a tree with your damaged knee.

Keep an eye on him while I get someone from the house." She turned to run inside, but halted when Lord Trelawney snapped her name in a tone she had never heard him use. His voice crackled like summer lightning, astounding her.

Looking over her shoulder, she gasped. Gil was crying and stretching out his hand toward her.

"Don't move!" she shouted.

"Want Maris," he cried.

She ran to the tree. "I am here, Gil. Hold on to the tree. Hold tight." Without taking her gaze from Gil as he followed her orders, she went on, "Bertie, go into the house and bring a footman. Fast!"

"I go," Toby offered.

"Bertie knows the house better than you do, and I will need you for other things." She added the last when she saw the superior look on Bertie's face. The boys were too competitive. "Go, Bertie! Quickly!"

The little boy ran toward the house as fast as his short legs could go.

A hand on her shoulder sent a warm tingle along her arm even before she realized it belonged to Lord Trelawney. She tried to smother her reaction. This was the worst time to allow his touch to thrill her.

"It will be fine," he said, standing so close his words caressed her neck along her bonnet ribbons. "Bertie will find someone quickly."

But he did not. Minutes passed, and the little boy did not return. Lord Trelawney murmured a prayer. Maris wished she could do the same, but she had to hope God would listen to the viscount's petition as He had not to hers. No one came out of the house, and a cool wind rose off the sea. It shook the branches, and Gil began to sob.

They had to do something before the child was knocked out of the tree. But what?

As if she had asked that aloud, Lord Trelawney said, "Miss Oliver, I can think of one solution."

She glanced at him before looking to make sure Gil had not moved. "What is it?"

"Climb onto my uninjured knee, and I will boost you up enough to reach him."

"That is madness!" She stared at him, shocked. "You could be hurt worse."

"Maybe, but not as badly as Gil will if he tumbles out of the tree while we argue about what to do."

Gil cried out her name again.

"I will be right there," she assured him. A motion caught her eye, and she turned to see Bertie coming toward them.

Alone.

"No footman to help!" he shouted. "Only maid."

Maris sighed. The children took everything literally. She should have said he needed to alert the first person he saw.

No time to think of that.

Turning to the viscount, she said, "Your suggestion is our best choice. However, you must promise you will do nothing to exacerbate your injury."

"I cannot promise when a little boy is in danger." His mouth was a straight line. "Do not ask that of me, Miss Oliver."

She wanted to lose herself in his incomparable eyes, but looked away while she could. "I am sorry, my lord. That was wrong of me."

"No, never apologize for your caring heart, which is a precious gift from God."

Unsure how to respond, because she could not tell him how she had given up on God helping her, she asked, "Shall we get started before the wind strengthens more?"

He nodded.

Again she warned the children to stay back. She did not want to topple over on them. They stepped away, their gazes glued to her. She saw fear and hope on their faces.

"Whenever you are ready, my lord," she said.

He went down to one knee beneath the tree. His face became a sickly shade of gray beneath its bronzing, and he grasped on to the trunk of a nearby tree to steady himself.

"Hurry," he ordered through gritted teeth.

She put her left foot on his light brown breeches and pushed herself up. His broad hands gripped her waist, holding her steady. They were strong and gentle at the same time.

Ignoring how his touch threatened to turn her knees to jam, she reached into the tree. Gil was a little above her, but close enough that she was able to convince him to drop into her arms. She wobbled as he fell forward against her chest, but Lord Trelawney's hold kept her from tumbling backward.

Maris stepped off the viscount's leg and heard a strangled moan. Even though she had tried not to cause him more pain, she had. Gil wept in her arms, so she held on to him while Lord Trelawney came slowly to his feet.

"I am sorry," she began.

"Say nothing of it," he ordered. "Both of us did what we had to."

She lost herself in his gaze, this time past the point of being able to look away. She wondered if Lord Trelawney could guess how much she needed his steadying now. As dappled light fell through the bare branches and across his face, she tried to pull her gaze away. She could not.

Worried voices came from the direction of the house, and he stepped past her. She released her breath in a whoosh. How long had she been holding it? She saw the children regarding her with uncertainty. Carrying Gil, she led them to the house. She did not look at the viscount as she passed where he was asking two footmen to have the lowest branches on the fruit trees pruned to prevent the children from climbing them.

If she locked gazes with him again, she would not be able to look away. She must remember he was going to marry another woman, a woman of his class, a woman who had not inveigled her way into his life with lies.

Chapter Five

Lord Trelawney must think she was a brazen hoyden.

Maris brushed her hair into a bun, but could not meet her own eyes in the glass on the wall. How could she have asked the viscount to join her and the children today? He had spent the past two days with them. His other duties usually kept him so busy he barely had time to spend with his family. Surely some of those obligations required his attention.

In addition, he was in pain. Rescuing Gil yesterday had done him no good. He had leaned heavily on the footmen as he returned to the house. The housekeeper, Mrs. Hitchens, had assured her that he had joined his family for supper without assistance, which had made Maris feel slightly less guilty.

She raised her eyes to her reflection, which was dim in the gray light before dawn. Guilt seemed to be printed on her face in glowing letters. Every day, she regretted lying to obtain her position in the household.

O send out Thy light and Thy truth: let them lead me; let them bring me unto Thy holy hill. The verse from Psalm 43 had been one of her parson's favorites when she was a child, and Mr. Nash had used it often in his sermons. A twinge of longing flickered through her, a longing for the simple faith she once possessed. That faith had been found wanting the night Lord Litchfield tried to force himself on her.

"Why did You leave me alone at my darkest hour?" she whispered.

She might as well ask herself why she expected an answer from God when He had other more important matters to consider than her problems. But she missed the connection with Him that she had once believed would never break.

Checking that she had made her bed properly—for how could she insist the children try when she left hers mussed?—she walked around the simple iron footboard, then lowered the small window. Even though it was sunny, the weather was always changeable along Cornwall's north coast. If the rain held off, she would reopen the window after the outing, so the cramped room with its slanted ceiling could fill with fresh air.

Her room in her parents' house had been larger. Even the antechamber where she had slept while staying with Belinda at Bellemore Court was bigger, but Maris would not trade either of those rooms for this one under the eaves. The room was hers alone, save for when one of the children needed comforting after a nightmare. Most important, she felt safe in it.

The early morning quiet was splintered the moment the children awoke. During her time at Cothaire, Maris had created a schedule that worked for her and the children, as well as Lady Caroline, who arrived after breakfast to collect Joy. Gil went with her some days. The other children showed no envy of the earl's daughter spending extra time with the two youngest ones. They were happy at the great house. Maris hoped they would be as content when they returned to their rightful families.

More than once during the morning, she considered sending a message to Lord Trelawney, letting him know she was canceling the outing. It was the coward's way out, but wondering what he thought of her unsettled her far more than it should. As she was collecting the children's toys before the midday meal, she thought— *again*, as she had during the night when sleep eluded her—of how the viscount's hands had felt so perfect at her waist while he had helped her rescue Gil.

Maris was settling the children at their small table, each drinking out his or her favorite nursery rhyme cup, when she heard someone approaching. She looked up, expecting a maid or footman. Instead, Cothaire's cook came into the nursery.

"Mrs. Ford! What are you doing here?" She pressed her hand over the bib of her apron. "Oh, dear, that came out completely wrong."

"No need to apologize, my dear girl. I wanted to bring these treats to the children, both here and in Lady Caroline's rooms, myself." The cook smiled before setting a tray with small cakes on the table. "A visit to the nursery is long overdue. I have never spent any time with the children here."

"You have a good excuse with your many duties in the kitchen."

"We all have our tasks to complete. May I?" Mrs. Ford gestured toward the window bench.

"Please sit. I should have suggested that immediately."

"My dear Miss Oliver, calm yourself." The cook sat on the cushioned bench and sighed. "Ah, it is always a pleasure to be off my feet."

Maris let the tension slide from her shoulders and sat beside Mrs. Ford. "I understand."

"I am sure these youngsters keep you busy, but it is a good thing you are doing, Miss Oliver. Helping Lord Trelawney become acquainted with them. He has spent his whole life taking care of Cothaire. For him to have an opportunity to enjoy the children's company is a wondrous gift, and I hope it will help him win Lady Gwendolyn's hand."

"You seem to approve of the match."

"If the earl thinks it is for the best, then so do I." The cook smiled. "When the earl was a young boy here, I was a girl working in the scullery. I have watched him grow and have a family. Never once have I seen him make a hasty decision. He cares deeply about his children and for his estate." She dabbed her finger at a spot of icing on her apron. "As for Lady Gwendolyn, I have not seen her in five years. The last time she called at Cothaire was shortly before she married Mr. Cranford. I made my seed cake for her. From the time she was no older than these youngsters, she was fond of it, especially if I mixed ginger into the batter. Even then, there was talk of a match between her and Lord Trelawney."

"The family must be fond of Lady Gwendolyn," Maris said, unsure how else to answer.

"Yes. The families visited each other often before Lady Launceston died. After her death, our family withdrew from Society." Mrs. Ford looked down at her folded hands. "It was during that time that Lady Gwendolyn was courted by Mr. Cranford. Before then, Lord

Trelawney was her escort to gatherings here in the West Country. A young woman can grow impatient, especially when she wants to attend a ball or a different sort of assembly." She looked up, worried lines threading her brow. "I am not saying her affections were inconstant, but a young woman must consider her future and her family's future." She was about to add more when Gil walked over to them.

He carefully cradled one of the cakes in both hands. Crumbs trailed after him as he crossed the rug. With a big grin, he held it out to Mrs. Ford.

"How kind of you, Master Gil," she said as she took the cake.

He grinned as he licked frosting from his fingertips. "Yummy!"

"I shall let Irene know. She made that icing."

"Make more. Yummy."

The cook looked at Maris and raised her brows. "He speaks clearly for such a young child. Is he two?"

"Somewhere between two and three is my estimation." She kept her smile in place so she would not upset the little boy. As soon as he went to the table, she sighed. "If one of their families could be found, we might learn more. As it is…" She shrugged.

"The poor dears! Set adrift in a sea of strangers. Oh, I should go before I get more maudlin. It makes me angry to know their futures are uncertain." Mrs. Ford stood and lifted the cake in her hands. With a chuckle, she said, "Thank you for your time, Miss Oliver. If I might, I would like to return occasionally to visit the children."

"You are always welcome."

The youngsters called their farewells as the cook went down the back stairs. In her wake, Maris was left with plenty to think about, but she kept coming back to the same question that had echoed through her mind during the past few days.

If Lord Trelawney cared so deeply for Lady Gwendolyn, why did he gaze at Maris with such warmth in his eyes?

Reaching for his hat, Arthur asked himself why he was bothering to bring it. If Miss Oliver did, indeed, intend to take the children up onto the hill overlooking the cove, the wind was sure to send it flying. He could hardly give chase when his knee and ankle were so stiff.

When he arose this morning, he had been relieved to discover most of his pain was gone. As Mr. Hockbridge had assured him, a short rest and then exercising his leg gently had helped. Arthur doubted, however, the doctor would consider letting Miss Oliver perch on his leg to get Gil out of the tree as gentle usage.

He paused, his hand hovering above his hat, as the memory of her slender waist between his hands and that luscious scent of jasmine filled his senses again. The simple ruffle on her gown's hem had brushed his cheek while her lyrical voice bade Gil to slide into her arms. Oh, how Arthur wished he could have been the one she asked that of!

He shook his head. Had he lost the good sense God had given him? He should not be thinking about her. He had promised to offer marriage to Gwendolyn, and his thoughts should be on her. And he needed to focus on the pressing matter of the odd letter she had sent. He would send another note in the morning, asking for her help in deciphering the strange code he could not break. Too many questions plagued him.

Was something wrong with her?

Had someone discovered her activities and intercepted the original message, sending another filled with gibberish to him?

Had someone discovered *his* activities, so she had written a worthless note to confuse the interloper?

And those questions were just the beginning of the long list he had.

No doubt his valet thought Arthur was losing his mind. After asking Goodwin at least a half dozen times if anything had been delivered for him, Arthur realized he was drawing unnecessary attention to his eagerness. The household knew of his correspondence with Gwendolyn. He could pretend he was eager for her next profession of love, but to do so meant lying. He would not do that.

For the past year, he had walked a fine line between his secret life as a courier and being the dutiful son of the Earl of Launceston. He had learned to answer questions in a way that did not require him to lie, though he seldom could reveal what he did while away from the house.

Lord, I trust You will help me find the right words to fulfill my vow to take over Cranny's obligations and protect my family from what could be dire consequences if the truth emerged. You have guided me on this journey for the past year. I pray You bring the war with Napoleon to a satisfactory ending that will allow me to set aside my duties as a courier.

Picking up his hat, Arthur tapped it into place and left his rooms. Sunshine flowed through the windows, making the corridor unexpectedly warm for an autumn afternoon. Glancing outside, he saw small whitecaps on the waves beyond the sheltered cove. That, as much as the tree branches swaying, told him there was a breeze. A windy day might be too dangerous to take little children along the hills edging the harbor, but the day looked perfect for a stroll through the remnants of the summer grass with Miss Oliver.

A door opened almost in Arthur's face, and he jumped aside. Carrie looked out and hastily apologized.

"No need," he said with a smile, as he glanced down at the baby she held. By her side, Gil clutched tightly onto her skirt. "After a lifetime in this house, I should know better than to walk close to the doors on this corridor." He did not want to admit he had been lost in a sweet fantasy of Miss Oliver. Without the distraction of the children.

Carrie asked, "Going out again with our young friends?"

"Yes." He was glad his sister had no inkling what he was thinking. "Miss Oliver thought taking them for a walk along the headland would be a good outing."

"You should heed her. She knows a lot about children." Carrie's smile wobbled as her gaze grew distant. "And on many other topics, as well."

"Such as?"

His sister blinked before asking, "Such as what?"

"You mentioned Miss Oliver is an expert on subjects other than children."

"She may be, but I cannot tell you a specific one." Carrie shifted the baby, who had begun to whimper. "But she is a patient listener when I ask her the same questions time and again."

"Most likely she is accustomed to doing so for the children."

Laughing, she said, "I never thought of that." The baby began crying. "Excuse us, Arthur. We were on the way to the kitchen for a feeding, and I have learned if I delay getting Joy to the wet nurse, my ears will suffer."

"Then by all means, do not let me keep you." He swept his arm in a courtly bow as he stepped out of her way. "Gil, would you like to come with me and Miss Oliver and the other children?"

"Who?"

"Maris, sweetheart," Carrie said. Over his head, she added, "He doesn't recognize her surname."

Arthur nodded, realizing he had never heard the children address her as anything but Maris. How different from the stern woman who had presided over the nursery when they were young! She was Nurse Broderick, a mouthful for a child to pronounce, so they had usually avoided using her name.

"Would you like to come with me and Maris?" Arthur smiled as he spoke her name casually.

"My baby," Gil replied, grabbing Carrie's skirt with his other hand.

"He wants to stay with Joy," she said.

"I understood." Anything else he might have added went unsaid when the baby let out a piercing cry, echoed by Gil.

Carrie calmed the little boy and tried to do the same with Joy. She hurried away at the best pace Gil's legs could manage.

Arthur followed, but went in the opposite direction when the hallway branched. He paused when he saw a footman going about his duties.

"Venton," he called.

"Yes, my lord?"

He asked the footman to explore the attics and search for the baby wagon. If Venton found it, he should send it to one of the carpenters working on the stable. Once it was checked for stability and repaired, it should be painted before Carrie was informed it was available for her use.

After Venton assured him he would make his best effort, Arthur went downstairs. He heard the children's eager voices before he saw them gathered at one side of the great staircase. The twins wore bright red coats he remembered Susanna wearing. Bertie's navy one might have belonged to Arthur or his brother.

Miss Oliver wore her unflattering gray bonnet and coat. He imagined her in clothing as bright as the little girls', tones that would complement her coloring, then halted himself. Thinking in that direction was wrong for a man about to ask another woman to be his wife.

"Are you ready to leave, my lord?" Miss Oliver asked.

He should tell her no. Tell her he had changed his mind. If he did, her lovely emerald eyes would fill with dozens of questions he was not sure he could answer and still protect the secrets he must hide.

"Whenever you are, Miss Oliver."

She picked up a large basket he had not noticed. Hooking her arm through the handle, she offered her hands to the children. The twins each grabbed one, but Bertie ran to Arthur.

"I friend of the bear," he announced.

With a laugh, Arthur took the boy's small hand. "That you are, Bertie."

The little boy chattered nonstop as they went out to where a small pony cart waited along with his horse.

After helping the children into the cart, Arthur held out his hand to Miss Oliver. She accepted his help up onto the seat, then set the basket on her lap.

As he took the reins from the stable boy and handed them to her, he asked, "What do you have in that basket?"

"A surprise for the children."

"And for me?"

She smiled, and he wished he could persuade her to keep wearing the expression. It lit her face and glowed in her eyes. "If you would like, I can keep it a surprise for you, too."

"I am not fond of surprises."

"Neither am I." The light went out of her eyes as if someone had blown out a candle. She looked away.

What was she trying to hide from him? She reacted like this at the oddest times. Perhaps if he took note of when she did, he might see a pattern. For now, he was baffled. He prayed God would ease her pain and send her someone to help, even if it was not him. That thought sent a sharp pain into his gut, though he knew he should concentrate on his duties to the estate and as a courier.

He swung into the saddle. A tightness in his ankle reminded him to be careful. He walked his horse alongside the pony cart and toward the gate.

As she did each time she drew away, Miss Oliver remained silent for several minutes, then began talking as if nothing had occurred. She steered the cart to the base of the headland. There, she lifted the children out of the cart and settled the basket once again on her arm. She told the little ones to climb the hill and calmed their excitement so they did not rush and hurt themselves.

And she never once looked in Arthur's direction, not even when he offered her his arm.

With a sigh, he lashed his horse's reins to the cart and followed the others up the hill. The twisting path was steep, but the children clambered up with ease. He watched where he stepped and did not realize how far he had fallen behind until, from higher on the hill, Miss Oliver called for the children to pause.

She hurried down to him. "This is too much, my lord."

"For you?"

"No, for you. Perhaps you should not be climbing like this when you are still limping."

"Allow me to decide what my own limits are, Miss Oliver."

Again she looked away, and he knew his tone had been too sharp. Her shoulders hunched as if she feared a beating. Who had treated her appallingly? Everything about her spoke of a gentle birth and rearing, but too often she acted like a kitten that had been kicked aside too many times. "Forgive me, my lord."

"Anything," he replied.

His quiet answer brought her eyes up, and he saw shock in them. She opened her mouth to speak, but no sound came out. When he offered his arm again, she put her fingers lightly on his sleeve. She said nothing as they followed the children up the slope.

As Arthur had expected, the wind at the top of the hill tried to pry his hat from his head. The children ran about, their arms outstretched like tiny birds ready to take flight for the first time.

Miss Oliver stepped away from him to get a better

hold on the basket, which rocked in the wind. "I can see why it was suggested I bring the children here."

"Who suggested that?" he asked, eager to keep her talking.

She counted off on her fingers. "Lady Caroline. Baricoat. Three of the footmen."

"That is quite a consensus."

"And an accurate one. It is beautiful here." Her eyes glittered like twin gems as she turned to take in the expanse of sea and land. "In one direction, it is as wild as the first day God created the world. When I look in the other, the village, the church and Cothaire show how the land has been tamed."

Arthur followed her gaze, trying to see the view as she did. Below to the left, the inner crag curved in to protect the harbor from storms. Yet the dual cliffs, facing each other like folded arms, created dangerous currents with every tide. Water shot with a thud out of a tunnel in the outer cliff. The sound and the eddies had fascinated him when he was a boy. In truth, they intrigued him still.

"Is that a beam engine I hear?" Miss Oliver asked.

He strained his ears. There! Beneath the pulse of the waves, he heard the deep, rhythmic sound of a beam engine. He shaded his eyes and looked inland toward the mines scattered across Lord Warrick's estate. Arthur could see smoke coming from the chimney of a beam house. Coal powered the steam turbines moving the great beam that pumped water from the earth so miners could dig more deeply into the seams of tin.

"You have keen hearing," he said.

"A handy trait when I need to keep track of active

children. Catching a whispered scheme can allow me to put a halt to the mischief before it starts."

"We often said Mother had the ears of a bat and the eyes of an owl. She seemed to hear us no matter how quiet we were, and I would have sworn she could see in every direction at once."

Miss Oliver faced him. "You miss her very much, don't you?"

"There are some wounds no amount of time can heal."

"Was she more like Lady Caroline or Lady Susanna?"

"Carrie. Susanna inherited many of Father's characteristics, such as his excellent financial sense. Carrie is more maternal." Arthur laughed shortly. "Though after seeing Susanna with the twins, I may have to rethink my appraisal. I sometimes wonder how different our lives would have unfolded if Mother had not died close to the same time Carrie's husband did. Mother was both a force to be reckoned with and a gentle spirit who brightened every room she entered. A light went out of our lives, but I know it is waiting for us when we rejoin her in heaven."

He told Miss Oliver a story he had not related in many years, of how his mother had chided him for eating all the jam one day, and how he had struggled to keep his stomach from erupting before the scold was done. When the nurse laughed, he realized how correct Carrie was. Miss Oliver had a true gift for listening to others.

"Thank you," he said when their laughter faded away.

"For what?"

"For listening while I prattled like a chatterbox. I don't do it often."

Her smile warmed him to his toes. "You should. You are a good storyteller."

He was astonished how her words pleased him. Compliments he received usually had to do with how smoothly he solved problems for others on the estate. He could not recall the last time someone had praised him for something personal.

Because you never share personal things, chided a small voice within him. *You have become so anxious not to reveal your work with Gwendolyn you cannot speak of anything in your heart.*

He could not argue with that voice.

"Look, Arthur!" Bertie tugged on his greatcoat. "Ship!"

Shielding his eyes, Arthur saw sails close to the horizon. He picked up the boy so he could see more easily past the rocks at the edge of the hill.

"Cap's?" asked the twin he was sure was Lulu.

Miss Oliver confirmed his guess when she smiled and said, "Lulu, be patient. One of these days, Cap will come back to Porthlowen."

"Soon?"

"Very soon."

The child's disappointment was clear on her face. Arthur felt compelled to comfort her, but he had no idea how. Later, he must speak with Miss Oliver about the best ways to offer solace to an unhappy child.

He realized he was getting his first lesson when Miss Oliver knelt and drew some items out from under the cloth tucked into the top of her basket. As she placed them on the ground in front of the children, who crowded around to see, she kept her hands on slender sticks and fabric so the breeze did not send them skittering away.

The children asked questions as Miss Oliver added a spindle of twine to the pile, but Arthur knew what she was planning. He watched as her nimble fingers put the pieces together. When she was finished, she held up a kite. In abrupt silence, the children stared at it, giving her a chance to explain what it was and what it could do.

She rose gracefully. "Shall we try to get our kite to fly?"

The children cheered in excitement and begged to be first.

Seeing the indecision on her face, because she did not want to choose one child over the others, Arthur admired anew how careful she was to keep the tots happy and show them they were loved.

He reached for the kite. "Let's go!"

"I think not." Miss Oliver put her arm in front of him. "Mr. Hockbridge would not be pleased to see you running about."

"I assure you I am fine." He held out his hand in a silent command for her to give the toy to him. When she did not move, he said, "If you don't mind, Miss Oliver…"

"But I do. I shan't have you harm yourself again because you refuse to see sense."

"Quite the contrary. I do not intend to chance injuring my leg anew." He held out his hand. "The kite, if you please, Miss Oliver."

For a long moment, he thought she would not give it to him; then, without a word, she held it out.

"Thank you," he said, as he took it and looked at the children. "First we run." At an easy trot that spared his ankle, he held up the kite. The wind caught it immediately, and it soared up into the sky.

"Look! Arthur flies kite!" shouted Bertie.

Arthur chuckled, amused by how the little boy treated him with respect, yet acted as if Arthur were his big brother. When had he last come outside to enjoy the day and do something as frivolous as flying a kite? Regret battered his heart when he realized he could not answer the question. It had been far too long since he had done anything but his duty.

Squeals of delight filled the afternoon. The children danced around, clapping while the kite dipped and rose on the breeze. Arthur gave each one a chance to hold on to the string with him. He had them stand in front of him while he held the twine with one hand and the child with the other. He laughed along with their giggles.

"Shall we give Miss Oliver a turn?" he asked, then corrected himself. "Shall Maris have a turn?"

Color rose on Miss Oliver's cheeks as he spoke her given name, but she shook her head. "I am happy to watch."

"Nonsense." He refused to let her stand aside and not be part of the fun. Drawing the kite with him, he walked to where she stood.

"Very well," she said, and he suspected she was eager to hold the kite's string, too.

"Are you ready?"

She laughed and reached for the taut string. "I think I am as ready as I ever shall be."

Instead of handing it to her, he raised his arms and brought them down on either side of her, so they both could hold the kite. Just as he had with the children.

But her reaction was completely different. She ducked under his arm and backed away, then looked at him, aghast. Her eyes were wide and her face ashen. Her fingers gripping her cloak shook so hard he could see that from more than an arm's length away.

"What is wrong?" he asked, confused.

"I must— That is, we must— The children..." She moved away and gathered the youngsters, telling them it was time to leave. They protested as she herded them ahead of her down the path toward the cart.

Arthur collected the basket and drew in the kite. That slowed him so much that Miss Oliver had finished placing the children in the cart by the time he was halfway down the hill. It was even tougher on his ankle to descend than to climb.

"Miss Oliver?" he called.

He would have thought she did not hear him, except she glanced in his direction as she climbed onto the front seat and picked up the reins. When she raised them to give the command for the horse to go, the children started yelling.

He could not hear their words, but they pointed at his horse tied to the back. She stopped the cart and got out. Untying his mount, she waited until he reached the bottom of the slope. Then she handed him the reins without meeting his gaze.

"Miss Oliver—"

"If you will excuse us, my lord, it is time for the children to return to the house." She added nothing more as she hurried to the cart and climbed up.

She drove past him. The children waved to him, but she did not look back.

With a halfhearted wave to the youngsters, Arthur

remained where he was. What good would it do to give chase and ask her why she had abruptly changed right in front of his eyes? Her laughter had become fright, but what had scared her?

Chapter Six

"My lord, this arrived for you." No hint of emotion colored Goodwin's voice.

Even so, Arthur whirled in his desk chair and stood. A hot sting ran along his leg from his ankle to his knee. He needed to take care, even after more than a week, not to jostle his leg or move it quickly.

Could it be a message at last from Gwendolyn?

The past week had been interminable. Not because he waited for Gwendolyn's answer. Not because he had no chance to seek information about Cranny's murder. In fact, Arthur had given far too little thought to his courier duties or his friend since the kite-flying outing. His thoughts were focused on why Miss Oliver had sped away with the children.

Getting an answer from her had proved as impossible as accepting that he had overdone it and set his recovery back. He had seen Miss Oliver on occasion in the house. The closest he had been to her was when she sat in the pew opposite his at church on Sunday. Every time he had aimed a surreptitious glance in her direction, she looked elsewhere. She had participated in the service, but he saw none of the heartfelt enthusiasm she showed with the children. That startled him, and he wondered why she seemed to draw into herself rather than reach out to the community under the church's roof.

Not that he had a chance to ask, even if he could have found a way to do so without overstepping the bounds of polite behavior. He was sure he had caught sight of her turning and walking in a different direction when their paths were about to intersect. He made excuses to himself and others not to go to the nursery. Even when his sister mentioned young Bertie thought his friend had abandoned him, Arthur could not bring himself to visit.

If he did, he would have to make conversation with Miss Oliver. How could he when the first words he needed to speak were *Why do you cringe when I am near?* She did not act that way with anyone else in the house. That she had been hurt by another man was the only possible explanation for her bizarre behavior.

Who was the cur? Neither Baricoat nor Mrs. Hitchens would allow such behavior in the great house.

What bothered Arthur even more than Miss Oliver not telling him why she had reacted as she did was that she feared he would treat her the same way. He could not reassure her he would never treat a woman so. Not when even bringing up the subject was impossible.

Now Goodwin had brought a missive from Gwendolyn. Arthur must turn his attention to his duties as a courier. Never before had that been so difficult.

He had done nothing with the letter she had sent last week. The instructions—assuming they were instructions—had been such a garbled muddle he had not risked leaving the enclosed page at one of the designated drop-off points. It invited disaster to leave any message in one place for long. Someone other than the next link in the courier chain might find it, and valuable information could be lost.

So he had waited, gladly spending time with Miss Oliver and the children. The reality of his obligations returned when he saw the black wax Gwendolyn used to seal her letters on the folded sheet his valet held. Though tempted to order Goodwin to take the letter away so Arthur was not drawn into the subterfuge anew, he took the page and waited until his man left the room before he broke the wax seal.

A quick scan of the contents sent waves of relief and tension through him. Relief that, even on first glance, he could see Gwendolyn had resumed using their familiar code. Tension because he had no doubts the contents must be sent onward without delay.

First, he needed to read the page folded around the message he had to convey to the next courier. Arthur never broke the seal on the inner sheet, though curiosity teased him to peek. The inner page was written in a different code that would be deciphered by the final recipient. A necessary precaution, because the information could mean the difference between life and death for the king's men who fought Napoleon's forces.

Arthur carried the letter to his desk. As he did each time, he placed the page he would not read under a porcelain box of blotting sand. There, it would be safe while he decoded the page with his instructions.

More than two hours later, Arthur leaned away from his desk and rubbed his eyes. The message was straightforward. As soon as he possibly could, he must pass along both sealed pages from the last two letters Gwendolyn had sent. They must be placed in his primary location so the next courier could continue the messages on toward London. The spot was a small opening between two stones in the ancient foundation of a circular structure on the moor.

Usually he took messages when visiting one of the tenant farms. Once he was far enough out onto the moor that nobody would see where he was bound, he sped to what his father believed was an original Celtic settlement.

Arthur's stomach growled, and he realized he had missed the midday meal. He rose, kneading his lower back. When he saw a plate of cold meats and cheese set on a table near one of the windows, he smiled. He was fortunate Goodwin kept track of time.

He ate as he returned to his desk to check one last time the information Gwendolyn had sent. He must code his own instructions to the next courier. It was far too simple to make a mistake, and Arthur did not want to delay the messages any longer.

Gwendolyn had been perfect in her use of the code until the previous communication. When they were younger, he would have looked forward to the opportunity to tease her about it. She would have known he was jesting and mocked him back. But the next time he saw her, he must be serious and ask her to be his wife. Every day, as the date for the hunt gathering grew nearer, the idea of marrying Gwendolyn became more bizarre.

Arthur could not let himself be distracted while he prepared his coded message. Sitting, he went to work, glad to clear his mind of anything but his task. It took him less than an hour to finish the note for the next courier. After the ink dried, he folded the page around the two unopened messages. He reached for the green wax Gwendolyn had given him to use. He could not use his regular seal. That would identify him as a member of the earl's family.

"Arthur?"

He recognized the hesitant voice. Looking over his shoulder at the door, which was ajar enough to let a small child peek around it, he said, "Bertie, come in and tell me what you are doing away from the nursery this time."

The little boy skipped across the room, grinning. Without waiting for permission, he climbed into an upholstered chair. He sat, his short legs not reaching the edge of the seat cushion.

"Come to see Arthur the bear."

"Does Maris know you are here?"

Bertie's smile fell away. "No."

"She will be worried, won't she?"

"Guess so." The answer was reluctant.

Putting the pages from Gwendolyn under his coat, Arthur stood and held out his hand. "We need to let her know where you are."

"Then go out?"

"That is for Maris to decide."

"We go? You tell Maris we go?"

Arthur fought not to smile at the little boy's attempt to get him on his side. He was pleased Bertie wanted to spend time with him; yet the child was in Miss Oliver's care.

"We must wait and see what she says."

Bertie sighed, his small shoulders rising and falling.

"It cannot be bad in the nursery," Arthur said. "You have friends there."

"Just girls." His nose wrinkled. "They play with dolls and the dollhouse."

"Is Gil with Carrie—Lady Caroline?" Arthur corrected himself when the little boy glanced at him with puzzlement.

"Yes. Gil go. Bertie stay with the girls. I want no more playing dolls."

"Ah, I see." He hid his amusement. To Bertie, his predicament was as important as matters of the estate were to Arthur.

Promising the boy could have an outing would be wrong without checking with Miss Oliver first. Would she even speak to him when he took Bertie to the nursery? She would, but only because good manners required it.

Patting the folded pages under his coat, he looked at Bertie, who stood on tiptoe to get a piece of cheese. Bertie wanted to go on an outing. Arthur needed to leave the house without anyone being curious where he was bound. Why not combine the two? Offering to show the children what was left of the ancient buildings would provide the perfect excuse. As many outings as he had taken with Miss Oliver and the youngsters in the past fortnight, nobody would take notice of another. The children could run about, and Miss Oliver's attention would be on them while he slid the pages between the rocks. His mission would be accomplished, and Bertie could escape an afternoon of playing with dolls.

Arthur ruffled the little boy's hair, astounded a child would provide the inspiration he sought. *Lord, thank You for bringing this child to me today. Watch over us while we try to save many lives.* He faltered on the prayer. Yes, getting the information to London post-haste could make a difference, but he must be cautious. Endangering Miss Oliver and the children would be a high price to pay for victory over the French.

He told himself not to be dramatic. No one save Gwendolyn knew he was a courier. No one but he and she could read their code. He knew there were French spies abroad in Cornwall, as well as those who wanted the government to think less about defeating Napoleon and focus on how poor harvests had left people on the edge of starvation. Any of them would be eager to keep the message from reaching London.

"Bertie, why don't you sit while I finish what I was doing?"

"What you doing?"

Arthur should have expected the question. With a laugh, he said, "A 'none of your bread-and-butter' task."

Bertie grumbled as he climbed into the chair. "Maris says that when she does not want our help."

"I will want your help." He held up a finger to halt the excitement bursting out of the little boy. "In a few minutes after I finish this."

As he sat at his desk, Arthur was startled how the word *finish* resonated through him like a hammer clanging on a bell. The burden of the secrets weighed more heavily on him each day. He had not guessed how much he wished to be done with his hidden life.

He melted the end of the stick of wax and let several drops fall onto the folded sheet. As it cooled, he pressed his finger into the green wax to seal it. He had promised Gwendolyn he would assume Cranny's duties, and he would not let her down. Either as the courier or as her husband, if she accepted his offer of marriage.

Whether he wanted to make that proposal or not.

Miss Oliver's face emerged from his thoughts along with the questions of what and who had hurt her, but he tried to ignore the images. He must in the future, so why not develop the habit before he saw Gwendolyn? He must do everything he could not to hurt either woman.

He wished he knew how.

"Lord Trelawney!" Maris pushed loose strands of hair toward her bun. How was she going to tell him Bertie had slipped away *again*? She could be dismissed for a lack of attention. The little boy had been sitting at the table, paging through a book, one minute, and the next time she looked up from her conversation with Irene, one of the kitchen maids, seconds later, he was not.

"No Bertie!" called Lulu as she stepped off the back stairs' landing and into the day nursery. She held Irene's hand.

The maid shook her head with a worried frown. She dropped into a curtsy when she saw Lord Trelawney in the other doorway.

"Not upstairs." Molly appeared around them.

"I believe I have found who you are looking for," said the viscount as he drew Bertie from behind him. He gave the child a gentle push into the nursery.

Maris took Bertie by the hand and marched him to the window bench. Picking him up, she sat him on it. She told him to stay there.

Bertie nodded, big tears in his eyes.

She wanted to comfort him, because she hated seeing the children cry. However, he must learn he could not wander away whenever he wished. Could that be what had happened to the children? Had they slipped away from their parents and found their way to the boat? No.

The older boys might have managed it, but none of the children was big enough to carry the baby or to boost Gil into a boat.

"I will watch the children while you talk with him," Irene whispered, glancing over her shoulder at the viscount. "You were kind enough to listen to my troubles, so I can repay the favor now."

"Thank you." She squeezed the kitchen maid's hand, then squared her shoulders.

Keeping her polite smile in place, Maris returned to where Lord Trelawney was talking to the twins. She waited for a break in their conversation about the dolls the girls were eager to show off. After sending the twins to play with Irene, she watched them scurry across the room to sit at the table.

"Thank you for bringing Bertie back," she said in lieu of what she really wanted to tell him. She could not forget the shock and hurt in his eyes when she had pulled away from him. The sight had haunted her for the past week. He had brought forth memories she yearned to keep buried forever, but he had not done so intentionally. She owed him an apology, but how could she say she was sorry without an explanation?

Lord Trelawney clasped his hands behind his back as a faint smile flickered across his face. "I should thank you for rescuing me from a discussion of dolls and the new gowns you apparently have made them."

"Mrs. Hitchens gave us some scraps."

"You should see if she has any more of this material in her cupboards." He held up a piece of green silk.

"She may have more scraps. Do you wish me to inquire, my lord?"

"No need." He handed her the tiny gown she had

sewn while the children napped. "Bertie asked if I would take him on an outing."

"I will remind him that he needs to wait for an adult to make plans for him." She kept her gaze on the doll's dress.

"I don't want to subdue the boy's spirit, so don't chide him. However, I agree he should not slip away from the nursery without alerting you."

"As you wish, my lord."

"And you?"

Surprise brought her head up, and her gaze locked with his before she could halt herself. Emotions flashed through his eyes, but she saw hints of happiness and anticipation she had not previously. Her heart did a flip in her chest. Had she helped lessen the sorrow that often dimmed his expression?

"You are asking me, my lord?" She did not want to make the mistake of thinking it was more than a rhetorical question.

"Yes."

"Of course I need to know where the children are. That is what I am supposed to do."

"And you always do what you are supposed to?"

"I try."

He chuckled, his eyes crinkling. That released her from his strange hold on her.

"There is a vast sea of difference between *yes* and *I try* when answering that question," he said.

Maris laughed with him. She was unsure if she could trust Lord Trelawney—or anyone else—fully ever again, but she appreciated his sense of humor. Before his first visit to the nursery, he had seemed grim, always rushing from one end of the estate to the other.

Had being with the children brought this change? If so, Lady Caroline had been wise to suggest he practice with youngsters in order to learn how to charm Lady Gwendolyn and her children at the hunt.

Something sharp cut into Maris's heart at the thought of him courting Lady Gwendolyn. *Don't be want-witted!* Lord Trelawney saw Maris and the time he spent with her as a means to an end.

Nothing more.

If she believed more was possible, then she was an even greater fool than when she had believed Lord Bellemore would heed her when she tried to countermand his guest's lies. Hadn't she learned the nobility saw everyone else as tools to get what they wanted?

No! That protest came from deep inside her. She did not want to believe Lord Trelawney was like that. Hadn't he asked her opinion? She could not imagine Lord Bellemore, who had known her since her birth, caring what she thought. He would have heeded Belinda's assertion if she had said Lord Litchfield was feeding him a feast of lies. Belinda was his daughter, not a charity case living under his roof.

But why hadn't Belinda come to Maris's defense? Her friend had stood there, not meeting her eyes, while her father raged at Maris for being an ungrateful wench. Belinda had said nothing even when Lord Bellemore demanded Maris apologize to the man who had attacked her. Unable to do that, she had fled with little more than the clothes on her back.

"If I may…" Lord Trelawney's voice freed her from the dark cloud of pain and grief.

"Yes?"

"I would like to take a walk."

"A walk? With the children?" Maris knew she sounded witless.

"And with you to help me keep them from running in every possible direction." He cocked his head and gave her the smile that set butterflies dancing a quadrille inside her. "You will come with us, won't you?"

"Most certainly."

"I thought the children would like to fly their kite again. Up on the moor the wind is always brisk, and we won't have to worry about them getting too close to the cliffs."

"Up kite!" Lulu stood, and her chair fell to the floor with a crash.

The other children, including Bertie, who jumped down from the window bench after a slight hesitation, crowded around him. They all talked at once. Who would fly the kite first. How high it would go. What speed they needed to run to get it into the air.

"Hush!" Maris said. "If you don't listen, you will never get answers to your questions."

Her request lowered the volume, but not the number of questions fired at her and Lord Trelawney. When she saw his grin, she could not help smiling. The children's joy was infectious, and she wanted to enjoy every moment with them and the viscount.

With Irene's help, Maris got the children ready to go. They convinced Bertie to stand still long enough to button his coat, but then he ran over to Lord Trelawney.

Irene bobbed a curtsy to the viscount, then looked at Maris. "Thank you again."

"Anytime."

"I appreciate that more than you can know." Color flashed up her face as her eyes shifted to Lord Trelawney. She whirled and rushed from the room at a speed that would have gotten the children a reprimand.

Maris saw the viscount's curiosity, but he did not ask why Irene had thanked her. She was glad, because she could not reveal how the kitchen maid had come to discuss a problem involving another young woman in the kitchen. Irene had not brought her concerns to either Mrs. Ford or Mrs. Hitchens, because she wanted them to believe she could handle a difficult coworker on her own. Maris had listened while Irene worked out a solution by talking about the situation.

Maris found herself willing to listen because no one at Bellemore Court had listened to her.

And as ye would that men should do to you, do ye also to them likewise.

The familiar verse from the book of Luke whispered in her head. She was amazed the words should come to mind after her loss of faith that night in the book room and afterward.

She had no time to ponder that puzzle as she took the twins by the hand, and Lord Trelawney did the same with Bertie. She tried not to think how they resembled a happy family as they walked out into the windy day.

A closed carriage awaited them. After assisting the children in, Maris was not surprised when Lord Trelawney held out his hand to help her. His excellent manners compelled him to hand in a woman, even a servant. As her gloved fingers settled on his palm, the layers of leather could not halt the bolt of heat leaping from him to her. She calmed the quiver racing through her and kept her eyes on her feet as she climbed in.

Perhaps Lord Trelawney had not felt the sensation.

He sat beside Bertie, facing backward, and began chatting with the children. Maris folded her hands in her lap while she listened to their excited voices.

As the carriage followed the curving road to the moor, the dull rhythm of the beam engine could be heard. "We are not going near the mines, are we?" Maris did not want the children chasing a kite in an area that might be pocked with the entrances to abandoned mines.

"In the opposite direction."

"Toward Dartmoor?"

He smiled. "Yes, but we will be many miles from the place where the prisoners-of-war are kept."

"I am glad to hear that." She rubbed her arms, suddenly cold, as she thought of how narrow their escape had been from the French pirates who tried to capture Porthlowen. Those men were now behind the walls of Dartmoor Prison and would be given no chance to slip away again.

"There is an open field that will be the perfect. As well, there are ancient foundations for the children to explore."

"Foundations?" Her brows dipped toward each other. "Won't it be dangerous?"

"Not these. They are at ground level. The walls themselves are no more than two or three feet high. Raymond and I spent many hours as children exploring the circular foundations."

"When you were older than these children?"

"Yes, but you and I are here to watch them."

"True. How many of these foundations are there?"

"We found more than a dozen hidden among the gorse and grass. When I asked my father how long they had been there and who built them, he said no one knew for certain."

"Did he know what they were for?"

"He guessed they were storage or shelters for shepherds whose sheep grazed on the common lands." Shifting, Arthur gave Bertie space to get on his knees and look out the window. "Father suggested I check the book room and see if there was something there to help me. It took me several days, but I discovered a history of the area written more than two hundred years ago. However, the author was baffled by the foundations, which were considered ancient even then."

"Have you learned anything else about them?" She put out both arms to keep the twins from sliding off the seat as they knelt like Bertie so they could see outside, as well.

"Only that there are other places in Cornwall with this type of foundation hidden in the weeds. Most are on the moors, not far from the sea. The book's author was far more intrigued by the old burial barrows and fogous."

"Fogous? What are those?"

"You will hear people call them *fuggy holes*, but they are properly called *fogou*. The word comes from the Cornish for cave. They are underground rooms where food once was stored. But you don't need to worry. We never found a fogou here."

"You sound disappointed."

"Not as much as when I was a boy and hoped we could find a tunnel to play in."

"I am glad there are no tunnels. I am sure at least one of the children would need to be retrieved, and I have no wish to crawl in among spiders and mice and who knows what else."

Lord Trelawney laughed. "True. If you wish to learn more, Miss Oliver, you are welcome to use our book room."

"No!"

At her sharp cry, the children stared at her. Lord Trelawney did the same before asking, "What is wrong, Miss Oliver?"

Why hadn't she thought before she reacted? She could not explain how the idea of entering a book room made her stomach twist. To say that would open the door to other questions and threaten the facade she had created for Maris Oliver, nurse. She could not endure the idea of Lord Trelawney regarding her with disgust, as Lord Bellemore had when he cast her out of the only home she had. Or watch him turn away as Belinda did, as if the sight of her were repulsive.

"I am sorry," Maris said, having no choice but to devise another lie. "I thought one of the children was going to slip off the seat."

That explanation satisfied the youngsters, but Lord Trelawney said, "As long as nothing else is wrong…"

"Other than me overreacting, no." How many more lies could she tell before her tongue turned to stone? But what good had telling the truth done her at Bellemore Court?

The viscount settled against the seat. "Why don't I have the book brought up to the nursery? When you have finished reading it, I would like to know your opinion."

"Thank you. I look forward to that."

"Good." He glanced out as the carriage rolled to a

stop. "Here we are. Or as close as the vehicle can take us. It is a short walk." He held up his hand. "And before you ask, Miss Oliver, I assure you I am more than capable of walking that distance as well as helping the children fly their kite. However, I would prefer if you don't tell my family or Mr. Hockbridge I was running about on the end of a kite string."

Warmth slid up her face when he gave her a conspiratorial smile and a wink.

"This color is charming," he said, brushing her cheek with his crooked finger.

She should look away, but she melted into his gaze. There was nowhere else she wanted to be and no one else she wanted to be with than him. He was kind. He was amusing. He made her feel as if she were an important part of his world.

As he leaned toward her, she held her breath. Was he going to kiss her? Oh, how she wished he would! His finger glided down her cheek to tilt her chin at the perfect angle for his lips to find hers.

Suddenly a small form pushed between them. Bertie! The little boy grabbed the door handle to open it. "Go! Go! Go!" His excited shouts were echoed by the girls.

Maris was unsure if she or Lord Trelawney or both of them pulled back, as if the thread tying them together had severed. She began to laugh. She could not halt herself, especially when the viscount joined in along with the children, who had no idea why they were laughing. In truth, it was beyond ludicrous a little boy should act as her conscience, reminding her of her place, which was not in the viscount's arms.

He soon would be marrying another woman. Maris could not forget again, no matter how much her lips yearned to feel his against them.

Chapter Seven

Circular foundations were scattered across the field, some on one side of a low ridge, the rest on the other. Each circle was approximately eight feet across, and a break in the wall marked a doorway. Grass had grown over most of the stones. Dried with the coming of winter, the blades crackled underfoot.

Bertie, Lulu and Molly ran to the first foundation. They raced in and out, chasing each other and laughing. They did not pause before they did the same in a second circle, then a third. As the girls moved to a fourth, Bertie climbed up the stone to stand on top. He raised his hands high as he jumped up and down.

Maris let them play with childish abandon. They might scrape a knee or a hand if they fell, but the walls were too low for them to hurt themselves more.

She entered the first circle and saw stones set into the earth in the center. Two bowls were cut into them, the right size for a pestle. She wondered if that was the purpose of the stone depressions.

"Can you feel it?" Lord Trelawney asked as he approached. He carried the kite and spindle of string.

"What?"

"The weight of time on this place. If the book I read is right, people were living here around the time of Jesus's birth and maybe before. Wouldn't it be amazing if the stones could tell us what they have witnessed through the millennia?"

Maris stepped out of the open-sided foundation. "I never imagined you to be a romantic about stones."

He set his foot on top of a low wall and rested his elbow on his knee. Watching Bertie dance along a nearby circle while the girls clapped to the tune he sang, the viscount said, "Not stones, Miss Oliver, but the people who placed them there. I am curious how they lived here, where they came from and why they left."

"We may never know."

Lulu ran over to Lord Trelawney. "Up kite?"

"You should not interrupt," Maris said, squatting so her eyes were level with the little girl's, "when others are talking. You must wait and take your turn."

She nodded. Barely a second passed before she asked, "Wuwu's turn?"

Maris could not keep from smiling as she heard Lord Trelawney try to conceal his laughter, turning it into an inelegant snort.

"Yes, Lulu," she said. "It is your turn."

Lulu spun to look at the viscount. "Up kite?"

"Go to the top of the hill past the stones," he said, gesturing beyond the foundations. "We shall fly it there."

Cheering, Lulu ran to the others. They sped up the small hill.

As she walked with Lord Trelawney, Maris was surprised when he asked, "How do you make Lulu feel listened to when she does not want to listen?" He stopped, so Maris did, too. "How do you offer a child comfort with such ease?"

"Simply remember how your parents comforted you. Learn from what they did right and from what they did wrong. Try to do as well and try to do better."

His brows shot up. "So simple?"

"Yes. If you would like my advice—"

"I do."

She began to walk toward the children, not wanting him to see her face after he had said the words he would repeat when he took Lady Gwendolyn for his wife. "No two situations and no two children are alike. What do you know about Lady Gwendolyn's children?"

"There are two. A girl and a boy, I believe."

"You don't know the games they play?"

He shook his head.

"Do you know their ages?"

"They are young like our children, but beyond that I don't know."

Maris's heart danced foolishly at his words. Saying "our children" was no more than a turn of a phrase.

Calming her rapid heartbeat, she asked, "Do you know their names?"

"No." His expression was half smile, half grimace. "It would seem I know nothing about them."

"You know more than you think. You spent time with Lady Gwendolyn from an early age, didn't you?"

"Yes."

"And her husband? Did I hear you met him when you both were at school?"

He nodded, his eyes narrowing.

"If you knew Lady Gwendolyn and Mr. Cranford as

children, remember how they acted then. Chances are good the children have similar temperaments."

"But what if they are different?"

"Listen to your heart. Go with your instincts. When Lulu looks unhappy, you can either give her a hug or do something to cheer her."

"And there lies my problem. What do I do?"

"Speak bolstering words."

"As I would to anyone?"

Maris laughed in spite of herself. "Yes. However, you must keep your response simple, so the child will understand you are offering solace. You must be sincere in what you say and do."

"I have no intention of being false with the children." He frowned at her. "I have no use for lies or liars."

Somehow pushing thoughts of her own lies aside, she said, "I am glad to hear that. Children have an uncanny sense of knowing when we are not honest with them." That was true, but these youngsters had not guessed she was not the nurse she portrayed. Or maybe they did not care, because they were happy to be loved.

"Maybe we should have the children help us discover where they came from then."

She bent to pick a late-blooming flower. Twirling the stem between her fingers, she said, "Someone knows the truth."

"I would like to know it, too. Not only for the children's sakes but for my sister's. Carrie is attached to the baby."

Maris opened her mouth to reply, then closed it again. She did not want to say anything disrespectful of Lady Caroline, who had let her loving heart welcome

Joy into it. And Gil's as well, because the little boy was spending more and more time with her and "his baby."

"Go ahead," the viscount said, as he paused out of earshot of the children, who were running around the top of the hill as they flew imaginary kites. "Say it."

"Say what?"

"What we both are thinking. I should be trying to find out who put the children in the boat and why."

"I was not thinking that."

"You should have been." He handed her the kite and began to unreel a length of the string from the spindle. "Nobody is going to come to Cothaire, knock on the door and give us the information."

She looked at him directly for the first time since they had started up the hill. "Captain Nesbitt and his men asked throughout the villages along the shore. They learned nothing."

"Then I need to ask questions elsewhere." Lord Trelawney reached up to pat his coat, then lowered his hand. Without saying another word, he took the kite and strode to where the children were bouncing about like drops of oil sizzling on a hot pan.

Maris followed and let herself be caught up in the children's high spirits. Her smile grew as the children guided the kite through the sky with the viscount's help. An unfamiliar feeling bubbled up in her.

Happiness.

When had she last been happy? No, she would not think of that. She wanted to wrap herself in the contentment of watching Bertie holding the string with Lord Trelawney, while the twins danced about in anticipation of their turn. Unbidden, her feet drew her closer to the quartet, who shouted instructions at each other and laughed and watched the kite flit toward the clouds.

"Maris fly kite!" shouted Bertie. "Maris fly kite. Maris fly kite."

The other two took up the chant, running to grab her hands and pull her toward Lord Trelawney.

When he looked over his shoulder, his eyes asked the question she had avoided answering for the past week: Why had she panicked last time? She could not satisfy his curiosity without explaining the truth, but she could keep that dark time in her life from overshadowing the day's joy.

"Step aside," she ordered in mock gruffness. "It is time for the ladies to show you gentlemen how a kite should be flown."

Bowing from the waist, the viscount held out the taut string. "As you wish."

Bertie copied his motion before passing the string to Lulu and Molly. They grabbed it in front of where Maris held it.

Letting more string unroll, Maris sent the kite even higher. The girls squealed, too excited to keep holding on. They ran to follow as the kite dipped and rocked on the breezes above them. She drew it away from the darker clouds, and they chased it like eager kittens after a mouse.

The youngsters were beginning to flag as the first raindrop fell on Maris's upturned face. She pulled the kite down, fighting to control it, while more drops struck her. She called to the children to come to her.

"Lord Trelawney, could you help?" she asked when the kite, caught on a gust, tried to tear itself from her hand. The string scorched her palm. She got no answer, so she raised her voice. "Lord Trelawney!"

"Arthur gone," said Bertie.

Gone? Where was he?

She scanned the open field, but could not see him. Had he returned to the carriage when the sky darkened? He would not leave them in the storm.

Busily wrapping the string around the spindle, she thanked Molly, who brought the lifeless kite to her after it hit the ground. The raindrops seemed as big as coins, and the children complained when they were struck. She hurried them down the hill. The dry grass was growing slippery as more rain fell.

Where was Lord Trelawney?

A motion caught her eye. There he was! She smiled, realizing he must have been investigating a stone foundation. As fascinated as he was by them, he probably had not even noticed the clouds overhead had thickened. He bent close to the stones. As he straightened, she saw something small and white flutter to the ground.

He turned to wave to them, then glanced skyward. "Hurry! We are going to be soaked if we don't get inside."

Rushing with the children to where he stood, she thanked him when he took the kite and spindle. He urged the children to run to the carriage.

As they obeyed, he said, "You, too, Miss Oliver! Hurry!"

"You dropped this." Maris bent and picked up the white item. A folded page sealed with green wax.

He whirled, looked at what she held out, and seized it. Her shock at how he had snatched it from her hand must have been visible because he said, "I will say my thanks, Miss Oliver, when we are in the carriage. Hurry!"

This time she did. By the time she had the children seated, Lord Trelawney was behind her. He tossed the kite to Bertie and picked her up by the waist. He set her in the vehicle, swung in himself and called to the coachee to get them to Cothaire with all possible speed.

The horses were whipped up so fast that Maris fell onto the seat. A sharp snap and the rip of fabric along with the children's horrified howls warned her that she had sat on the kite. She shifted enough so she could pull the pieces from beneath her.

Lulu burst into tears, followed by the other two. Maris spent the ride consoling them and promising to build another kite soon. Their sobs eased as the carriage halted by Cothaire's front door.

Lord Trelawney jumped down and lifted the children out. The door opened, offering them sanctuary from lightning striking the cove. Thunder threatened her ears as Maris climbed out.

"Leave the kite," the viscount ordered when she reached for it.

"The children will want—"

"Leave it!"

Rain burst from the sky as if a dam had collapsed. Instantly she was soaked.

He grabbed her hand and pulled her into the house as the driver shouted to the horses to go, so they could get out of the storm, as well.

"Maris wet." Bertie laughed, pointing at them as the footman closed the door. "Arthur wet."

She glanced at the viscount, who was dripping on the floor. Knowing he could have gotten inside before the rain came down if she had not insisted on retrieving the kite, she started to say how sorry she was.

He waved aside her words. "I should apologize. If I had gotten us out of the carriage faster, neither of us would be drenched."

"I should take the children to the nursery and get them out of these dirty and damp clothes."

When he nodded, she grasped the girls' hands in one of hers and Bertie's in the other. She climbed slowly up the stairs, listening as they discussed every detail of their afternoon.

At the top, she looked down to where Lord Trelawney stood in a widening pool of water. His gaze collided with hers so strongly she almost reeled. Again she saw an emotion missing from his eyes a week ago. The same emotion she had lost in her life.

Happiness.

With her? With the children? With something else entirely? Those questions she could not answer, and she would be wise not to try.

A broad smile felt comfortable on Arthur's face the next morning when he awoke shortly after sunrise. He had passed along the communiqué, albeit with the complication of Miss Oliver discovering it had fallen out of the crevice where he had placed it. He was grateful, though he could not tell her. If she had not seen it on the ground, it could have been blown heaven knows where. Mending the bridge between him and Miss Oliver seemed like his reward for a job well done. He could not imagine anything he wanted more than spending a few hours with her every afternoon, listening to her sweet voice and seeing her smile.

Walking into the breakfast parlor with its dark furniture and pale blue walls, he saw his father at the table, a newspaper opened by his plate, which held the remains of his meal. Another reason to smile, because he must feel well if he had had his breakfast here rather than in his rooms.

Looking up, Father said, "Good morning, Arthur."

"Good morning. How are you feeling today?"

"Well, thank you. With the good Lord's blessing, I may be able to join you and Caroline at Miller's house for the hunt."

Did his father intend to be there to make sure Arthur did as he promised? He scolded himself. Father was not devious, and he trusted his children. Arthur wished he could trust himself, but as the time of the hunt approached, he found it more and more impossible to imagine Gwendolyn as his wife. Perhaps because his thoughts centered on Miss Oliver and a collection of small children.

"I am pleased to hear that."

"As I can see. You look pleased this morning."

"It is a sunny morning." He walked to the sideboard where food steamed after its arrival from the kitchen. In the past when he was bothered by a problem, he had found his father to be a good sounding board. But he could not speak to him about how his mind was filled with thoughts of their nurse rather than Gwendolyn.

"Try the eggs," Father said. "Mrs. Ford has outdone herself this morning."

"I shall." He spooned food onto his plate, not taking note of what he selected. Carrying his plate to the table, he nodded his thanks when a cup of coffee was set in front of him. He bowed his head and gave quick thanks for the food as well as the ones who had prepared it. He picked up his fork. Taking a bite, he glanced at his father.

"You are right," Arthur said. "This is good."

"Caroline tells me you have been spending time with the children."

He explained his sister's suggestion to ease any concerns Gwendolyn might have about his suitability as a father to her two little ones. "Yesterday, we flew a kite on the moor until we were chased home by the storm."

"I heard you looked like a drowned dog." His father laughed. "Many a time I ended a journey across the estate soaked to the skin. Your mother would chide me, reminding me that I would scold you children for being careless. Each time, I said I would be more careful. But too many times, I failed because I thought I had time for one more stop along the way."

"I have done the same myself. Too often."

Father leaned forward, resting his elbow on the table. "With you spending time with the little ones, it would appear you are not opposed to the idea of marriage and children."

"I never have been." Arthur chose his words with care, wanting to hold on to the light feelings that banished the darkness. It had surrounded him since his mother and Carrie's husband had died. For more than five years, he had lived in shadow, going through the motions of life. "I have been busy."

"I know well how obligations can consume one, but you have done well. I trust you will do as well when you meet with Lady Gwendolyn. Have you made a plan of attack?"

Arthur arched a brow. "An odd way to describe courting a woman."

"It is a battle, my boy. In the case of Lady Gwendolyn, I daresay it will be a battle of wits. She has been known to have a sharp tongue."

"So I have heard." He recalled Cranny mentioning more than once how his wife did not hesitate to scold him when she was in a pelter. When his friend had mentioned her threatening to strike him over the head with a teapot, Arthur had been dumbfounded. As a child, she always was even-tempered, more likely to laugh than to cry.

You have changed. Why wouldn't she?

His father folded the paper and set it by his plate. "If you are averse to this match, son, the time to say so is now."

Arthur hid his surprise. He had not guessed his father would offer him a chance to rethink his promise.

Or maybe he did not hide his astonishment, because Father went on, "I know my request shocked you, but it is vital for the future of Cothaire that you marry someone who knows how to handle a household like ours. She must be able to oversee the servants, leaving you free to concern yourself with the estate issues."

"I understand, Father."

"I know you do, but you have seen your siblings follow their hearts to someone beyond the *ton*. I am happy to see them happy, but you are the heir." He rubbed his hands together, and Arthur realized for the first time how ill at ease his father was with the topic. "Lady Gwendolyn fits the criteria well, and if I am not mistaken, you were considering asking for her hand before Cranford did."

"I was too young then to take any important matters seriously." It was too late to tell his father he had thought of Gwendolyn as a sister, as annoying at times as his own.

"Now you must be serious."

"Yes," Arthur said, though every word tasted bitter as his short-lived joy drained away, "now I must."

Arthur surveyed the new stable. The work was going even faster than he had hoped. The building should be ready for use by the end of next month, and the horses would be protected through winter in comfort instead of crowded into cramped spaces in the other outbuildings.

The tack must be replaced, along with several carriages. He had arranged with the tenant farmers to purchase hay to replace what burned in the stable fire. He made sure he spread the offers to buy evenly among them, so nobody felt left out or too obligated. Before she left on her honeymoon, his sister Susanna had worked out fair payment. She handled Cothaire's accounts with the skill of an estate manager.

Sanders, the head groom, was talking with one of the carpenters, but halted when he realized Arthur was behind him. "My lord, you should have let me know you were here."

"You are busy."

"What can I do for you today?"

"I wanted to let you know how pleased my father and I are at how swiftly the stable is being rebuilt. And at no cost to quality, if my eyes judge accurately."

Sanders smiled. "The boys have worked hard and with skill."

"Under your supervision." He put his hand on the head groom's shoulder. "Well done."

"Thank you, my lord." A flush rose from the man's open collar.

Arthur could not keep from thinking of how a blush looked much prettier on Miss Oliver. His own face grew hot at the discovery of how easily she came to mind, especially in the wake of the conversation with his father a few hours ago. Hoping he was not turning red, too, he mumbled another hasty thanks to the head groom before walking away.

Somewhere between now and the hunt, he must learn to control his thoughts. If Gwendolyn discovered he was thinking of another woman while he asked *her* to be his wife, she would be hurt. That he must avoid.

Somehow.

Snuffing out thoughts of Miss Oliver was not as easy as pinching out the light of a candle.

As he edged between two weatherworn barrels, Arthur heard a childish shout. Miss Oliver was in a nearby field. She held the hands of the two older boys. He grinned. Was she trying to keep Bertie and Toby separated? The two were fine when apart. Together they were flint and steel, sparking off each other with every word and action.

The gentle sway of her skirt was like the melody of a song he could not quite hear. When the children laughed, he knew her beautiful eyes would crinkle as her full lips framed her smile.

He wished she was looking at him. Seeing her gentle smile lifted his spirits. He wanted to be with her, to hear her laugh, to see her eyes sparkle, to take her hand in his and hold it as long as propriety allowed. Like the two boys, there was an undeniable spark between Miss Oliver and him. It grew stronger each time they were together. Yet staying away condemned him to the shadows of unhappiness.

Lord, I need Your guidance more than ever. Please help me, I pray.

Arthur forced himself to look at the stable. He had put aside his estate duties for too long. He no longer had the excuse of an injured leg. He had delivered the latest coded messages as instructed. Putting distance between him and the temptation of spending even more time with Miss Oliver would be best.

Wouldn't it?

"Good afternoon, brother." Raymond clapped him companionably on the shoulder.

Arthur had not noticed him approaching. "Good to see you, Raymond."

"The progress on the stable is marvelous."

Arthur let the conversation focus on the rebuilding for a few minutes before he said, "I doubt you came here to ask me my opinion how many stalls we should have in the new stable."

"No, I came to collect Toby for tea."

"I would like your opinion on that subject."

"Tea?"

Shaking his head, Arthur said, "No, on the children." He glanced at where Miss Oliver was skipping across the field with them. "I have been thinking we need to ask more questions about how they came to be in that little boat in the harbor."

Raymond sighed deeply. "I must admit I had hoped this would not come up soon, even though it is the right thing to do. Elisabeth says she will readily give Toby to his rightful family, but I see the pain in her eyes when she mentions it. Does Caroline know you plan to start inquiring about this?"

"I have not told her yet, but in spite of her love for the children, she wants to know the truth. I don't want to go over the same ground covered previously. Do you have any idea where I should look?"

"None. Every village along the shore was visited and everyone asked about the children. Susanna even took them to one of the mining villages on Lord Warrick's estate, hoping they might have come from there, because of the message in the note pinned to Joy's shirt."

"Message? What message?"

"I thought Susanna had showed it to everyone."

Arthur grimaced. "If she showed it to me, and she probably did, I have forgotten. What did it say?"

His brother reached under his coat and pulled out a piece of paper that had been folded and opened dozens of times. "I copied this from the original note, which Susanna has."

Taking it, Arthur opened it and read the few words:
Find loving homes for our children.
Don't let them work and die in the mines.

"That is pretty specific." He gave the page to his brother. He glanced toward where Miss Oliver danced in a circle with the children. Their light voices lilted through the air, but the distance obscured the words. "But Susanna found nothing at the mines."

Raymond slipped the note under his coat. "No one has discovered any clues to what happened before the children were rescued." He paused, then asked, "Are you listening to me?"

"Of course! Why would you think otherwise?"

"I don't have your complete attention."

"Excuse me?"

"I am here." He tapped his chest. "You seem to be more interested in who is over there." With a chuckle, Raymond leaned his hand on a nearly empty barrel of nails. "Miss Oliver is extraordinary with the children, isn't she? Elisabeth never frets when she hands Toby over to her."

Arthur knew it would be silly to act as if he did not understand. Even as he debated how to put her out of his mind, he stared at the nurse like a child looking at freshly baked treats.

"Carrie is pleased she was hired also."

"And you?"

Arthur frowned. "If you and Carrie and Susanna are pleased with Miss Oliver, why would I have any reason not to be?"

"I did not intend to suggest you were not pleased with her." His brother rubbed his fingers against his chin as the two of them watched Miss Oliver lift the boys, one at a time, to look at cows at the far end of the field. "I am curious if you are more than *pleased* with her."

"You are being absurd," he replied automatically, unsettled by his brother's insight.

Raymond shrugged. "I don't believe so. Speaking as your parson, I would caution you to be careful, Arthur, for, though God forgives us as a loving father should, it is not as easy for us earthly creatures to be forgiving when our hearts are involved."

"You are wasting your breath. There is nothing to be forgiven for."

"Yet." Any hint of humor vanished from Raymond's voice. "Speaking as your brother, I wonder if getting to know these children for the sake of Gwendolyn's is the real reason you continue to spend time with them and their nurse."

"I confirmed to Father this morning I plan to ask Gwendolyn to become my wife."

"Then let me give you one more piece of advice. This is man to man. Make sure you and everyone else knows that." He pushed himself away from the barrel. "Give my words some thought, Arthur. If you want to talk, you know where to find me. I need to collect Toby and return him to the parsonage before Elisabeth wonders where we both have gone." With a wave, he strode toward where Miss Oliver squatted in the grass, holding up her hand while the children peered into it.

Arthur went to a side door into the house. He thought about what Raymond had said.

All he had to do was ask Gwendolyn to marry him as soon as they both reached Miller's house. That gave him the fortnight before the gathering to clear his mind of Miss Oliver. A short time, but he must put it to the best use.

In the meantime, he needed to continue to search for answers. Who had murdered Cranny? Who had put the children in the boat and pushed it into the sea? Arthur had depleted almost all his venues for information about the first question.

He planned to check one more tonight when he spoke with a man of the lowest repute, a meeting he had spent a long time arranging.

As for the questions surrounding the children, he knew where to start.

With the same man.

Chapter Eight

Cold rain pelted Arthur as he drew in his horse in front of the tumbledown building that served as a tavern and carriage stop along the shore road. Swinging down, he ignored the pain searing his ankle. He hoped the trail he was following had not grown cold.

He turned up the collar of his greatcoat as he walked through puddles to an overhang where his horse could wait out of the storm. Once he was sure his mount was secure with others beneath the roof, he walked to the door.

Faint light came through filthy windows where streams of mud traced the uneven panes of glass. Opening the heavy plank door, he entered. He shook rain off his coat, but did not remove his hat. The brim dipped down, concealing his face. He hoped nobody recognized him. Otherwise, word would spread rapidly that Lord Trelawney was seen at the tavern called The Spider's Web.

The low ceiling threatened to knock his hat off, so Arthur kept his head bowed. The tavern was well named because webs hung, thick with dust, from every beam and in every corner. Men sat at long tables, some with their heads down. When one snored, another slapped his shoulder. The man roused enough to turn the other way before falling back to sleep.

Crossing the room to where the publican stood behind his bar, Arthur put his hand on the wooden top.

"Something to drink?" asked the barkeeper.

"No." Drawing back his hand slightly, Arthur let the man see the coins beneath his fingers. Gold and silver caught the light from the lantern overhead. "I am here to meet someone. In private."

The barkeeper made the coins vanish before he motioned with his head for Arthur to follow him. No one glanced at them while the publican shouldered aside a ragged cloth and opened a door behind it. He stepped aside to let Arthur enter.

Nodding his thanks, Arthur went into a chamber even more dimly lit than the outer room. There was enough light, however, for him to see a lone man sitting at a small table. In front of him were the remnants of what looked to be a generous meal, if Arthur judged by the platters and bowls.

"Ye be late," the heavily bearded man said. Gray twisted through his ginger hair and drew two parallel lines down his beard on either side of his mouth.

"I am here at exactly the agreed upon time. You are early." He drew off his gloves as he crossed the narrow space between the door and the table. Not waiting for the man to offer, he pulled out a chair and sat. "That is, you are early if you are Mick Higbie."

"Aye, that be me." He eyed Arthur coolly. "And I know who ye are, my—"

"No need for formalities." He took off his hat and set

it on his lap. "I have been told you are the man to talk to if one wants to know about the activities of the knights of the pad in this area." He refrained from using the term *highwaymen*. He had been warned that the criminals who sought their victims along the shore did not call themselves by the name the law had given them.

"Ye were told right. Were ye told as well such knowledge can cost dear?"

"What I need to know should not come dear because it involves nothing more than a dead man." His stomach clenched at his own indifferent tone, but he must not allow Higbie to guess how desperate he was for information about the night of Cranny's death.

"As my *mamm-wynn* was fond of sayin', 'dead men tell no tales,' but that does not mean that information comes cheap."

"*My* grandmother," Arthur said with a cool smile to let the highwayman know he spoke Cornish as well as English, "was fond of saying only fools buy a pig in a poke."

The man stared at him for a long minute, then another. Finally Higbie chuckled. "Tell me what ye need t'know, and I will tell ye how much it will cost ye."

Arthur outlined what he knew about the night Cranny died. The man across from him held up a hand to halt him.

"I remember." He spat on the floor. "One of m'boys was questioned about it." With a snort, he said, "Ye be askin' the wrong man. None of us play the sports ye Smarts do."

"What do you mean?"

"If we have a matter t'settle, we do it with our fivers." He held up his fists. "That is how poor men fight. We don't face each other over pistols."

Cranny was killed in a duel? Arthur asked himself why he had not considered that possibility. His friend was hotheaded, even though Cranny complained about Gwendolyn having the worst temper in their household.

If it had been a duel, who else was there? Such a secret could not be kept forever, even if the other participants swore to say nothing. A guilty man with a secret usually had a tough time hiding it.

"But ye are interested in more than a beefhead gettin' himself killed in a duel. I hear ye be asking about some children."

"Ye were told right," he said, as Higbie had.

The highwayman's smile appeared amidst his bushy beard, then he leaned forward. "If ye want m'advice, m'lord, ye need look no farther than yer own cove."

"Are you saying someone in Porthlowen put those children in a boat and set them adrift?"

"I am sayin' nothing. Just repeatin' what I heard."

"Where?"

"Can't say. Might've been here. Might've been there." He leaned back, clasping his hands behind his head. "Take the free information for what it be worth."

Arthur was not deceived by the highwayman's pose. "Why are you forthcoming?"

"No one should leave babies in a boat that be ready to sink." Higbie sat up again, his boots striking the floor. "I once had a woman and a child. If someone had put m'child in a boat, I would ne'er rest till I made that person pay."

Arthur nodded even as he wondered what had happened to Mick Higbie's wife and child. Were they the reason he had turned to robbery? Or had he begun that life after they were gone? No matter. Higbie would not want his sympathy. Yet he had to respect the highwayman who cared about children. Pulling out a few more coins, he dropped them into one of the bowls.

Higbie glanced at them, but did not grab them as the barkeeper had. He said nothing as Arthur stood and turned toward the door. When Arthur put his hand on the latch, the highwayman said, "I wish ye good huntin', m'lord."

"Thank you." He walked out, crossing the main room without looking either right or left.

He paid no attention to the rain that was threaded with sleet as he rode to Cothaire. The ice scoured his face, but Higbie's words echoed in his head.

If ye want m'advice, m'lord, ye need look no farther than yer own cove.

Questions had been asked in the village and in the great house, and everyone denied knowing anything about the children.

Someone was lying.

But who?

"Am I intruding?"

Maris looked up from the thick history book she was reading in the day nursery. Until the book on the ancient foundations had arrived, she had not guessed how much she missed the chance to lose herself in a story. She once had been an eager reader, but since the violent encounter with Lord Litchfield in the book room, she had not turned a page other than while reading to the children.

"Lord Trelawney, what are you doing here at this hour?" She put her hand up to her hair, which she had unbound before going to bed. She had come downstairs to read so the light creeping out beneath her door would not wake the children. Glancing at her legs drawn up on the window bench, she made sure her dressing gown covered them completely. Only then did she say, "Forgive me. I should not have asked such a question."

"Of course you should." He remained in the shadows by the doorway. "My being here is unexpected. May I come in?"

"Certainly." She stood and put the book on the cushion. Again she brushed hair from her face, wishing it did not curl wildly when she released it from its proper bun.

She forgot about her appearance when Lord Trelawney stepped into the light and she saw him. From the top of his head, where he was taking off his tall hat, to the tips of his boots, he was drenched. Water dripped off his dark hair and the hem of his greatcoat. Mud splattered his dark breeches.

But it was his face that caught her eyes and held them. For once, he wore his emotions openly. Grief, pain, anger, disbelief. They battled for precedence as if he had seen something so terrible no words could describe it.

Her first instinct was to hold out her arms and draw him into an embrace. She could offer the children such comfort, but not Cothaire's heir, most especially when she was in deshabille. All she could do was step away from the window bench so he might sit there.

He shrugged off his greatcoat, looked at it, grimaced and then carried it into the hallway. He dropped it and his hat on the floor. The coat he wore beneath his great-coat was damp, but clung to his wide shoulders.

Maris got a towel from the pile she kept to clean the children. Handing it to him, she stepped back as he rubbed his hair. He lowered the towel, and she could not keep from smiling. His hair stood on end, pointing in every direction.

"Pardon my appearance," he said. "I am afraid the storm left me worse for wear."

"If you will pardon mine."

"Yours? You look beautiful." He picked up a tress from her shoulder. "You should not hide this spun-gold silk as you do." He dropped her hair and draped the towel over his head again. To dry his hair more or to cover his embarrassment at his untoward words?

Pleasure at his compliment warred with her good sense telling her to put a quick end to the conversation. No one had told her she was beautiful since before her father died, and his comments were usually self-satisfied ones of how her appearance might obtain her a titled husband to raise the status of their family.

"Please sit," Lord Trelawney said as he continued to run the towel through his hair.

She did, but flinched when the wind banged against the window behind her. Rain clattered on the glass, and she guessed it was turning to sleet or snow.

When the viscount picked up the book and sat beside her, Maris resisted the warning alarms sounding inside her. Nobody was nearby except the sleeping children, and she had vowed she never would be alone with another man. But she could not flee up the stairs to her room without him asking why. She locked her fingers together in her lap and pressed her feet to the floor, ready to rush away.

"Let me begin by saying I am sorry I interrupted your reading." He looked at the book's spine. "Are you enjoying this?"

"I have only begun reading it."

"The children keep you busy, I know."

"Yes."

Silence fell, smothering and uncomfortable. Rain struck the window again, driven by the frantic wind. Maris waited for him to speak, unsure why he had come to the nursery. Was it connected to where he had gone? Her breath caught. Had he discovered the truth about the children? If so, he might ask her help in telling his sister.

"I apologize again for intruding," Lord Trelawney said with a sigh. "The truth is I needed to talk to someone. My father would listen, but telling him of my actions tonight could anger him. With his fragile health, I want to avoid adding any stress to what he bears." He looked at her directly. "I have heard you are an excellent listener."

"I try."

"That is all I ask. That you listen."

"I know how difficult it can be when you feel as if there is no one who will listen." She reached up and smoothed a spike of his hair. Jerking her hand back, she looked away from the astonishment on his face.

He caught her wrist. Not like a manacle as Lord Litchfield had, but gently, as if her arm were a fragile bird. As he slowly lowered her hand, she held her breath. It burst out of her when he released his hold and set himself on his feet. He began to pace the long room. No, not pacing. Prowling, like the bear Bertie believed him to be.

"What I am about to tell you," he said, his back to her, "no one else knows. You must promise me you will keep this secret."

"Yes."

He looked over his shoulder, his eyes narrow slits. "Promise me you will keep this a secret. Say the words."

She wondered who had betrayed him by leaking a secret. "I promise I will keep this a secret as long as doing so will not harm the children."

"I would never do anything that would cause them harm." He faced her. "I thought you knew me well enough to know that."

I don't know you at all, and you know even less of me. She kept those words unspoken.

He prowled like a bear on the hunt, intent and unstoppable. "We have spoken of Lady Gwendolyn Cranford, but what I am about to say has to do with her late husband, Louis Cranford."

Maris listened in shocked silence as Lord Trelawney spoke of Mr. Cranford's death and his own suspicions. No wonder he had looked sad when she first found Bertie in his rooms. He was carrying a burden he had not shared with anyone.

"I have been searching for answers for more than a year," he said, "and I may have found something tonight."

"That is wonderful!" She put her fingers to her lips. "I am sorry. You asked me to listen, and I should listen without comment, Lord Trelawney."

Again he paused and faced her. "I think that is no longer appropriate."

"That I should listen about Mr. Cranford?" She came to her feet. "As you wish, my lord."

He held up his hands in astonishment. "Must you always obey the canons of Society?"

"I don't understand."

"You are always polite to the point it can become aggravating."

Her eyes widened. "Would you have me be otherwise?"

"At times, yes! The *ton* did not collapse when the children began to address me as Arthur. It feels absurd when you continue to call me 'my lord.' Why don't you do as they do?"

"They are children. They are excused from making such a faux pas."

"How can it be a faux pas if I ask you to address me so?"

Maris had no quick answer to give him. To let his name form on her lips… If other servants or members of his family heard, would they be as accepting as they were with the children? The household thought it cute that the children called him Arthur, especially Bertie, who wondered if he was really a bear. It would not be the same for her. There would be whispers of an inappropriate relationship, perhaps even a love affair. She could not face those false accusations again.

As if she had aired her thoughts aloud, he said, "It would be only when we are with the children or when we are having a conversation like tonight. Could we at least try tonight?"

"Yes."

He raised a single brow.

"Yes, Arthur," she said with a faint smile. How sweet

his name tasted on her lips! Would his lips feel even sweeter on hers?

She sat again, so she could avoid Arthur's gaze. Even though he had granted her permission to use his name, she must keep a tight hold on her wayward thoughts. No matter what they called each other, nothing had changed. He was the heir and planning to marry Lady Gwendolyn. She could not forget that. Not for a moment.

"Now that is settled, Maris…" His smile sent another wave of warmth over her. "Let me tell you what I discovered tonight."

"Please do."

She tensed as he began to speak of how his friend had not died at the hands of highwaymen, but in a duel. A shiver coursed down her spine. Belinda had spoken about men dueling, sometimes satisfying honor by firing in the air as cooler heads prevailed. Other times the ending was more tragic.

"Can you imagine?" Belinda had asked, lying on her tester bed in her elegant bedchamber. "A man willing to die to protect your honor. What could be more romantic?"

"The man alive and at your side?" Maris frowned at her friend.

"Oh, Maris! You don't understand. Of course, I would not want him to die, but a small flesh wound would be romantic, wouldn't it? I could be by his side as he healed, and he would profess his undying love and ask me to be his wife. It would be like that new poem by Walter Scott." She pursed her lips. "What is it called?"

"The Lady of the Lake." Maris had read the poem

and found the writing beautiful, but some of the events illogical, including how no one recognized the king disguised as a rival for the heroine's hand.

"When Ellen and her beloved Malcolm marry after her father nearly gives his life for honor..." Belinda sighed and draped her arm melodramatically across her eyes. "Oh, to have such a poem written about me."

Maris had changed the subject. Then, as now, when Arthur spoke of duels, she felt sick at the idea of men throwing away their lives.

"I must find the person who slew him," Arthur said. "At least three men know the truth of what happened that night."

When he paused, leaning his hand against a wall, Maris asked, "Who told you this tonight?"

"A knight of the pad."

"A highwayman?" She surged to her feet. "Why would you accept his word on something like this?"

"Because I saw the truth in his eyes when he asked about my search for the children. He said he would not rest, if one of the children in the boat was his. Not until he knew who had abandoned them to the sea."

She measured the man in front of her as if seeing him for the first time. His eyes flashed with resolve, and even with his hair sticking up as it dried, he looked every inch the earl he would someday be, ready to lead his people to protect their beloved Porthlowen Harbor. He believed the highwayman because his words echoed what was in Arthur's heart. He was determined to find out the truth about his friend's death, and he would not stop until the man who had killed Mr. Cranford was brought to justice.

"I understand," she said softly.

"What?"

"Why you need to solve the mystery of Mr. Cranford's death. He was your friend. You are doing this to honor his memory."

Arthur regarded her through narrowed eyes, appraising her as she had him. Not on the outside but within. In a voice as quiet as hers, he said, "Thank you, Maris. It means more than you know to have you understand as nobody else has."

When he closed the distance between them, she did not move. She wanted to be nearer to him, though every instinct warned her to flee. He paused a hand's breadth away. When he reached out his finger to bring her face up toward his, warnings rang through her head. She ignored them as she touched his sleeve.

The arm beneath it was as strong and brawny as a laborer's, and she wondered how many different ways he helped when he visited tenant farms. She had never imagined a lord's arm could be so muscular.

With his fingertip, he drew her toward him. Her hand slid up his damp sleeve, savoring each plane along his arm. As he slanted toward her, she closed her eyes. The alarms in her mind grew louder, but not too loud to drown out footfalls on the nursery stairs.

Bertie came into the room, rubbing his eyes. "Arthur!" He flung himself forward.

Scooping the child up at the same time he gave Maris a regretful glance, Arthur held Bertie so they were eye to eye. "Aren't you supposed to be asleep, young man?"

Bertie giggled. "Yes."

"So why are you here?"

"Thirsty."

Maris went to the pitcher that was always kept filled in the day nursery. Her hands shook as she poured a cup. She should be grateful Bertie had arrived when he did. She had been about to kiss a man who was as good as betrothed to another woman. No reason she could devise excused her behavior.

And worst of all, what did Arthur think of her when she willingly came into his arms after they had discussed Lady Gwendolyn's husband seconds before?

As she held the cup out to the little boy, she said, "Bertie, you know there is water in the cup by your bed." Her voice was unsteady, but it was the best she could do.

He ducked his head and sipped, not as thirsty as he claimed.

Maris lifted him out of Arthur's arms and carried him to the window bench. Sitting, she took the cup and put it on the sill. She did not need to persuade Bertie to lie down with his head in her lap. He curled up beside her and shut his eyes. His soft breaths seeped through her dressing gown to warm her leg. When Arthur brought a small blanket to put over the little boy, she thanked him quietly.

Arthur sat on her other side, because no chair in the room was big enough to accommodate a grown man. In a husky whisper, he said, "I appreciate you listening, Maris."

"I wish I could do more."

"You may be able to. Not with my search for Cranny's killer, but by using the other information I was given."

"Other information?"

"I told you my contact said that if one of his children had been in the boat, he would not rest until he found the person responsible. I agreed, and he suggested I look more closely in my own cove."

"In Porthlowen? But everyone in the village and along the shore has already been questioned." She glanced at the little boy who slept with his head on her lap. "Where do we even begin?"

"I like how you say 'we.'"

"As much as anyone else, I want the truth."

"More than some."

She tried to quell the shudder aching across her taut shoulder blades. "Do you mean the person who put them in the boat?"

"Yes, but not only him or her. I worry about what will happen when we uncover the truth. My sisters have become attached to the children."

"As you have."

He drew in a deep breath, then released it, nodding. "That is true. We all will miss them when they are returned to their families."

"Do you intend to ask everyone in the village the same questions again?"

"I had hoped you would help." He stretched his arm along the windowsill. He did not touch her, but she could sense the heat from his skin close to her hair. "You are easy to confide in. You listen. If you turn a conversation to the topic of the children, who knows what you might learn?"

"I can do that."

He nodded again. "I am sure you can." He fisted his hand on his knee, then stood. "I must know the truth, Maris!"

"I know. I want to know the truth, as well."

He strode to another window and looked out at the raging storm, which seemed mild in comparison to the one in his eyes.

"What if you call the villagers together?" she suggested. "Maybe for some other reason, but that will give us the opportunity to chat with them."

"A brilliant idea." He smiled. "There has been some discussion in the past year about buying a new bell for the church. After the attack by the French pirates, there is renewed interest in a way to alert the villagers about danger."

"That should work."

"I will arrange with Raymond to have a meeting in the next two to three days. He can spread the word to his parishioners. Elisabeth will put up a notice in her store, and I will talk to the fishermen down at the water. If we tell everyone to tell others about the meeting, the news should reach every household."

When Bertie shifted, Maris looked at the little boy, then raised her eyes to Arthur. He was gazing again out the window. His fingers gripped the molding so hard his knuckles bleached.

"But what if it is worthless?" he asked.

"We have to try to find the truth."

"There is nothing more important than the truth. I have no use for liars. They are cowards as they spread their tales for whatever purpose they have. They need to be honest."

She was glad his back was to her, so he did not see her flinch at his taut words. "For some people, it may not be that easy."

He snorted in derision as he faced her. "You need not tell me that, Maris. Odd that the most honest man I have encountered in the past fortnight is a renowned highwayman. It reminds me of the verse from Proverbs."

"Which one?" she managed to say, though her throat was clogged almost shut.

"'The lip of truth shall be established forever, but a lying tongue is but for a moment.'"

Maris lowered her eyes. The lies she had told might have been told quickly, but her guilt resonated through her like thunder against the house. There was no comfort or forgiveness in knowing that if only Lord Litchfield had been honest, she would not have to live with her lies every day.

Arthur crossed the room and lifted Bertie off the bench, cradling him in his arms. "I will put him to bed, if you wish, Maris, and leave you to your reading."

Standing, she said, "Thank you, but it is not necessary."

"Trust me when I say it is. If I want to do something as innocent as tucking a small child into bed, then maybe the taint of learning my friend died needlessly can begin to diminish."

The pain in the viscount's voice was so raw she put her hand on his arm once more, though she should stay away from him. She could not when she heard his regret and grief. "I am sorry, Arthur."

"Thank you." He bent and pressed his lips to her cheek. "For everything."

She did not have time to react before he went up the stairs to the night nursery. Touching her fingertips to the spot where he had kissed her, she stared after him, torn between delight and dismay.

Everything had changed tonight when Arthur opened himself to her. What if he expected her to do the same the next time they talked?

Chapter Nine

"**A**rthur come soon?" asked Lulu as she skidded to a stop next to the sand castle Bertie and her sister were building. As Maris had warned, all the children had begun to use the viscount's given name. Maybe nobody would pay any attention if she slipped and called him Arthur, too.

She had been disappointed when she had walked with the children into the entry hall before their outing and found it empty. She had hoped Arthur would join them today. She had a few ideas about the meeting scheduled for tomorrow evening. Ideas about how to bring up the topic of the children, and thoughts of how he might be able to get people to talk about what they had seen or heard. Usually she spurned gossip, but some bit of hearsay might contain information that could lead them to answers.

When Baricoat drew her aside, the butler lowered his voice so the children would not hear him. "Are you waiting for Lord Trelawney, Miss Oliver?"

"Yes."

"He has been called away on critical business."

"I see." And she did.

As his injuries healed, she had sensed his impatience to continue his work. Or had he gone in pursuit of another clue about Mr. Cranford's death? She hoped he would find what he sought.

She understood why he was away, but the children did not. They had chattered about spending time with Arthur. She had looked forward to another pleasant afternoon with him. The hours up at the ancient foundations had been the most carefree she had enjoyed in so long. She could not recall the last time she had been as lighthearted. Even days later, she smiled when she thought of one of Arthur's amusing comments or when she recalled how safe she had felt as he took her hand in his much larger one and helped her into the carriage.

Lulu tugged on Maris's coat, intruding on her thoughts. "Arthur come?"

"He is busy, but maybe once he returns he will join us."

"Tell Arthur come! Tell Arthur come!"

When the other children took up the chant, fishermen along the strand looked in their direction, frowning. Maris calmed the youngsters by piling more sand on the mound they had collected. Telling them it looked like St. Michael's Mount, she answered their questions about the island in Mount's Bay. She told them about how it was separated from Cornwall twice every day when the tide was high. She related the ancient legend of how a giant had lived on the island before it was an abbey. A young man built a trap for the giant, and all that remained was a heart-shaped stone on the path up to the house.

By the time she finished the tale, interrupted over

and over by the children's questions, it was time to return to Cothaire. Maybe she should not have told them about the giant, because they kept asking if he would come to Porthlowen. She assured them there were no more giants in Cornwall.

"Bear beat giant!" exclaimed Bertie, holding up his hands like paws and growling. "Bertie help."

Maris bent to brush sand off his coat. "I am sure if Arthur ever has to fight a giant, he will want your help."

"Me, too!" shouted Lulu and Molly at the same time.

"You are all so brave," she said as she shook sand off the girls' skirts.

The children continued to babble about how they would fight any giant. They borrowed examples from the story of Jack the Giant Killer, which Maris refused to read to them at bedtime because the tale made them too excited to sleep.

She waved to Elisabeth, who was shaking out a rug in front of the parsonage. The parson's wife had asked her to bring the children to visit on Friday, but Maris had not told them yet. She had learned it was best not to reveal any treat too early. Otherwise, the children refused to nap. Fatigue made them cranky. When the time arrived for the treat, they were not interested in anything but crying or quarreling.

The sky lowered as they climbed to Cothaire. She tried to get the children to move faster, but Lulu began to complain and begged for Maris to carry her. No sooner had Maris picked her up and settled her on her left hip than Molly began to whine. Maris propped the little girl on her other hip, then found herself lagging behind Bertie, who proudly marched up the hill.

At a distant rumble of thunder, Maris set the girls

down and urged them to hurry. Both protested, but a flash of lightning and a louder crack spurred them to catch up with Bertie. Maris gathered her skirt and chased after them. The children darted through the gate to the front courtyard ahead of her.

"No!" a man shouted.

"Get back!"

"Look out!"

The warnings came from every direction. Maris burst through the gate. She looked in every direction. What was happening?

She cried out when she saw Bertie racing toward a horse. The girls were on his heels, but they stopped at her shout. Bertie kept going.

Thunder clapped. The horse shrieked, rising on its hind legs. Bertie halted. He was too close to the terrified animal. Maris ran forward.

A man pushed past her, almost knocking her from her feet. She started to protest, but light flashed off his face. Spectacles! Lord Warrick, the baron on the neighboring estate! He seized Bertie, swinging him away from the horse. One hoof struck the cobbles right where the little boy had been standing.

Bertie shrieked, and the horse reared again.

Arthur grabbed the animal's halter at the same moment Bertie was shoved into her arms. Maris hugged the child, and he buried his face in her shoulder. Hurrying to the edge of the drive, she knelt and held him close. The twins leaned against her, so she put her arms around them, too, drawing all three children into an embrace.

"Bertie not hurt." Lulu patted his arm. "Good. Bertie not hurt."

Molly nodded so hard her black curls bounced. Her bright eyes were wide, and she pushed her thumb into her mouth as she did whenever she was scared.

"Yes, it is good," Maris said, wiping the little boy's tears away with her apron. "Bertie, you must not go near the horses unless an adult is with you."

"Adult?"

"A big person."

"Horses bad," he pronounced.

She shook her head. "No, the horse was scared. Just like you were."

The children stared at her as if she had lost her mind.

Arthur hurried to where she knelt on the uneven stones. "Are you unharmed?"

"We are fine." Maris tried to stand, but her knees refused to hold her. Now that the crisis was past, they wobbled like a sapling in a high wind.

His hand under her elbow assisted her to her feet. Her breath caught when he put his arm around her waist so she could lean against him. Knowing she might be playing with fire, she rested her head on his chest. His rapid heartbeat told her he was frightened for Bertie, too.

Calling for the children to follow, he steered her into the house. Servants crowded into the entry hall. Baricoat instantly took charge, sending the household staff off to do their duties.

Maris, loath to leave Arthur's side, started to step away, but the viscount's arm tightened around her. She began, "I must—"

"Let someone else handle the situation for once."

"I should get the children upstairs before it is time for tea." Any chance for a nap was gone. Even if the horse had not almost stamped on Bertie, the approaching thunderstorm would keep them from sleeping.

"Baricoat," Arthur said, keeping her within the arc of his arm, "have someone take the children to the nursery and watch over them."

The butler looked at her as he said, "Yes, my lord."

"Irene would be good." Maris was unsure if she should offer a suggestion, but many of the younger maids would rather gossip about the footmen than keep an eye on the children.

"Ask Irene," Arthur ordered. "Mrs. Ford surely can do without her for a short time."

"Mrs. Ford, like any of us, would do anything for the children, my lord." Baricoat drew himself up to his straightest posture.

"I am pleased to hear that."

Maris urged the children to go with Baricoat and have fun with Irene. Promising she would be with them soon, she watched them follow the butler upstairs.

"I believe I insulted him and the kitchen in one fell swoop," Arthur said quietly so the words would not go past her ears. He suppressed a laugh. "Fortunately, he is a forgiving man."

Maris looked at the bespectacled man standing near the front door. Lord Warrick wore a troubled frown.

"Thank you," she said, walking to the baron. "Bertie is safe because of you, Lord Warrick."

His frown deepened. "Have we met?"

"I am Maris Oliver, the children's nurse. I was with them when they visited one of your mines a month or so ago."

He nodded. "Yes, I remember you being there, though we were not introduced."

"You were busy that day working on the beam engine." Heat rose along her cheeks. She had spoken as if they were long-standing friends. What must Arthur think of her lack of propriety when she was supposed to provide a good example for the children?

If he was annoyed, she saw no sign of it. He offered his hand to Lord Warrick and welcomed him to Co-thaire.

"What about you?" Arthur asked. "How are you, Warrick?"

"Other than my nerves, I daresay I shall survive."

"I am glad. You obviously are here for a reason."

"To speak with you, Trelawney." His face remained grim.

Maris dipped in a curtsy. "I will ask you to excuse me."

The baron shook his head. "Miss Oliver, I think you should hear what I have to say, as well."

"Me?" she squeaked, sounding no older than Bertie.

She was given no chance to ask another question as Arthur took her arm and led her and Lord Warrick toward the small parlor the family favored. As always on chilly afternoons, a fire burned on the hearth. Arthur closed the door behind them and suggested she sit on a chair by the fireplace. She did, after removing her coat and folding it over the back.

Lord Warrick chose a chair while the viscount pulled a third one from near the glass doors. The panes shook as thunder exploded close to the house.

"Our timing is better this time, and we did not get soaked." He smiled at Maris. Turning to his guest, he said, "I can see something is wrong, Warrick. What is it?"

"Have any other children been found in Porthlowen?"

Arthur glanced at Maris, shock naked on his face. "Not that I have heard of."

Lord Warrick sighed. "When I thought of the children found in the cove, I hoped the one that has gone missing would be here also."

"A missing child?" Maris choked the words out, even though she should remain silent.

The baron nodded. "Yes."

"Who? From where?" asked Arthur.

Lord Warrick pushed his brass spectacles up his nose in a motion that looked habitual. "One is missing from the biggest mining village on my estate. No one knows where the child is." His mouth worked, then he added, "Nobody can even tell me the last time the child was seen."

"How old?"

"Two."

"Like Lulu and Molly," Maris murmured, but Arthur must have heard because he patted her arm.

Lord Warrick cleared his throat, and she guessed he had not missed the motion. "The missing child is a little girl. Her grandmother says she was wearing a pale blue dress and her hair was in a single braid."

"Have you talked to her parents?" Arthur asked.

"Her father is dead, and her mother is accused of theft at the house where she worked. If she is convicted, and it seems likely she will be, her punishment will be transportation to a penal colony. That is why the child was in the care of her grandmother."

Maris drew in her breath sharply. Lord Bellemore had warned if she continued to accuse Lord Litchfield, she could be arrested for slander. He did not say what punishment she might face, but she had nightmares about being sent away to a strange and untamed land, far from everyone and everything she knew. When she had fled from the betrayal and lies in tears, she had heard Lord Litchfield laugh and call, "Bon voyage!"

She blinked back tears for a mother she did not know. Even if the woman were a thief, punishment should not separate her from her child. That was too cruel.

The door opened, and Lady Caroline stepped into the room. For once, she was not carrying the baby. Instead, she held a book.

"Oh, I did not realize anyone was in here," she said.

Arthur and Lord Warrick had risen as soon as Lady Caroline entered. Maris did, as well. Even though she was invited to be part of the discussion, she could not forget her place in the household.

With a tight smile, Arthur said, "You are not interrupting, Carrie. Please sit here while I get another chair."

Lady Caroline held out her hand as she crossed the room. "Lord Warrick, to what do we owe the pleasure of you giving us a look-in?"

He took her fingers and bowed awkwardly over them. As he straightened, he said, "I am not here for a call, my lady."

Her smile dissolved into distress as he explained why he had come to Cothaire. Lady Caroline grasped Maris's arm, her nails biting into her sleeve. Maris put her hand over the lady's, saying nothing.

"Carrie, we need to decide what we can do to help." Arthur put another chair into the arc in front of the hearth.

"There must be something, Arthur!"

He seated his sister in the chair beside where Maris had been sitting. His glance urged her to sit, as well. Maris withdrew her handkerchief and handed it to Lady Caroline to blot away the tears rolling down her cheeks.

"Forgive me," Lady Caroline said. "I cannot stop thinking about the pain the family is suffering. To lose a child and have no idea if he or she is even alive…" She pressed the handkerchief to her lips.

Again Arthur looked at Maris. She understood his silent message as surely as if he had shouted it. He worried about his sisters if—no, *when* he discovered where the children living in the nursery belonged. They would agree to return them to their grieving families. However, even knowing they were doing the right thing would not lessen the sorrow at being parted from the tiny castaways.

Sitting, Arthur folded his hands between his knees. "I can promise, Warrick, we will spread word of the missing child through Porthlowen. We are gathering tomorrow night to discuss other matters, but we will make sure everyone who has not heard learns about the child then."

"We will pray," added Lady Caroline. "We will ask God to guide our search and return the poor child to her grandmother."

Maris envied the lady her certainty that God would protect the missing girl. Once she had been as sure of God's presence in her life. She hoped He would be there for the child. *Please.*

She listened to the others discuss the best way to find out who was behind children disappearing and appearing where they did not belong. When Lord Warrick suggested they try to get further information from the children at Cothaire, Lady Caroline vetoed the idea.

"I cannot imagine we will discover anything new," she said, her voice as taut as her lips. "You must understand, my lord, that the children are little more than babies. What information they have given us is from a child's point of view. Asking them to describe people in their lives gains us words like *tall* or *laughing*, but no clue where to look for their families."

Lord Warrick sighed again. "It is obvious that you are struggling to find answers for yourselves. To be honest, I felt as if I were invoking the Spanish Inquisition to obtain information about the missing child from her grandmother."

"But," Maris said, shocked, "if she reported the child missing—"

"She didn't. A neighbor did. The child's grandmother reluctantly admitted the little girl was gone. I don't know if she was afraid of being labeled a poor guardian for the child or if there was another reason for her reticence. I find you Cornish baffling at times."

"The miners are a clannish lot," Arthur said. "They squabble among themselves, but stand as a united front against outsiders."

"And I am an outsider to them. Perhaps if I had spent more time on the estate when I was younger, I might find them easier to puzzle out. I assumed my cousin would inherit, but he died a short time before my uncle did, and suddenly the estate became my responsibility, when I would have preferred to continue teaching." He stood. "Pardon me for babbling."

"Don't worry about it. We all are upset about the children," Lady Caroline said.

He looked at her and nodded. "Keep your children close to you. I must return to the mine and make sure the repairs on the beam engine are progressing. The fool machine seems determined to find as many new ways to fail as possible."

Arthur frowned. "But beam engines are simple. Why is it failing over and over?"

"Another thing I wish to find out. Every day it is not working, the men cannot go into the mines because we cannot risk the tunnels flooding. When the men cannot go into the mines, they become frustrated."

"Can they work on the machinery?"

"Few have the skills." Lord Warrick pressed a smile on his lips. "However, that is my problem, and I will not punish your ears, ladies, with a recitation of such matters. Good day, Lady Caroline, Miss Oliver." He bowed his head to them, then turned to Arthur. "Trelawney."

"I will see you out," Arthur said, surprising Maris, because she had thought he would remain to offer solace to his sister.

As the two men left, Lady Caroline sighed. She returned the damp handkerchief to Maris as she said, "If you don't mind, Miss Oliver, I will go to the nursery with you. I feel a great need to be with the children."

"I understand." And she did, because Lord Warrick's news warned that the children could vanish from their lives as quickly and mysteriously as they had appeared.

As Arthur followed the baron out of the parlor, the soft voices of his sister and Maris wove together in a lovely melody he would have liked to listen to far longer. He pushed that from his mind as he walked with Warrick toward the entry hall.

Abruptly the baron stopped and faced him. "Is there somewhere we can talk alone?"

"Yes." The question startled Arthur. He had thought Warrick could speak frankly in Maris's and Carrie's presence. "Third door on your right may provide what you are requesting." He opened the door to his father's smoking room.

As Arthur expected, it was deserted. Motioning for Warrick to enter, he followed him in and closed the door. He twisted the lock on it and on the one opening onto the formal dining room. He did not offer Warrick a seat. He doubted the man could have sat still for even a moment. Stepping to one side, Arthur watched as the baron paced from one end of the smoking room to the other.

As he himself had done in the day nursery two nights ago when he went to seek out the one person he wanted to listen to him. When he had seen Maris sitting there, the lamplight aglow on her golden hair flowing around her shoulders, he had almost changed his mind about staying. He was unsure if he could keep from pulling her into his arms. She was lovely, and her emerald eyes too often mirrored his own, filled with sadness and loneliness. He should have listened to his own good sense, because if Bertie had not interrupted as he did, Arthur would have discovered every inch of Maris's lips. He should be grateful to the child, and he was, but he yearned for the kiss that had been denied them. The memory of the sweet flavor of her cheek lingered on his lips.

Warrick stopped. "Trelawney, I did not want to say this in front of the women, but the child reported missing may not be the only one that has vanished." He glanced toward the parlor. "Those children found in Porthlowen Harbor…"

"Disappeared from somewhere. I have been thinking much the same myself. Since my younger sister married, the search for their families has languished. I have begun to ask questions, though I have not learned much other than I should concentrate those questions on Porthlowen." Without saying where he had obtained the information, he shared what Higbie had told him. "At the meeting tomorrow night, the main topic is not the children. I had wondered how to introduce the subject without looking as if it truly is the real reason for the gathering. I suspect people will be talking about the child missing from your village. Miss Oliver and my brother and I are going to see what we might learn by talking with those who attend."

Warrick's cool smile matched his voice as he said, "Ingenious, Trelawney.

"If I learn anything, I will let you know."

"And if I can help, do not hesitate to call upon me."

"Thank you. I plan to send footmen into the village to tell those who are already sharing the news of the meeting to let everyone know about the missing child." He told himself to be certain one footman's first stop would be the Winwood twins' cottage.

Shaking the baron's hand, he rang for the butler while Warrick took his leave. Arthur was not surprised when Baricoat arrived even before the last clang of the bell had faded. He asked the butler to send footmen into the village as soon as possible with the news.

"I will arrange it," Baricoat said, but did not move.

"Did you wish to speak to me about something, Baricoat?"

"Rumors reach my ears, my lord."

"Such as?" Had someone seen him alone with Maris in the nursery? When he had gone to seek a sympathetic ear, he had not paused to think how he could ruin her reputation.

Arthur realized his worries were misplaced when Baricoat said, "Low places such as The Spider's Web are never without those who will reveal what they know for a price. Especially when they can spread stories about those of a class far higher than their own."

"I was there on business."

Baricoat looked him straight in the eye, something he had not done since Arthur was a mischievous child and needed to be reprimanded for sneaking into the silver room and leaving his fingerprints on every recently polished item. The butler had reprimanded him, but agreed to say nothing to Arthur's parents if he repolished every piece before a grand dinner the following night. It had taken Arthur more than twelve hours to finish the task by working that day and the next. When he was done, he received no more than a nod from the butler.

Now the butler wore the same disappointment, but Arthur was a grown man and capable of making good decisions. Baricoat knew that, too, because deference remained in his voice as he said, "I have no idea what would compel you to go to such a place, my lord, but may I remind you there are many within these walls who would gladly go in your stead?"

"I appreciate that, Baricoat. However, there are some things I must do myself. I will not risk someone else when the obligation is mine."

"Very well, but keep what I said in mind."

Arthur put his hand on the butler's shoulder, momentarily shocked at how bent it was, because Baricoat showed no outward signs of growing old. "Thank you. I will remember what you have told me. In return, I ask that you remember me in your prayers until I finish what I must."

"This family and this household are always foremost when I ask God for blessings," he said with the dignity that was his hallmark. "If you will excuse me…"

As the butler walked away, his steps were a bit slower, but not much, Arthur noted. He respected the butler and the vital role he filled at Cothaire. Like Arthur, Baricoat had assumed duties the earl once had done.

Arthur looked across the room to where his father usually sat. While he could not talk to him about the search for Cranny's killer, he could discuss trying to unravel the mystery around the children's arrival and get his father's insight. It was long past time.

Chapter Ten

"This arrived for you, my lord." Goodwin walked across Arthur's sitting room. He held out a folded page as he had many times before.

Arthur put down the book he was trying to read. The words would not stick in his brain. His thoughts were whirling in too many other directions: the missing child; the six children found in the harbor; Cranny's death and the duties Arthur had assumed in its aftermath; how he must ask Gwendolyn to be his wife. And most often, thoughts of Maris and how much he longed to hold her…just once, even though he knew once would not be enough.

He saw the black wax sealing the page closed. After Gwendolyn took so long between messages last time, he should have guessed the next note would come soon. That often was the case, because information was carried to Cornwall by smugglers. They could sail only when the sea and wind allowed it.

Thanking Goodwin, he added, "That will be all for tonight."

The valet retired to where he slept in a room beyond

Arthur's bedroom and dressing room. Arthur suspected Goodwin stayed awake as long as he did, feeling it was a valet's duty. Telling him to sleep had done no good, so Arthur did not bother.

Carrying the folded sheet to his desk, he broke the wax. He brushed the shards into his hand, opened the window beyond the desk and threw them out into the chill night.

He started to close the window, then saw a light flash higher in the other wing of the house. It must come from the nursery. He had not realized its windows would be visible from his.

Someone moved in front of the light. Even from the distance, he recognized Maris's silhouette. Not with his eyes, but with his heart, which began hammering against his chest as if it could batter its way out and go to her. His mind sought any excuse for him to go up to the nursery. He halted those thoughts. Or he tried to, because his hands ached to sweep up through her lush, golden curls in the moment before he pressed his face to it, breathing in her jasmine scent.

The draperies closed on the nursery window, and the light blinked out like a star consumed by clouds. He leaned forward, and his shoulders sagged. He felt as if he were in a great tug-of-war, his yearning pulling him toward Maris and the promise he had made to his father holding him back.

I know my request shocked you, but it is vital for the future of Cothaire that you marry someone who knows how to handle a household like ours. She must be able to oversee the servants, leaving you free to concern yourself with estate issues.

Father's words resounded through his head day

after day. Even if Arthur broke the vow he had made to him, he was unsure if the earl would give his blessing to Arthur courting Cothaire's nurse. He knew what Cranny would have said. Marry as Father wished and set up Maris as a mistress, and then Cranny would have laughed when Arthur told him that was not the way to live a Christian life. Arthur's attempts to persuade his friend to open himself to the faith Gwendolyn treasured as well had been futile.

But he should not judge Cranny when he had faults of his own. He glanced at the letter on his desk. Hypocrisy. There was no other name for it. He had proudly proclaimed he had contempt for liars and had quoted Proverbs to Maris, but he had told more half-truths than he could count since assuming Cranny's duties. If she knew of his dishonesty, would she turn away from him? He would never know because his secrets had to remain hidden.

Arthur latched the window before lighting the lamp. Sitting, he opened the letter from Gwendolyn. He frowned when he saw there was no page folded inside it, the page he passed along to the next courier. Had it fallen out? Or was the message in the words on the hastily scribbled page?

He had his answer after an hour of struggling to decode the words, not even looking up when he heard doors open and close. His valet knew not to disturb him. Gwendolyn's handwriting had never been illegible before. Blots of ink concealed some letters completely. He hoped his guesses were correct as he filled in the words he could not read. The last two sentences caught his eyes and held them:

Place this message in your primary hiding place in the next three days. If you cannot, alert me immediately.

So there should have been another message inside the folded page, but it was gone. Bending over his desk, he took another piece of paper and coded the words: *No message included. Lost. Resend.* He sealed it by pressing his forefinger into the soft green wax.

He leaned away from the pool of light on his desk. Rain splattered on the window. Sending the message tonight would be foolish. Higbie and his men were not the sole highwaymen who loitered beneath the trees, waiting like spiders for a victim to be snared by their web.

Blowing out the lamp, Arthur crossed the room to the slit of light visible beneath his bedroom door. He opened the door and walked past the grand tester bed with its dark red curtains. A single lamp shone on the small table beside the bed, where a glass of water waited beside his well-thumbed Bible.

Another glowing light shone beneath Goodwin's door. Arthur knocked on it.

Goodwin opened it immediately, and Arthur wondered if the valet listened for his footsteps. The valet was fully dressed, but fatigue weighted his eyes.

"What may I do for you, my lord?" he asked.

Arthur held out the sealed letter. "Would you see that this is taken to Lady Gwendolyn Cranford as soon as the sun rises? Remind the messenger it is to be delivered into her hands only." He had given the same instructions with every note he sent to Gwendolyn.

"I shall." Goodwin took the note. "Will there be anything else?"

"No. Go to bed." He grinned. "Really to bed this

time. Dawn is not too many hours off, even at this time of year."

"Good night," Goodwin said, then shut the door.

Arthur returned to his own bed. He hooked a finger in his cravat and loosened it. Pulling it off, he tossed it and his collar onto a chair in front of the window. His coat followed as he sat on the chest at the foot of his bed. He yanked off his boots and set them beside the chair. Stretching when he stood, he unbuttoned his waistcoat and folded it carefully before laying it atop the other clothing.

He stifled a yawn as he went to the head of his bed to draw back the covers. Goodwin had readied the bed every night until Arthur told him he would prefer to do the task himself. He wanted time alone to read the Bible and say prayers without his valet bustling about the room.

As he reached to toss the covers aside, Arthur saw an unusual lump at the foot of the bed. It moved. Who was there?

He shifted the lamp so its light spread across the covers, which matched the bed curtains. There, curled up on the dressing robe Goodwin had left for his use, was Molly. The little girl, the quieter of the twins, was asleep and sucking her thumb.

How had she gotten into his room without being noticed?

He smiled as he recalled how he had not paid any attention to the sound of doors opening. He had been too focused on decoding Gwendolyn's message. His inattention to anything else had allowed the child to sneak in.

Arthur stood, his smile vanishing. Maris must be looking for Molly, and he doubted she would consider looking in his rooms, because until now, Bertie was the only child to come here. More than an hour had passed since he had first heard a door opening. Maris must be frantic.

Leaning forward, he slipped his arms under Molly and his dressing robe. Lifting both, he tucked the robe around the little girl. The corridors would be chilly and damp. She nestled against him with the trust of a young pup curled up with its littermates, and his heart filled to overflowing.

The corridors were silent. Most of the servants were abed and so was his family. No wonder Molly was able to slip through the house unseen.

He turned the corner toward the stairs to the nursery. A light, like a lost star, was coming down them at a rapid pace.

"Arthur!" Maris ran toward him. "Have you seen—?"

"Shhh," he warned, then looked down at the little girl.

Relief swept over Maris's face. "Where did you find her?"

"At the foot of my bed."

Her eyes widened so far he could see white around the brilliant green. "Without her sister! They usually stay close to each other."

"Is the other one missing?" He was careful not to use Lulu's name.

"No, she is asleep upstairs." Maris walked toward the stairs with him, keeping her steps slow to match his as he tried not to jostle Molly. "How did she slip in without anyone noticing?"

Trying not to laugh, because that might wake the little girl, he told her. He did not mention Gwendolyn's message. Only that he had been writing a letter.

"I am sorry she interrupted you." Maris held out her arms.

A single step would carry him into her embrace, but she was reaching out for Molly rather than him. How he envied the little girl as Maris took her from him and cuddled her close!

She looked at him in surprise when he followed her up the stairs. Asking him to remain in the day nursery, she disappeared up the stairs to the night nursery, where the other children would be asleep, unaware of Molly's adventure.

Arthur sat on the window bench, which was the only seat large enough for him. He listened to Maris's light footsteps overhead and the creaks and groans of the old house settling for the night. Outside, the shapes of the inner curve of the cove were silhouetted against the sea.

Solutions to his puzzles were out there. One of these days, he would find them. He had to believe that. He could not give up his search for the truth about Cranny's death. Now he had taken on the herculean task of finding answers about the children, the ones here and the one missing from Warrick's village. Tomorrow night's meeting might help if he and Maris could uncover a secret that someone had kept hidden.

As if he had spoken her name aloud, Maris walked into the day nursery. She wore her unflattering gray dress, and her glorious hair was in its severe bun. He would rather see her in a soft dressing gown, her feet bare and her hair curling around her.

She must not have guessed his thoughts because she smiled and said, "You didn't need to wait, Arthur."

"I know, but I also know you are curious about the search for Warrick's missing child."

"Very."

He stood and motioned for her to take his place. He could not sit beside her, breathing in the scent of jasmine. He would be able to think of nothing but bringing her into his arms and sampling her lips. He almost laughed. That was all he could think of whether he was in the same room with her or halfway across the moor.

"Neither of the footmen I asked Baricoat to send to the village and the nearby farms discovered any news about the missing child. I did not expect they would sniff out anything, because having another child appear in Porthlowen would set every tongue wagging."

"Unless someone is hiding the child, and no one knows of it."

"You have a macabre imagination."

Maris smiled. "I read widely when I was young, and I honed my imagination then."

"Do you have any ideas where to look?" He wondered why he had not asked her before.

"Has anyone talked to the youngsters in Porthlowen? Adults seldom think twice before talking when children might overhear. They believe toddlers will not understand or be interested, but one thing I have learned is they are interested in *everything*. Even if they don't comprehend what they have heard, they often can repeat it back."

Arthur leaned his shoulder against the wall and smiled at her. "Another brilliant idea, Maris. We should talk with them as well as the adults after the meeting at the church tomorrow night." He did not add that the suggestion might work as well for obtaining information about Cranny's death. Small children would not have been abroad at the hour when duels were held, but older ones might be. If they were not supposed to be out, they would not admit to what they had witnessed unless asked directly.

"I hope it helps."

"It has already, reinvigorating my conviction the truth will eventually be known."

Her voice took on a playful tone as she flicked her fingers toward him. "Then go forth, my lord knight, and seek the wrongdoers and rescue the meek babes who look to you for deliverance from those who have stolen them from their rightful homes." Maris laughed, and the sound twirled in him like the sweetest music he had ever heard.

"Your wish is my command." He picked up her hand and bowed over it. "I, dubbed Arthur the bear, do so pledge to do everything in my power to make your wish come true."

He bent over her hand again, but this time raised it to his lips. As he brushed it with a light kiss, her eyes widened in surprise before softening in an invitation he ached to accept.

He must not, not when he had just finished a desperate note to the woman he was going to marry. Dropping Maris's hand, he wished her a good night's sleep. He was unsure if she replied as he left the nursery. The pounding of his heart urged him to pull her into his arms. It was too loud in his ears to hear anything else. He must not listen to his heart, but he had no idea how to silence it.

Maris watched the door at the back of the church. The meeting was ready to begin. Past ready, for she had seen the parson check his pocket watch more than once.

The church was filled with restless people. The pews were crowded, and more parishioners stood along the walls. A half-dozen children sat on the steps leading up to the altar rail. They were giggling, but stopped when a woman leaned forward to remind them to mind their manners in the church. By Maris's count, almost everyone from the village and the nearby farms had come to the meeting. That spoke of how important the topic of a bell for the church tower was.

But where was Arthur? He was the one who had asked for this assembly, and he had failed to arrive, even though the meeting was supposed to start at least a half hour ago.

A rustle of whispers from the rear of the church alerted her to Arthur's arrival. He strode in, his great-coat flapping behind him. Mud stained his boots and breeches, and it was clear he had ridden hard and fast. She wondered if he had been chasing information on his friend or on the children. He might have been busy with estate business.

He was so handsome, her heart shuddered through a pair of beats before racing. As he took off his hat and his dark hair fell forward into his pale eyes, she thought of how she had filled with joy when he pressed his mouth to her hand. She wanted to comb her quivering fingers through his hair. Instead, she clasped her hands in her lap and looked down at them. She must be careful, or she could find herself in as tenuous a situation as at Bellemore Court. Arthur was not beastly like Lord Litchfield, but entangling her life with his could be as disastrous when in a fortnight he could be announcing his betrothal to Lady Gwendolyn Cranford.

"Lord Trelawney!"

At the imperious voice, Maris looked at where Arthur had paused in the aisle. To his left, Mrs. Thorburn was regarding him with her usual frown. Charity Thorburn was, in Maris's opinion, inaccurately named, for she could find something to complain about in any situation. She had few friends in Porthlowen because of her sour comments.

"Good evening, Mrs. Thorburn." He bowed his head toward her.

The woman's frown deepened, adding lines to her thin face. "Is this meeting truly about the church bell, or is that an excuse to put those six boat urchins in front of everyone again?"

Maris drew in a sharp breath. Did anyone else share Mrs. Thorburn's suspicions?

Arthur kept his smile in place. "As you can see, none of the children from the boat are in attendance tonight."

"They do not have to be here for them to be the topic of the meeting."

"The topic I am here to discuss is a bell for the church."

She made a harrumphing sound as she sat beside Peggy Smith, the young woman who worked at the store in the village. The girl looked dismayed, but wisely said nothing.

Arthur continued along the aisle. When he glanced toward Maris, he looked away swiftly. Was he regretting he had kissed her hand last night?

Another question for which she had no answer.

As soon as Arthur sat beside Elisabeth in the front pew, his brother welcomed everybody and thanked them for coming. He led them in a prayer to keep their hearts and their ears open; he asked for the first comment.

To Maris, it seemed as if the congregation was in

agreement about raising the money for the bell. Someone asked if the bell would be ready to hang before the war was over. Its main purpose beyond announcing services and marriages and funerals would be to alert the village to French pirates. When Parson Trelawney reminded them not all pirates were French, heads nodded.

Maris listened closely to all that was being said. Arthur got up to answer a question. From the way he scanned the crowd, she knew he wanted to demand that the person who knew the truth about the children stand and admit it. She could not imagine a single reason why anyone in Porthlowen would conceal the truth.

Arthur also told the gathered people about the missing child. Maris saw a few shocked faces, and some parents held their own children closer, but the majority of the villagers had already heard the news. He thanked them, but she knew he was disappointed nobody had any information to share.

"Do you have anything else for us, my lord?" asked Mrs. Thorburn in her usual sour tone. "If not, may I suggest this meeting be adjourned? Many of us need to rise early on the morrow."

"One last thing." Arthur stepped aside to allow Raymond to invite the parishioners to join him in a prayer for those in need, especially the little girl whose family longed to have her home with them.

As Maris raised her head when the prayer ended, with a blessing and gratitude to all who had attended, she noticed Mrs. Thorburn was the first out the door.

Maris rose and smiled when she heard Arthur tell his brother he had handled the meeting with the flair of a politician in Whitehall. Seeing how many of the people were leaving, she decided it would be best to talk with them outside. She hurried up the aisle, but stopped before she ran into the Winwood twins.

"This meeting was an inspired idea, Lord Trelawney," Miss Hyacinth said, and Maris realized Arthur was right behind her.

"We are stronger when we come together to discuss a subject," added her sister.

"Actually," Arthur said, "the idea for this meeting was Miss Oliver's."

"Your idea, Miss Oliver?" asked Miss Hyacinth. She exchanged a glance with her twin. "My, my!"

"I told you, sister, there was more to Miss Oliver than what we see at first glance," Miss Ivy hurried to say.

"Having a chance to air our opinions to our parson and to you, my lord, is a true pleasure. And may I say it would appear you have a true treasure in Miss Oliver?"

Miss Ivy refused to be outdone, even when heat seared Maris's face at the effusive compliments. "I daresay you are a diamond of the first water, both inside and out."

"True, sister." Miss Hyacinth gave both her twin and Arthur a brilliant smile. "You, Miss Oliver, have a gentle heart. We have seen how protective you are of those dear children."

"A gentle heart, but a lioness's heart, as well."

"Exactly."

"Exactly."

"Exactly," Miss Hyacinth said again.

Before Miss Ivy could repeat the word, Arthur said, "Thank you, ladies, for coming tonight. Forgive us for hurrying away."

He placed his hand gently on Maris's elbow and steered her toward the door. Behind them, the elderly twins continued the conversation as if she and Arthur had not moved. Maris wondered if Lulu and Molly would become like the Winwood twins as they grew older. Lulu prattled, and Molly spoke far less. However, Molly had dared to leave the night nursery on her own and go to Arthur's room after dark.

People milled about the churchyard in the light of the quarter moon. Most were chatting. Maris wanted to stay beside Arthur and ask him what had kept him from arriving on time, but when he urged her to talk to as many villagers as she could before they left for home, she joined a conversation with the blacksmith and his neighbor's family.

She found it easier than she expected to move from one discussion to the next and introduce the subject of the children, both the one lost and the ones found. The village youngsters and those from the tenant farms were delighted when she asked their opinions. Some were amusing; others were serious. None provided her with any new information.

When Lady Caroline walked toward her, talking with Mr. Hockbridge, Maris said with a smile, "Mr. Hockbridge, everyone in town must be doing well if you had time to sit through the whole meeting."

"With most of the residents of Porthlowen in the church, it was the obvious place for me to be."

Lady Caroline laughed lightly. "Forewarned is forearmed."

"A clever way of putting it, my lady." He bowed his head to her. "Well said."

"I cannot take credit for the words, Mr. Hockbridge. My father uses them often. He said he read them in an old book." As a tall form stepped out of the shadows, she turned. "Father has many adages he likes to use, doesn't he, Arthur?"

"Most often when he is trying to teach us a lesson." His voice was lighthearted, but Maris sensed tension beneath it. Did the others?

She realized Mr. Hockbridge did because the doctor asked, "How does your leg fare, Lord Trelawney? Is it giving you problems?"

"It seems fine except when I do something stupid. Then it does not hesitate to remind me of my foolishness."

"It sounds as if it is healing as it should." The doctor laughed before saying, "Be cautious for another month. After that, those painful reminders should fade away." He tipped his hat toward them. "Good evening, my lord. My lady. Miss Oliver."

Arthur waited until Mr. Hockbridge reached the lych-gate, then asked, "Was he able to tell you anything, Carrie?"

"Nothing. He was disturbed by the news from Lord Warrick and agreed to ask about our misplaced children while making calls." Lady Caroline sighed. "Even though when he is tending the sick and hurt may not be the best time to be asking questions."

"If he can uncover something new," Maris said, "it may be the clue we need to lead us to the truth."

Lady Caroline smiled. "You have spent too much time with Arthur. You sound just like him. Always on the trail of the truth."

Grateful the darkness hid her face, which must be scarlet, Maris listened when Arthur admitted he had learned nothing more than his sister or she had. He added that he needed to let the parson know of their fruitless evening, so he would see his sister when he returned to Cothaire. When Lady Caroline offered Maris a ride in her carriage, Arthur said he would escort her to the house.

"I suspect Maris wants to see Toby," he said.

"At this hour?" his sister asked, startled. "Won't he be asleep?"

"Actually, I intended to speak with Elisabeth about him coming to play with the others later in the week," Maris said.

Lady Caroline glanced from her brother to Maris. "Very well." She went to where her carriage waited and soon drove toward Cothaire.

"Can your conversation with Elisabeth wait, Maris?" Arthur asked.

"Yes." She was curious where he had been, and she could arrange at any time for the children to play together.

"Mine with Raymond can wait, as well." He offered his arm. "Shall we walk while we talk?"

She nodded, knowing he wanted to be far from any eager ears. Putting her hand on his, she was surprised when he led her toward the church. He said nothing as he picked up a lantern someone had left on the steps. They walked through the lych-gate, and he held the lantern so it lit the way ahead. Moonlight spread a white path over the sea to the distant horizon.

He paused by a single tree twisted by the gales it had weathered. Hanging the lantern on a broken branch, he said, "This should be far enough. No one else will be out here now."

Looking at the wooden fence edging an area as big

as the orchard at Cothaire, she asked, "Is that used to keep animals from the cliffs?"

"Only human ones. After a tragedy nearly one hundred years ago, a fence was raised so nobody could tumble over during our fall festival."

"I didn't know there was a fall festival in Porthlowen."

"In about ten days."

She was startled. Why had nobody mentioned it to her? They must know she was unfamiliar with the cove's traditions. Bits of conversations popped out of her memory, and she realized the other servants were discussing the festival, but had called it by another name. "Is it connected to the blessing of the boats?"

"Yes. Like many manors, we have customs that reach back into the Middle Ages, including the blessing of the fishing fleet each year. No one remembers why or how those customs came into being, but everyone enjoys the feasting and games and silliness. It is our biggest celebration each year, in addition to New Year's Eve, when Cothaire holds an open house. Everyone in Porthlowen and beyond comes for the games and races and plays."

"Like on Twelfth Night?"

"Yes."

She smiled. "Both the New Year's Eve party and the festival sound like great fun."

"Most of the festival is."

"Most?" She laughed. "What is not fun at a festival?"

He grimaced. "Certain absurd duties the Earl of Launceston or his representative must undertake."

"And you have that role this year?"

"Yes."

Maris laughed at the annoyance in his voice as she

scanned the area, imagining how excited the children would be to attend a festival. "It cannot be horrible."

"Wait and see. Then you will understand."

"I cannot wait."

He leaned against the tree, and she gazed up through its branches to the stars. She did not want to look at his pose, which brought to mind how he had stood in the nursery last night before he kissed her hand.

Her skin tingled anew. She had not guessed her teasing would lead him to take such an outrageous—and wonderful—action. From memory, she could hear Belinda giggling while sharing every detail of having her hand kissed for the first time. Belinda's words had failed to describe the explosion of sensation from the simple touch.

"Why are you looking in every direction?" Arthur asked. "What do you expect to see in the darkness?"

"The children."

"But they are in the nursery at Cothaire."

"I know, but it seems odd not to be constantly watching that they are not wandering off or getting into mischief. I don't know what to do with myself."

He opened his mouth to reply, then closed it. When he answered, she wondered what he had planned to say originally, but his words pushed other thoughts from her head.

"Maris, you could help me sort out what I learned tonight."

"I would be happy to try."

"Thank you."

She waited for him to add more, but he became so silent she could hear the hushed waves against the sand in the cove. Knowing she might be courting trouble, she took his hand between hers. He glanced at their fingers pressed together, then raised his eyes to meet hers. His gaze burned through the dim light from the lantern as his other hand touched her cheek as lightly as the faint breeze coming off the sea.

"Tell me," she whispered. "A burden shared is a burden you no longer have to carry alone."

"You sound like Father."

"Tell me, Arthur," she said, refusing to let him change the subject.

He did not look away. "I was late to the meeting because I had another. With someone I thought might be able to help me learn the truth of what happened to Cranny. I did not learn anything new other than Cranny, a man I have long considered a good friend, may not be the man I believed him to be." He pushed himself away from the tree, but did not slide his hand out of hers. His fingers tightened around her palm. "The duel he fought the night he died was not his first. It may have been closer to his tenth. In every case, he was challenged because he wronged someone else."

"I am sorry. I know how painful it is when someone you admire has feet of clay. I have learned their faults are not mine." She smiled sadly. "I have enough weaknesses of my own. I don't need to assume theirs, too."

When his arms came up to draw her close to him, she leaned her face against his chest and drew in his wonderful scent, a mixture of wool and linen and his horse and the night air. She should not be in his arms; that place belonged to another woman. Even so, she lingered for one precious minute, then another, listening to his heart's steady beat and his deep breaths as he fought the hurt in him.

He released her, and she stepped back. "I am truly sorry, Arthur."

"I know. I am sorry, too." He took down the lantern and held out his arm as he had before.

Again she put her hand on it. As they walked toward Cothaire, she wondered if when he spoke of being sorry he was referring to his disappointment with his friend's shortcomings. Or if he meant his words to mean he was sorry he had to release her because of his vow to his father.

Chapter Eleven

"They are here!" Bertie rushed into Arthur's room, the door slamming into the wall behind him.

Goodwin popped out of the dressing room. He moved to intercept the little boy before he could reach the desk where Arthur was working on another coded message to Gwendolyn about the missing pages in her last letter. Four days had passed since he had last written to her, and he had received no answer so he was writing again. He would see her next week at the hunt hosted by Miller. That might delay the missing message too long, because he would not be able to leave it for the next courier until he returned to Cothaire.

Arthur waved Goodwin aside and gestured to Bertie. "Who is here?"

The little boy's eyes were as wide as platters. "Cap is here! Susu, too!"

He smiled. His sister had married Captain Drake Nesbitt as soon as the banns could be read, and they had sailed on his ship for their honeymoon. *The Kestrel* must be moored again in Porthlowen Harbor.

Opening a drawer, Arthur swept the pages into it. He

closed the drawer and locked it. Once he had thought doing so was an unnecessary precaution, but that was before Molly slipped into his rooms. If an innocent toddler could do that, someone far less virtuous might, too.

He stood and reached for his coat. Shrugging it on, he said, "Goodwin, I will need my evening clothes laid out for tonight's dinner. Mrs. Ford is certain to be preparing a feast already to welcome the newlyweds home."

"Of course, my lord." Goodwin's smile was almost as broad as Bertie's.

The household staff was especially fond of Susanna, who had been born many years after the other children. She, like the six foundlings, was cherished by the servants.

"Come along, friend of the bear," Arthur said as he held out his hand to Bertie, who was bouncing from one foot to the other.

The little boy grasped his hand, and Arthur swung him up into his arms. Bertie crowed out a laugh. "Go, bear! Go! Go! Go!"

"We are go-go-going." He strode to the door.

By the time they reached the entry hall, the house was in an uproar. Arthur followed the sound of voices into the small parlor filled to overflowing as his family and the staff welcomed the newlyweds back to Cothaire. Drake and Susanna smiled at everyone, but their first hugs were for the children, especially the twins, who had won a special place in his younger sister's heart.

Arthur held on to Bertie and waited patiently while others greeted his sister and her husband. Captain Nesbitt had proved both his courage and his love for Susanna before asking her to become his wife. Arthur at first had worried when his younger sister fell in love with a sailor. Carrie had lost her beloved John to the sea, and Arthur did not want Susanna to suffer the same grief. But as he came to know Drake and saw the love they shared, he had heartily approved of the match.

People shifted, giving him a clear path to reach his sister. Setting Bertie by his feet, Arthur reached over his little head to give her a big hug and a kiss on the cheek.

"Welcome home." He offered his hand to Drake. "Are you going to be able to stay for a while?"

"Long enough to set up housekeeping on the other side of the cove," Susanna said, smiling.

Arthur remembered how their father had built what he called a dower house across the cove. The idea at one time was his parents would retire there when Arthur married. Instead, it would be Susanna's first home as a married woman.

"How are you, Bertie?" his sister asked.

The little boy tapped his chest. "I friend of bear."

"Are you?" Susanna tried to hide her confusion, but looked toward Maris.

Arthur smiled as Maris explained, before she gently moved the children away so he could speak to his sister without interruption.

"So you are the bear, Arthur?" Susanna asked, tilting her head. "I have to say you have had more than your fair share of grouchy days when you growled like a bear."

"Very funny." He tapped her nose as he had when she was younger. When her husband turned to talk to Raymond, he went on, "Marriage seems to agree with you, baby sister."

She kissed his cheek as she gave him another hug.

"You might consider giving it a chance one of these days."

"Not you, too!"

Susanna regarded him with a frown. "What have I missed?"

Arthur told her about their father's request. As he had expected, his younger sister bristled at both the request and the deadline Father had given him to propose to Gwendolyn.

"Not that she would make a poor wife for you, Arthur, but Father should not ask that of you."

"As Carrie has said, daughters have faced such requests since time immemorial."

"Even so," Susanna murmured, deflating as she recognized the truth in their sister's words, "Father should not ask such a thing of you. I want you to be as happy as Drake and I are."

"I am not sure that is possible." He kept his eyes from cutting to where Maris talked to Drake and the twins. He pasted a smile on his face and hoped it did not look as hideous as it felt. "You and Drake have found something rare."

"I disagree. Do you think Raymond is any less happy with Elisabeth than I am with Drake? Do you think Caroline and John loved each other less than Drake and me? What about our parents?"

Arthur held up his hands. "I surrender, Susanna. Our family has been given many blessings. Don't you think it is greedy to ask for another?" His heart contracted at his own question. Was he trying to convince himself or Susanna it was not necessary for him to have a marriage filled with love?

"God has never limited the number or breadth of his blessings. You know that."

"Yes, but I am saying we should be thankful for what we have."

His sister's silver-gray eyes became slits as she frowned. "You are hiding something. Or trying to. What is it?"

"A topic for another day. Let's enjoy your homecoming."

"As you wish, but don't forget, big brother, you have only a few days left to convince yourself that you are worthy of such a blessing." She gave him one more penetrating appraisal before being drawn into another conversation.

Arthur glanced at where Susanna looped her arm around her new husband's. Anyone looking at them could not doubt the depth of their love.

Lord, am I wrong to want that for myself? I know I have given my word, and I will not break that vow, but is it wrong to want real love? A love like I could have with Maris?

He must be patient. God responded to every prayer, but God's answer might not be the one Arthur wanted. He must accept that, though it would be hard for his heart.

Abruptly he felt like an island of melancholy in a sea of joy. Not wanting to dampen everyone's high spirits, he edged toward the door. He stepped into the corridor and released a deep sigh.

"That sounds profound."

Maris stood framed by the doorway. He craved the warmth of her in his arms. He had enjoyed that briefly by the sea cliffs, and his arms had felt desperately empty since.

When he continued to stare at her without speaking, she said, "This should be a happy day."

"It is."

"You don't look happy."

"I have too many not happy matters on my mind."

She glanced over her shoulder, then moved closer. "Have you learned more about your friend?"

"No, but I did not expect to quickly."

"Then why do you look a portrait of gloom? What are you not telling me?"

I fear I am falling in love with you. No, he could not say that. How many times had someone come up to him in recent days and mentioned it would be nice to have a celebration at Cothaire at Christmastime? No one used the word *wedding*, but he knew exactly what the comments meant. How so many people knew of his father's request for a marriage ceremony for his heir by year's end could be explained by the fact most secrets swiftly became un-secrets in Porthlowen.

"This is not the place for this sort of conversation," he said when he realized she would not accept silence as an answer.

"If you need to talk, you know where you can find me." She touched his arm, then went into the room to watch over the children.

Yes, he knew where to find her when the house grew quiet and the children were asleep. She would be in the day nursery, snatching a few minutes to read. He need only go up the stairs. No! He must not seek her out after the family gathered for dinner tonight. He should think only of Gwendolyn!

Yet he knew he would eventually return to the nursery when the house was quiet. It might be his final chance to spend time alone with Maris before he wed.

Maris gave up on the idea of the children taking a nap. They were too wound up to lie down. When she persuaded one to rest, another was up and running around with excitement. She tried to get them to play with their toys, but they were more interested in racing from the door to the windows, hoping for a sight of Lady Susanna and Captain Nesbitt.

She finally lifted them up onto the window bench and pointed at where Captain Nesbitt's ship, *The Kestrel*, rocked in the cove. That set them to chattering as they told her about their visit to it. They seemed to have forgotten she had been with them, and she did not remind them. As they listed what they had seen, she smiled at their childish impressions of the vessel and its crew.

She was unsure how long they would have gone on if the sound of footsteps had not reached the nursery. A man's footsteps, she realized, and her heart did a somersault.

Was it Arthur?

When Venton, one of the footmen, appeared in the doorway, Maris submerged her disappointment. She should have guessed Arthur was busy with his family. It was as it should be.

"Venton, can I help you?" she asked, motioning for him to come in.

He carried a wagon painted in bright greens and yellows. "May I leave this here for Lady Caroline?" He set the small wagon with its extra-long handle on the floor in front of Maris.

She kept the children from swarming over it. "What is that for?"

"It is a baby wagon. So the infant does not have to be carried all the time. I thought as a nurse you would recognize it instantly."

She did not look at him. "I have heard of them, of course. I never have seen one."

"Lord Trelawney had it brought down from the attic because he thought Lady Caroline and you would want to use it for Joy."

"It is wonderful." She gave him a genuine smile. "I know Lady Caroline will be delighted."

He nodded and left without another word.

Maris let the children examine the wagon, but did not let them climb into it. "This is for little Joy. You are big boys and girls, not babies."

"My baby." Gil patted the side and stuck out his narrow chest.

"Yes, for your baby." She kissed the top of his head, amazed at the devotion such a young child could show for another. It spoke well of Gil's warm heart and the man he could become.

The hours passed quickly as the children played. Maris opened a window when the air became heavy in the nursery, but more humidity came rushing in along with the cooler air from outside. Everything began to feel clammy, and the children grew fussy because they were uncomfortable and tired.

She was considering another attempt at naps before tea arrived when suddenly Lulu let out a shriek. Spinning to chastise whoever had upset her, Maris had to leap aside as the twins burst to their feet and ran past her toward the door.

"Susu!" they both shouted.

The girls flung their arms around Lady Susanna. The boys did the same. The lady greeted each of them with warmth, but it was clear by the way her fingers lingered on the twins' heads that she had a special place in her heart for the two little girls.

"I would like to speak with Miss Oliver." When the children continued chattering exuberantly, she frowned.

Maris said, "They know me as Maris, not Miss Oliver."

"Ah," Lady Susanna said, her smile returning. "Children, you need to play now with your toys while I talk with Maris. Once we are done, I will sit with you. I want to hear about everything—absolutely everything—you did while I was gone."

"Up kite!" Lulu shouted, too excited to wait.

"Play now," Maris said, echoing the lady's words. "Or why don't you practice the song we learned about boats? Then you can sing it to her later."

That suggestion diverted the children. As they raced away, mangling the words to the song, Lady Susanna smiled more broadly.

"They seem so happy," she said. "I believe we have you to thank, Miss Oliver. Or should I call you Maris as the children do?"

"It would make it easier for them and for you." Realizing she held an armful of blocks, she put them in their box. "I do not mean to rush you, but they will not stay distracted for long."

"Very well. I shall get right to the point. Drake and I have discussed it, and we would like to bring Lulu and Molly with us to our new house. It will not be a problem, will it?"

"Of course not, my lady," Maris said, even as her heart cramped. She loved the little girls, and the nursery would not be the same with them gone.

From the beginning, she had known the children could depart at any time and with no notice. But she had thought they would leave only when their true families were found. She never imagined the youngsters would be separated before then. Toby had lived with the parson and his wife since the children's rescue, and now the twins were going away. Gil spent most days with Lady Caroline. That would leave Bertie without a playmate.

Maybe Lady Caroline would bring Gil and the baby to the nursery more frequently, or Toby could come and spend more time. Even though the boys squabbled like brothers, Bertie otherwise would be the sole child in the nursery.

If she had not had Belinda to play with when she was young, her days would have been tedious. To be alone, day after lonely day, made time pass slowly. She did not want that for Bertie.

"I know this may be difficult for the children when they have been living together since their arrival at Cothaire," Lady Susanna said, warning Maris she had not hidden her thoughts well.

"It will, but it is good for the twins to be with you and Captain Nesbitt. Each time a ship came into view, they wanted to know if it was his."

"I assure you we will invite the boys to the house often, and when Drake is at sea, I probably will spend most of my time here at Cothaire. In addition, we will be here regularly because Arthur asked if I would handle Cothaire's accounts until he can hire an estate manager. I want to make this transition as easy as possible for the children. I know they are going to be unsettled by another change."

"Children are more resilient than we give them credit for."

The lady put a hand on Maris's arm. "And I suspect it will difficult for you, as well."

Wishing her face did not display her thoughts and reactions, Maris replied, "Of course I shall miss them. They are delightful. However, they will be happiest with you."

"Drake and I are the ones blessed to have them in our lives. That is why we want to have them with us for as long as God allows."

Maris nodded, wishing she could speak as easily of God and His will. *Are You there? Can I reach out to You as I once did?* She longed to feel God in her life again.

"When would you like them to be ready to join you, Lady Susanna?" she asked.

"Now if possible."

Every inch of her rebelled at losing even one of "her" children, but again Maris submerged her feelings. She bent to pick up a toy, positive she could not conceal how her eyes flooded with hot tears.

Looking at the floor, she replied, "It will take me a few minutes to pack their things. If you don't want to wait, my lady, I can have them sent to your house."

"I will wait."

"Yes, my lady." She gave a half curtsy before rushing toward the stairs leading to the night nursery. As she went up, she dashed away the silly tears. The girls would be on the other side of the cove. It was not as if she would never see them again.

Though it felt like that.

The upstairs nursery was quiet, and she heard distant thunder. She glanced out a window. Ugly clouds blotted out the sunshine. Trees whipped, their colorful leaves scattering. At that rate, the branches would be bare by nightfall.

She wrapped her arms around her as she dropped to sit on one of the small beds. Molly's. More tears leaked from Maris's eyes. Two pieces of her heart were being ripped away.

Until that moment, she had never guessed how deeply she longed for a home and a family of her own. Truly of her own, not one borrowed for a time. She had no yearning for a grand house as her parents had. She had seen the dark side of such a life. She wanted a life she could share with a man who loved her and would delight in their children as much as she did. A man who would have time for their children, as her father never had because he was too worried about the next rung on the ladder leading up to the heights of Society where he longed to be.

A man like Arthur.

She pushed herself up from the bed and found a wooden box. Trying not to make a mess of everything in her haste, she put the twins' clothing and favorite toys in the crate. No matter how she focused on making sure she did not forget a single item, she could not escape how want-witted she was being.

Arthur would leave for the justice of the peace's house in a few days. Once he was there, he planned to ask Lady Gwendolyn to be his wife. Did he love the lady? It did not matter, because it was a match both families desired. He was the heir, and that was his duty.

Knowing that and repeating it over and over in her

head did not lessen her sorrow. Maris was unsure when she had begun to fall in love with Arthur. She must keep her feelings a secret. She did not want to burden him more. Nor did she want to hear him say he did not love her.

Maris picked up the box, which was heavier than she had expected. With careful steps, she went down to the day nursery. She paused in the doorway. Lady Susanna was on her knees, watching Bertie place another block on a tall tower. The lady would be an excellent mother, and Maris must put aside her own grief and envy that Lady Susanna had the family and the love she longed for.

She must be strong. If she fell apart, she would frighten the children with her tears. She should be grateful the twins would not witness how her heart shattered when Arthur proposed to another woman.

Keeping her voice to a cheerful chirp, she said, "I believe this is everything." She set the box on the floor and went to ring for a footman.

Venton stepped into the nursery before she could pick up the bell. He must have been waiting in the corridor. With a nod to her, he picked up the box as if it weighed nothing. He told Lady Susanna it would be waiting in the carriage, then left.

Lady Susanna stood and smoothed her lovely gown. "Before we leave, I wanted to discuss your place in my father's household, especially now that the number of children in the nursery is lower."

Maris stiffened. Was she going to be dismissed? Who would watch over Bertie? He and Arthur had grown close, but Arthur had many duties that often took him far from the house. Bertie needed someone with him when nightmares stalked him or he wanted a lap to cuddle on after he scratched his finger.

That and more raced through her head, but she said, "Of course, my lady."

"I want to be sure you never worry about having a position here in Cothaire, Maris. I spoke with my family, and they agree with me wholeheartedly. For as long as you wish to work at Cothaire, we would be grateful to have you in our household. The work may not be in the nursery after Arthur is married, but I will make sure Lady Gwendolyn knows how important it is to us that you have a position here commensurate with your station."

"Thank you, my lady." What else could she say to such a generous offer? She could not admit the idea of remaining at Cothaire after Arthur married was abhorrent.

Lady Susanna's smile never wavered, and Maris knew the lady believed she had done her a great favor. It would have been, save every day brought them closer to the time when Arthur brought his new wife and her children to Cothaire. Lady Gwendolyn would want her own nurse for her children, and Maris would be given work in the kitchen or as an upper maid, the tasks her parents had struggled to keep her from having to take.

"Lulu, Moll," Lady Susanna called. "It is time for us to go."

"Go! Go! Go!" chanted Lulu as she bounced around the nursery.

"Say goodbye to Maris," the lady continued.

That stopped the little girl in midstep. "Bye Maris? No bye Maris."

Before Lulu started crying, which was sure to send

the rest of the children into tears, Maris took her tiny hands. "Lady Susanna and Captain Nesbitt want you to stay at their new house. I have packed your toys and your pretty dresses. Go with Lady Susanna, and we will come to visit you."

"Soon?" Lulu asked, her bottom lip quivering.

"Very soon." Maris was glad when the lady confirmed it.

Lulu was obviously not satisfied with that indefinite answer. "Tonight?"

"Very soon," she repeated before she kissed each twin's cheek. "Be good girls."

"Go with Susu," announced Molly, amazing her because the little girl seldom spoke. Had it been because she missed Lady Susanna?

When the lady held out her hands to the twins, they clasped them. They did not look back as they walked out.

Bertie grasped Maris around the knees and moaned, "No go, Maris."

She was unsure if he meant he did not want the twins to leave or he wanted to remain with her or he feared she would abandon him, as well. Kneeling, she drew both boys into her arms. She put her head against their soft hair as she let them weep the tears she must not cry.

Chapter Twelve

Maris dropped to sit on the window bench and looked around the day nursery. She was tempted to blow out the lamp and seek her bed. The children had been rambunctious all day. The return of Lady Susanna and Captain Nesbitt yesterday, combined with the twins departing, had left her as unsettled as they were. Bertie and Gil had bickered, something they had never done. The more she tried to quiet the boys, the louder they got. She could not take them outside because cold rain had begun with a thunderstorm last night and did not let up until long after dark tonight. It was as if the heavens mourned, too, that their small family was broken apart.

Arthur had not come near the nursery, and she had not spoken with him since the brief conversation in the hallway after the Nesbitts returned. When Irene brought the children's supper, she mentioned how sorry she felt for Lord Trelawney, who had ridden out at first light in the rain. Maris was curious where he had gone and why he had not mentioned anything about going out to her.

Why should he keep you *informed of his whereabouts?* asked her mind's most reasonable voice.

That voice was annoying, but right. She had no claim
on his time, and she should not expect Arthur to come
and entertain the children with his silly stories and
games that seemed to make sense only to the males of
the species. Still, she had been hopeful he would give
her a look-in tonight, because he had not the previous
evening. Irene had informed her that the family had
gathered to dine last night and had spent long hours at
the table, talking and laughing.

Finally, when nothing else worked to calm the boys,
Maris had resorted to having warm water carried up to
the night nursery. She bathed each child, singing softly
as she did. That had soothed them enough so she could
persuade them to go to sleep after their prayers, two
stories and four more songs.

She needed to repair the damage to the day nursery
before she could go to sleep herself. It looked as if a
tempest had passed through. Toys were scattered everywhere. Not a single one remained on any shelf or
in the toy box. Only one book sat on the shelf between
the windows. Anything that could be spilled, smeared
or crushed during supper was spilled, smeared and
crushed. The tabletop was a bizarre pattern of dried
food, half of it glued to the wood with jam.

She leaned her head against the cool glass and sought
any remnants of energy within her. To delay picking up
the toys and cleaning the table would be foolish, because
that would mean she must rise earlier in the morning.
Maybe tomorrow would be sunny, and she could take
them out to the garden and let them run about until
they grew so exhausted they would happily take a nap.

She closed her eyes, telling herself it was for a moment. She let her thoughts drift, and they pulled her to-

ward Arthur. He had not said he wanted answers about Mr. Cranford's death to share with Lady Gwendolyn when he saw her, but Maris guessed that was why he pushed himself relentlessly.

Her thoughts shifted to when she and Arthur were alone, and the barriers of class temporarily fell away. She smiled as she remembered how close they had come to kissing. She treasured the memory, knowing it must never happen again.

"Maris…" His voice was so real she longed to put her arms out and gather him close. "Maris…"

Her eyes opened, and she saw the face from her dreams in front of her. Her gaze traced the lines drawn by wind and worry in Arthur's tanned skin. Dark whiskers shadowed his jaw and accented his lips. His hair was wet and curled across his forehead. When she reached up to push a strand from his eyes, her skin against his sent a delightful shock through her.

This was no dream.

It was real.

With a gasp, Maris sat. She had not realized she had curled up on the window bench as fatigue pressed upon her.

Arthur smiled. "I am sorry if I startled you, but I was afraid you would move in your sleep and tumble off to the floor."

"Th-th-thank you," she stammered, as she came to her feet. "You are back."

Oh, this was going from bad to worse. First she had brazenly touched him as she had longed to do in her dreams. Now she was spouting the obvious.

His smile dropped away. "Yes, and none the wiser."

"You found out nothing?"

"I spent a long day in the cold rain, and I know no more about either Cranny or the children than I did when I got into the saddle this morning."

"I am sorry, Arthur. I am sure you chased every clue as far as you could."

"Your faith in me is invigorating. Thank you, Maris." He glanced around and chuckled tersely. "It would appear you had a busy day."

"The boys were on edge, and they were not satisfied until they had pulled every toy out. I doubt they played with a single one."

"They miss Lulu and Molly."

Maris nodded, her throat suddenly tight.

"You miss them, too," he said.

"Yes, I do. I knew from the beginning my time with them could be cut short at any moment. Knowing and having that moment actually come are two different things."

"If you want me to talk to Susanna about allowing the children to come back—"

"No!" Her face heated as she added in a calmer tone, "King Solomon found it a challenge to solve the problem of a single child and two women who claimed to be its mother."

"And I am not as wise as King Solomon." He sat on the window bench she had vacated and locked his fingers around one knee. "I am sure Susanna would be willing to let the girls come and play with the boys. Maybe once a week."

"We have already spoken of that. After she and Captain Nesbitt are settled in their new house and the twins have had a chance to adjust to another new home, she plans to bring them here regularly. As well, I will take

Bertie and Gil to Lady Susanna's house to see the girls. Mrs. Trelawney will have Toby join the others whenever she can."

"It would appear you have solved a problem that nearly confounded Solomon."

Maris did not have to force her smile. "I am happy for Lulu and Molly. They adore your sister and her husband, who love them in return. How much better it is for the girls to have a doting family! It is just...just..." Her words came out in a rush. "Poor Bertie will be here alone when Gil is with Lady Caroline and the baby."

"You make that sound like a terrible fate."

"It is. I know because I was an only child."

"That must have been lonely."

"My parents arranged for me to spend time with another girl so I had some companionship close to my own age. We became bosom bows. Unfortunately, some friendships cannot endure as we change from children to adults."

"Yet you think of her often."

"Is it obvious?" She sighed. "I wonder how she fares. Has she married? Does she have a family of her own?"

"If you were to write to her..."

"That is not possible," she said before she realized what she was revealing with those four words. "Please don't ask why."

"As you wish, but I am curious if it has to do with the sadness that dims your eyes far too often."

"It does, but do not ask me any more."

"I will respect your request." He shook his head, making that stubborn lock fall into his eyes again. He pushed it away as he said, "Though I have trusted you with my deepest secret."

"I know."

He set himself on his feet. "If you change your mind, Maris, you are welcome to invite your friend to Cothaire."

She was astounded at the generous offer he was making to a servant. "Thank you, but I will not change my mind." *Not as long as I remember how betrayed I felt when Belinda turned away as her father was tossing me out.* "Even if I did, her visit would be inconvenient for everyone." She did not explain her friend was a member of the Polite World, because that would elicit more questions she did not want to answer.

"Shall we change the subject?" Arthur asked, his eyes beginning to twinkle.

"Yes."

He laughed at the relief in her voice. Asking her to wait where she stood, he went into the hallway. He returned almost immediately with a bolt of bright green fabric that looked like the scraps of silk Mrs. Hitchens had given her to make doll's clothing.

Placing the material in her hands, he said, "I did not expect there to be much of this available, but I thought you could put it to good use."

"It is beautiful, Arthur." She balanced the bolt on her left arm while she stroked the fabric with her right hand. "The girls will look charming in it, and they will be delighted to be able to dress like their dolls."

He put his hand on the fabric. Even though she knew it was impossible, heat seemed to spread from his palm through the layers of silk to where her fingers touched it. "I did not bring this for Lulu and Molly."

"The boys will not want to wear—"

"I did not bring it for them, either." His voice remained even, but she sensed strong passions beneath his everyday words.

"Then...?" Her eyes rose to lock with his gaze. "Arthur, I cannot accept such a gift. This fabric is not for a nurse."

"Why not? You considered it appropriate for the children."

"They are your father's wards. Their position in Society is higher than a nurse's."

"But it is the perfect color to match your eyes, and you would look stunning in a gown made from it."

She pushed the fabric against his chest, and his arms came up to take it. "That is neither here nor there. I cannot accept such a gift from you, Arthur. It would give the wrong impression."

"It is not only from me. My sisters asked that I bring you this. They thought you could make yourself a gown for when you bring the children to the New Year's Eve gathering."

She looked from his earnest face to the beautiful fabric. "Lady Caroline and Lady Susanna asked you to bring it to me?"

"Are you suggesting I am not being honest with you?" He put the growl in his voice that had persuaded Bertie that Arthur was a bear.

Laughing, Maris said, "I know better, but I am overwhelmed."

"Does that mean you will take the fabric and use it for yourself?"

She desperately wanted to agree. "No, Arthur."

"What?"

"Arthur, you have to look at the situation from my point of view." Sensing the frustration roiling through him, she clasped her hands in front of her so she would not reach out to take his. She swallowed hard because the next words she must say tasted bitter. "What would Lady Gwendolyn think if she learned you had given me such a gift?"

"I told you it is also from my sisters."

"Even so, Lady Gwendolyn could be hurt and humiliated. I know you don't want that."

Reluctantly, he nodded. "You are right, Maris. You always think of others before yourself, but this once, I wish you would think of yourself. You are important to my family, and we only intended to thank you." A sad smile creased his face. "You don't need to remind me where good intentions can lead one." He looked around the day nursery. "Do you want help cleaning up this mess?"

"No, I am fine, thank you."

"Then I should bid you good night. I will see you tomorrow at church."

"Yes." She hated how they sounded like the most casual of acquaintances. "Good night, Arthur."

He nodded and walked out of the nursery with the beautiful green silk under his arm.

When she was sure he was far enough away that he could not hear her, she whispered, "Thank you for being kind. That is one of the reasons I love you."

In the pew set aside for the Cothaire's upper servants, Maris sat between Bertie and Gil. Letting the two boys sit together was an invitation for them to misbehave. Across the aisle from them, Lulu and Molly, whom Lady Susanna called 'Moll,' were perched on the pew beside the lady and Captain Nesbitt. They were the image of a perfect, happy family.

Would that ever be more than an illusion?

Even though she tried to halt herself from looking at Arthur, Maris's gaze settled on his profile. He was disappointed that she had refused the family's gift. She could gauge his feelings with a skill that astonished her, but she guessed anyone who saw how his fingers tapped his knee would discern his disquiet. He seemed focused on his brother, who was climbing the steps to the pulpit; yet Arthur acted as unsettled in his pew as the little boys beside her.

Too late, she realized it had been a mistake to turn down his generous offer. Talking with Irene this morning while getting the boys ready for church, she had discovered it was not uncommon for the Trelawneys to open their cupboards to the household staff. She was surprised. That never happened at Bellemore Court. Belinda had shown off her newest gowns, but never offered anyone, even Maris, her discarded ones. Maris had been shocked to discover that they were cut up and used for cleaning rags.

When she had asked Belinda about it, her friend repeated what Lord Bellemore had said about not allowing the servants to take on airs above their birth. Maris had never imagined the earl might be talking about her…not until he chose to believe a nobleman's lies rather than the truth. His dismissal of her as beneath his contempt had hurt her as deeply.

But she could not tell Arthur any of this. If she did, her tapestry of lies would fall apart. She had worked hard to hide the truth after she had fled from Bellemore

Court. Very hard, and she was proud of what she had accomplished.

Pride.

It had caused her parents' downfall when they tried to maintain a life beyond their means. Now she was letting pride keep her from being honest with Arthur. She could not bear the thought of him reacting as Belinda's father had. Not when she loved him so much.

Far too much, she realized, because Arthur would be leaving for the hunt two days after the Porthlowen festival. He would ask Lady Gwendolyn to be his bride. By Christmas, if the rumors were true, he intended to bring her to Cothaire as his wife.

"Our lesson today is from Hebrews 13." The parson's voice drew her eyes to the pulpit as he opened his Bible. When he spoke, even though he was not even looking at her, it seemed as if the words were meant specifically for her. *I will never leave thee, nor forsake thee. So that we may boldly say, The Lord is my helper, and I will not fear what man shall do unto me. Remember them which have the rule over you, who have spoken unto you the word of God: whose faith follow, considering the end of their conversation. Jesus Christ the same yesterday, and today, and for ever.*

He continued, but she repeated the verses in her mind. Not fear what any man did to her? The words seemed simple. All she needed to do was turn to God and her fear would be taken from her. She longed to believe that was how it worked, but it had not when Lord Litchfield had put his face close to hers while he kept her from escaping. His breath, tainted with wine, had filled every breath she took as she cried out for help. None had come.

Should she ask for God's help to face what was ahead? Would He hear her? His promise was clear. *I will never leave thee, nor forsake thee. So that we may boldly say, The Lord is my helper, and I will not fear what man shall do unto me.*

But she did fear. Not about having her reputation ruined beyond redemption, as she had when she had fled from Bellemore Court. She feared she could not live in Cothaire along with Arthur and Lady Gwendolyn, but she had no idea where she might go. To another house where they needed a nurse? Lady Caroline would likely give her a good recommendation, but that would mean leaving the children and never seeing them again.

Could Maris live without knowing if they were ever reunited with their families?

She felt utterly and irrevocably lost.

Arthur strolled among the colorful festival booths, each one decorated with braided strands of wheat in unique designs. He had no idea why the braids were hooked to the stalls. It was the way they had always been adorned, and nobody wanted to break the tradition.

The weather was perfect. A breath of breeze wafted over the headland, and the sun shone almost as warmly as on a late summer afternoon. The field was crowded with excited families and flirting couples. Children raced between the booths, their faces covered with sugar and other treats.

He greeted people he passed and assured them that his father would be arriving later. If he had ever had any doubts how respected and loved his father was in Porthlowen, they would have been swept away by the many questions about the earl's health.

Shouts came from the direction of a pole that had been raised overnight and lathered with lard. Arthur walked to where he could watch young men attempting to climb it and win the guinea in the box nailed to the top. He had won the contest when he was sixteen after he convinced a trio of friends in the village to work with him. He had one get down on all fours, and the next one clamber onto his back on his own hands and knees. Once the third one was in place, Arthur was able to climb atop them and pluck the guinea from the box. He wondered what ideas the young men would come up with this year to retrieve the coin.

When he saw a familiar gray bonnet, he walked faster. Maris might wear dreary colors, but she could not hide her beauty. Not from him, and not from several young men loitering near her. Was she unaware of them? She did not look once in their direction as she squatted to hear what Bertie and Gil were saying.

"Are you having fun?" Arthur asked when he stood beside her and the boys.

"Climb, climb, climb!" Bertie repeated over and over, until Maris put her finger to her lips and urged him to be quiet so she could answer Arthur.

How he envied that finger! Close to her sweet lips, which had been near his…in his dreams. He thought of her words about making sure Gwendolyn was not embarrassed even before she came to Cothaire, and he knew Maris was right. He did not love Gwendolyn, but she was his dear friend, and he would do nothing to hurt her.

"We are having a lovely time," Maris said with a smile. "The others will be joining us later, but Lady

Caroline wished for the baby to have a nap before they left Cothaire."

"Climb, climb, climb!" shouted Bertie again.

Gil joined in as one of the lads who worked on a fishing boat made a running start to jump as high as he could on the pole. When he slid to the ground with a thump, the onlookers jeered and yelled for the next youth to try.

"Does anyone ever make it to the top?" Maris asked.

"Eventually, but first the young fools have fun showing off." Arthur chuckled. "After they have slid down a few times, they will work together, as they decide to do every year."

"Why don't they work together right from the beginning?" she asked.

He laughed again. "And miss the chance to be the first in the history of the festival to make it to the top on his own? A lifetime of boasting rights are worth ruined clothes and rattled bones."

They watched a little longer, then began to wander from booth to booth. They had not gone far before someone called Arthur's name.

Warrick rushed up to them, his spectacles bouncing on his nose. "Ah, Trelawney, just the man I was looking for." Without giving Arthur a chance to answer, he continued, "I wanted to let you know the little girl reported missing has been found."

"Where?" Arthur asked as he saw a smile blossom on Maris's face. "How is she?"

"Alive and well. As to where she was found, I cannot ascertain." The baron grimaced. "To say these Cornish miners are closemouthed is an understatement. I have been assured in the most patronizing way that I need not worry about the matter further."

"What are they hiding?" Maris asked.

Lord Warrick arched his brows. "Exactly my thought, Miss Oliver. I had hoped you, Trelawney, with your far vaster knowledge of these people, could offer me some insight."

"In this case," Arthur replied, "I have none. I have asked everywhere about missing children. People act sympathetic, but claim they have no information. Even though they might believe you, as a new arrival to Cornwall, would swallow such a clanker, they should know I would not. No tidbit of gossip gets overlooked here. A missing child—or six—should be a nine days' wonder. That is what bothers me."

"We should be thankful the mystery of one missing child has been solved," Maris said quietly, "even if not to our satisfaction. One little girl is home and safe with her family."

"Trust you to get to the crux of the issue," Arthur said, before looking at Warrick. "Still, the lack of answers is dashingly bothersome."

"Agreed. I..." He stared past Arthur's shoulder.

Arthur turned and saw Carrie strolling toward them. She pulled the baby wagon. In it, Joy was chewing on a toy.

"Such serious faces during the fair." Carrie stopped beside them, drawing the wagon close to her. "I hope there is not more bad news."

"Quite the opposite, my lady," Warrick said as he bowed his head toward her. "I bring good tidings. The missing child has been found safe."

"Wonderful!" Her smile wobbled, and Maris guessed

it took the lady every bit of her strength to steady it. "Has anything been found out about the children from the harbor?"

"I am sorry, my lady, but it seems the two incidents are not related." He glanced at the wagon. "Is that one of the children from the boat?"

He bent closer to Joy. Sun glinted off his lenses, and the baby reached for them, excited. He stood to keep her from pulling them off his face.

"She knows what she wants," Carrie said.

"I see." The baron's gaze swept over them before he said, "I am glad I was able to share the good news before I take my leave."

"You are not staying for the blessing of the boats?"

He shook his head. "Though I would like to, I will have to wait until next year. I actually came to Porthlowen today to talk to your blacksmith about making some replacement parts for a beam engine."

"The one that was not working before?" asked Arthur, hearing the sudden undertone of tension on Warrick's voice.

"No, that one seems to be working. Thank God. However, one of the others has a broken cylinder, and I need to get it repaired so the mine can reopen."

"I don't recall your late uncle having such trouble with beam engines."

"Apparently neither does anyone else, but when I arrived, they were in poor repair, and I have done my best to keep them working since then. A thankless job, I must say, when a week's work can be destroyed in seconds." He tipped his hat to Carrie and then to Maris. "Good day, ladies."

"Thank you for bringing us welcome news," Arthur said.

"Let's hope I don't have to bring you any more bad news." He sighed, then walked away.

"He was grim, wasn't he?" Carrie shook her head. "It seems as if he goes from disaster to disaster. Poor man."

Arthur offered one arm to her and the other to Maris. "Enough of Warrick's gloom. Today is our festival. Shall we enjoy it?"

He was glad when both women laughed, though his happiness tempered when only Carrie took his arm. Maris held the boys' hands and followed the baby wagon as they went in search of the fun the day could offer.

Chapter Thirteen

Maris was having a wonderful time, and the children grew more excited with every booth they passed. Arthur bought Bertie and Gil some cakes, which soon had the boys' faces covered from top to bottom in frosting. Cool cups of cider quenched their thirst as they met the Nesbitts and the twins, who were eager to see some animals perform. Lady Caroline excused herself to take the baby to a shady spot, but the rest of them hurried to keep up with the youngsters.

They found a man was playing wooden pipes while a black-and-white terrier twirled about on its hind legs. When a monkey wearing a jeweled collar like the dog's climbed onto the terrier's back, the children applauded. They cheered when the dog finished its dance, and the monkey climbed onto the man's shoulder. Arthur dropped coins into the hat the monkey held out.

As they turned to go and see what other entertainment they could find, Gil said, "Want a monkey."

"We will see the monkey dance again," Maris said, taking his hand.

He jerked away and stamped his foot. "Want a monkey!"

Astonished because the youngest boy was usually the calmest, least demanding one, Maris knelt in front of him. She folded Gil's tiny fingers between her palms.

"So do I," she said.

"You do?"

"Of course. A monkey is fun, isn't it?"

"Yes! Want a monkey!"

She sighed. "But that is the only monkey here, and if we took it home with us, none of the other children would have a chance to see it dance with the dog. You wouldn't want that, would you?"

On the little boy's face, she read the thoughts rushing through his head, much as the monkey had scurried from person to person while collecting farthings and pennies. It was a risky question because Gil might well answer he did not care about the other children.

"No, but want a monkey." Gil's voice was sad instead of petulant.

"What if we make a stuffed monkey for you?" she asked. "Then you can make him dance. Or maybe we will make two. One for you and one for me."

The little boy grinned. "Yes. Want a monkey for Gil. Want a monkey for Maris. Make now?"

"Let's enjoy the fun here. We'll make monkeys later."

Gil ran to where children were watching a puppet show.

"That was brave of you," Arthur said.

"I had to take the chance so he would stop fussing. I have seen Gil cares much about the other children, especially little Joy. I was sure he would choose correctly."

"And if he did not?"

She laughed. "I figured I would cross that bridge when I came to it, and fortunately, it looks as if I will not have to."

As the time grew closer for the ceremony that had given rise to the festival, people began to gather by the cliff overlooking the harbor. Arthur led the way through the crowd to where his brother was waiting.

"What happens now?" Maris asked, as she tried to wipe stickiness from the boys' faces with a cloth she had dampened in one of the buckets of water scattered around the grounds.

"The fishermen must pay the Earl of Launceston or his representative one pure white oyster shell for the rights to fish from Porthlowen. The shell cannot have any colors in it other than white. It is their quit rent."

"Quit rent?" She looked up at him. "I should know what that means, but I don't."

"A quit rent is something 'paid' in lieu of money or service to one's feudal lord."

"Why a pure white oyster shell?"

"I have no idea." He chuckled, and she drew the sound into her memory so she could recall it later and savor it. "I cannot imagine why any earl would want a heap of whitewashed shells, but someone thought it was an inspired idea. So the payment for each boat is one white oyster shell."

"What do you do with them?"

"Usually they are handed out the next day at dawn to the village children. They vie to see who can throw a shell the farthest. The one who does wins a prize."

"Is that done so the same shells cannot be used again the following year?"

He shrugged. "I never thought about the reason, but

you may be right. The fishermen say the opened shells must provide good feeding for fish, so it makes for a better haul on their next time out to sea. Everything has become connected through the centuries. To omit a single step would make the whole fall apart."

"You like this!" She laughed and pointed a finger at him. "No matter how much you pretend otherwise, you like being part of the tradition."

"Guilty as charged." He winked at her before he moved forward to stand in front of the crews of fishermen who called Porthlowen their home harbor.

Nothing was announced, but nobody spoke while, as solemn as criminals walking to the gallows, the crew of the first boat stepped forward. One fisherman held out a white oyster shell, and Arthur nodded in acknowledgment. The man set it on the ground, then stepped back to allow the next crew to repeat the process. At last, after about ten minutes, the final crew's representative set their white shell atop the others. The man abruptly grinned, and cheers erupted along the strand.

Maris applauded along with everyone else, while the children bounced up and down with excitement. They had no idea of the significance of the tradition, but they could not fail to sense the excitement.

His part done, Arthur picked up the shells so they would not be crushed beneath the crowd's feet. He then moved aside so his brother could offer the blessing that was as much a centerpiece of the festival as the quit rent ceremony. After Parson Trelawney called out for everyone to bow their heads so he might bless the boats pulled up on the sand, he began the prayer.

"Heavenly Father, we ask You to look down this day upon the boats in Porthlowen Harbor and on the men who take them to sea day after day. We ask You to keep these men safe upon Your vast sea and to guide them to the harbor. Let them feel Your comforting presence when the waves are at their worst. We ask this in the name of Your son, Jesus Christ."

A chorus of "Amen" was followed by more cheers as the crews climbed over the fence and raced down the hill. Arthur must have seen Maris's bafflement, because he explained tradition held that whichever boat was the first to reach the sea beyond the cliffs would have the largest and most profitable catch during the next year.

As the crowd surged forward to watch, Maris held tightly to the boys' hands so they did not get separated. She smiled when Arthur swung Bertie up to sit on the fence, then did the same to Gil. Soon the twins were beside them. As she kept her arm around Gil, while Arthur made sure Bertie did not fall, they yelled and hooted for the crews. The noise became deafening, resonating off the hills edging the cove as the boats were pushed out into the water. Shouts announced when the first boat made its way out of the cove, and the crews turned toward shore so they could join the rest of the day's festivities.

Maris wondered if she had ever been happier than she was at this moment with Arthur. The weight of his friend's death seemed gone from his shoulders, and he appeared almost carefree. She was not going to think beyond this minute when she could leave the past in the past and not worry about the future.

"Are you enjoying the day?" he asked as they lifted the boys off the wall.

"Yes." She did not add that was because he was with

her. When he smiled at her with his amazing light blue eyes, she knew he understood what she did not say.

And that seemed the most wondrous part of the whole day.

"Climb?" asked Bertie as Maris tucked him into bed a third time. In the bed beside him, Gil was listening eagerly.

"No one is climbing the pole again." She patted his covers. "Not until next year."

"Long time?"

She smiled. "The time will pass faster if you go to sleep."

The two boys squeezed their eyes shut.

"Good night," she whispered, kissing one, then the other on the forehead.

As she blew out the lamp, leaving the room awash in moonlight, she could not keep from looking at the spot where the twins' beds had stood. The room seemed too empty after the girls' beds were moved to the house on the other side of the cove.

She stepped out of the room and paused by the door, listening for sounds from within. In the central room of the nursery, the baby slept in her mahogany hanging cradle. She checked that Joy was covered with a light blanket, then, hearing nothing from the boys' room, crept down the stairs.

Tonight, the day nursery would be easy to clean. The children had spent most of the day at the festival. It had been fun for all of them, and she guessed the boys would be talking about it nonstop for the next week.

Maris halted in the doorway when she saw Arthur in the day nursery. He wore an expression she had never seen on his face—a haunted hollowness mixed with a desperate yearning. Hurrying in, she asked, "Has something happened? Did you learn something about your friend? Or about the children? Arthur, what is it?"

"Maris, I am sorry."

"Sorry?" Shock pierced her. "What is wrong?"

He shook his head. "No, that is not what I wanted to say. I am not sorry. No, that is not what I mean, either. By all that's blue, why are words failing me *now*?"

Not caring that she was being too forward, she stepped closer to him. She put her hand over his heart. It leaped at her touch, and hers fluttered to echo it as if they were connected.

"Don't worry about words, Arthur," she whispered, gazing up into his hooded eyes.

"You are right. I should not worry about words."

His arm curved around her, and he tugged her to him. She held her breath. Not that she could have released it if she tried. Every bit of her was focused on how his face was lowering toward hers. Knowing she should tell him to stop before they both did something foolish, she let her thoughts fade into a luscious warmth when his lips brushed hers. Gently but urgently, as if she were as fragile as dew upon a rose petal.

His gaze searched her face, but she had no time to think as he captured her mouth again. This time, his kiss was deeper, more tender. His fingers caressing her back invited her to be as bold. She lifted unsteady hands to his broad shoulders. Lightning seared her. When he cradled her against his strong arms, she let the tempest sweep her even closer. The thunder of her pulse careened through her, banishing every sensation but joy.

His lips left hers and sprinkled kisses across her face.

In between each one, he whispered her name as if it were the answer to his most heartfelt prayer. Her hands framed his face, and she guided his mouth to hers. His kiss was everything she had ever wanted, even though she had not known until this perfect moment.

With a groan, he cupped her elbows and drew her arms away from him. Not looking at her, he said, "Maris, I am sorry. I should not have kissed you." His eyes locked with hers as he growled, "No, I am not sorry I kissed you. I wish I could again and again and again for the rest of my life."

"Arthur, don't say that. Please."

"I told you I would never lie to you. It is the truth, sweetheart."

The endearment undid her. She wrapped her arms around herself as tears welled up in her eyes. She blinked them away as someone came into the nursery.

Lady Caroline! What if she had arrived a moment earlier and found Maris in her brother's arms? Suddenly Maris understood why Arthur had pushed her away abruptly. He must have heard his sister approaching. Maris had heard nothing but the exultant beat of her heart.

"Arthur, did you tell her?" the lady asked with a frown.

"No," he replied.

The siblings exchanged a look that told her they were not in agreement about whatever had brought the lady to the nursery at such a late hour. Strain underscored Lady Caroline's voice when she said, "Miss Oliver, I would like to know if you can be ready the day after tomorrow to travel with us to Mr. Miller's house."

"Me?" She pressed her hand to her chest where her

heart suddenly felt as dead as a lump of coal. "You want me to go to the hunt?"

Again Lady Caroline glanced at her brother, and again he said nothing.

The lady stepped forward and smiled. "Arthur does not agree with my plans, but I don't want to be separated from Joy for the length of time we will be calling on the Millers. Neither would I separate Gil from his baby, and if I bring Gil, I cannot in good conscience leave Bertie behind in the nursery."

"Elisabeth could bring Toby to play with the boy." Arthur clipped off each word in a staccato tempo.

"But I cannot ask Elisabeth to watch Bertie, as well."

Maris looked from one to the other. "Why would she need to watch Bertie? I will be able to, as I always do."

"No," Lady Caroline said firmly, "you will not be able to, because I will need you to come with me to take care of Joy and Gil when I am otherwise occupied."

"You really want me to go to the hunt?" she asked, as she had before.

No! No! She wanted to shout those two words over and over until Lady Caroline listened. To go to the hunt where Arthur would be asking another woman to marry him was the cruelest torment she could imagine. Far worse than when Lord Litchfield had tried to force her to submit to him.

"I trust you can have the children and yourself ready to travel first thing in the morning the day after tomorrow," Lady Caroline said.

"Yes." *No! No! No!* Maris glanced toward Arthur, comprehending why he had told her he was sorry.

"Good." She patted her brother's arm. "See? I told you the matter would be resolved easily. Thank you,

Miss Oliver." She walked toward the door. "Coming, Arthur?"

"In a moment. I want to find out how much luggage must be added to the mountain you are bringing. I doubt children travel any lighter than you do."

Lady Caroline laughed. "I suspect you are right."

As the lady's footsteps faded away down the stairs, Maris did not move.

Arthur closed the distance between them. Or he tried to, but she backed away. "Maris, I could not persuade her to change her mind. I am sorry. For that. I am not sorry I kissed you."

"You are going to ask Lady Gwendolyn to marry you at the hunt." Her voice was flat even in her own ears.

"Yes. I promised I would, and I cannot break a promise."

As if from a great distance, she heard herself say, "I would not ask you to."

"I wanted you to know—"

"No more." She backed toward the nursery stairs. "Please do not say anything more, Lord Trelawney."

Shock and dismay warred on his face in the second before she spun away and ran up the steps. She sought the refuge of her own room. Collapsing on her bed, she pressed her face to the covers. She should have heeded her own warnings. Lord Litchfield had hurt with his cruelty, but Lord Trelawney had hurt her with his love. That was far worse.

The two days that followed were the most miserable of Arthur's life. A void from not having Maris and the children as part of his daily routine left him on edge and uncertain. Now he was the one turning around and going a different direction if he saw Maris. No amount of apologies could atone for his toying with her affections. He was a cad, the exact type of man he had despised in London. Even sorrier than those fools, because Maris worked for his family. She must be concerned her position at Cothaire was in jeopardy. He wanted to reassure her, but to do that, he would have to talk to her.

And how could he talk to her when he wanted to tell her how much he loved her? She thought he was dallying with her, that his heart yearned to belong to Gwendolyn. If he told her the truth, his words might reach Gwendolyn and hurt her. Maris would not repeat them, but there was no place where they could be sure nobody was listening to their conversation.

His regret that he had wounded her, along with the knowledge that he was desperately in love with her, sent him to his knees. He laid out his emotions for God and, as before, sought guidance.

Arthur hoped God would send him an answer to his quandary before the hunting party at the justice of the peace's house. He waited while arrangements were finalized for the journey. He waited as he again tried to talk Carrie out of taking the children and Maris, but relented when he brought his sister to tears.

He was still waiting for an answer to his prayers when the carriages and carts, laden with their trunks, pulled up to the front door. More than ever, he wished he had that answer when Maris walked past him without a glance in his direction. To anyone else, it would seem she was absorbed in the task of herding two small boys into the second carriage, but he knew better.

She was avoiding him, too. He had realized that yesterday when, unable to stay away any longer, he had gone to the nursery ostensibly to spend time with the children. Somehow, through the invisible lines of communication the servants used, she had known his intentions before he arrived, and was gone on some errand, leaving a maid to oversee the nursery in her absence.

As she stepped into the carriage, Maris looked serene, but he saw the truth in her eyes. She thought he considered her an easy conquest because she had let him kiss her when he was planning to marry another woman. If only she would give him a chance to tell her how wrong she was.

There was nothing easy about this.

He walked past the servants' carriage to the one where he would ride with his sister. He opened the door to see Carrie had arrived before him and was already seated. The baby was asleep on her lap. The wet nurse must be in the carriage with Maris and the boys.

Gazing up the hill that rose steeply from the cove, he could not keep from thinking of how he had taken Maris and the children to the ancient settlement. That outing on the moor, they had laughed and flown the kite and gotten drenched, which made them laugh more. He had fallen in love with Maris that afternoon, wanting to spend the rest of his days and nights with her beside him.

He sighed. He would never return to the old foundations. Being there would break his heart all over again. If it ever healed. He would have to arrange another place to leave messages for the courier who transported them farther east.

"Are you going to stand there as if you are posing for a statue?" Carrie asked with a smile. When he did not respond, she grew more serious. "Are you having second thoughts, Arthur?"

Second and third and four and fifth thoughts, and all of them about Maris.

He shook his head as he climbed into the carriage and sat facing her. He pulled the door closed, then slapped the side of the carriage to direct the coachee to get them under way. "I gave Father my promise, and I will fulfill that vow."

"You sound like an ancient warrior setting off to his doom. If you think you cannot be a good husband to Gwendolyn, put an end to this before you ruin her life and yours."

"You were the one who said I am facing what generations of daughters have faced."

"But you are not a daughter. You are Father's heir. You can stop this, Arthur."

"It is too late for second thoughts," he said with finality.

For once, his older sister did not persist.

He looked out the window, but the only thing he saw as the procession of carriages and carts drove through the gate was Maris's lovely face in the moment before his lips found hers. A sight he must forget, though he had no idea how.

Chapter Fourteen

Arthur stood in the hallway outside the rooms Gwendolyn had been given for her stay at Miller's house. When the carriages arrived from Cothaire, a message had been waiting from her. She had asked him to call in the hour before the evening meal, which barely gave him enough time to clean off the dirt from the road and dress appropriately for the grand meal Miller was planning for his guests.

He would have preferred to spend his time making sure Maris and the children were settled into the nursery set up for any youngsters accompanying the guests. Perhaps having to turn his attention to Gwendolyn was for the best. Maris had not looked in his direction once as she had helped the wet nurse and the boys out of the carriage. However, he had watched her until she was out of sight in the house. Her posture suggested she was a creature beaten one time too many.

How he wanted to run after her and take her hands and beg her to look at him as he apologized for hurting her. Would he have gone after her if Gwendolyn's message had not been waiting for him the moment he stepped into the house? He liked to think he would have, but he also knew he did not want to do anything more to cause Maris pain.

When a maid walked past and gave him a curious glance, Arthur knew he could not remain in the corridor. He knocked on the door. A muffled voice called for him to come in.

Gwendolyn did not rise from the white tufted settee when Arthur entered the well-appointed sitting room decorated in shades of gold and white. Compared to the last time he had seen her, standing by her husband's grave, her face had a much rosier color. Her gown was no longer black, but a warm purple that flattered her dark hair and brown eyes. The lines he had seen drawn around her mouth were gone.

She smiled as he came toward her.

"Good afternoon, Gwendolyn," he said. "You look well." Hardly a profession of undying love, but she had known him for too long to let him hide his heavy heart behind a facade of gleeful anticipation of her accepting his offer of marriage.

"I am well, Arthur." She held up her cheek for him to kiss it, as she always had when they met. Her smile was warm, but no warmer than when they were younger and they, along with Raymond, had explored every inch of Porthlowen cove and the moor beyond her home. "And you? How do you fare?"

"I am fine." It was not a lie unless he counted his broken heart. He must never speak of that to her, because she had suffered enough hurt when Cranny died. Nor would Arthur ever reveal what he had discovered about her late husband and his apparent habit of dueling, for it made no difference.

On the ride from Cothaire, he had considered delaying this conversation, but postponing the inevitable would gain him nothing. When he received Gwendolyn's message, he had hoped it would say she wanted no part of their fathers' scheme. It seemed odd that, after more than a year, her words were not in the code she had developed. Her note had suggested an urgency he could not feel when he considered marrying her.

Was her father pressuring her more than his had, to make the match? Gwendolyn would be dutiful, as Arthur was, but could he make her happy when he longed to be with Maris?

"Do sit, Arthur." Gwendolyn motioned to a chair facing her.

He was surprised. He had thought she might ask him to sit beside her as a proper suitor should, but he complied with a smile he hoped did not appear as strained as it felt.

"How are the children?" he asked before silence could fall between them.

"A joy." She smiled. "I understand you have a houseful yourself. It is not easy to imagine the bachelor viscount who once was every matchmaking mama's dream with a boatload of children and still unwed."

Was she giving him an opening to present his suit? Even as he asked himself that question, Gwendolyn continued talking about her children and encouraging him to tell her about the ones at Cothaire. He tried to without mentioning Maris's name in every other sentence, but it was impossible. She had become too much a part of the children's lives.

And his.

Gwendolyn's eyes narrowed after he mentioned

Maris for the fifth time, but she made no comment as she told humorous stories about her toddler and baby.

"Caroline tells me one of the boys calls you Bear." Her voice gave no hint to her true thoughts, but he could read them in her eyes. She wondered how close he had become with Maris.

He resisted blurting out he would be true to his wedding vows, because he was an honorable man. Instead, he said, "Yes, Bertie decided I was a bear because I growled when I twisted my ankle."

"I remember when you banged your chin painfully on your knee in a jump from the stable's second floor." She chuckled, banishing any hint of darkness in her words. "You were determined your parents would never discover you had hurt yourself, but you could hardly chew for several days. You grumbled and growled out every word. I am sure it hurt even to talk. Raymond asked me why you had become grouchy."

"Did you tell him?"

"You asked me not to tell anyone, and I did not. I learned from you that staying silent is better than telling a lie." She put her hand to her forehead as if she had a sudden headache. "I have not thought of that in a long time. I should have remembered that lesson once I was a woman. Maybe I did, because I saw how you suffered nobly in silence because you did not want your parents to think less of you for your escapade. Maybe I learned that lesson far too well."

"Gwendolyn, what—?"

"Forgive me, Arthur." She did not let him ask the question. Instead, she affixed a smile on her face, a smile that struggled to escape and let her expression reflect the tension in her brown eyes. "I am babbling because I have something to tell you that I am not sure how you will respond to."

Sympathy filled him. This was as difficult for her as it was for him. He reached out and took her hand. "We have known each other too long for you to be hesitant about anything."

"I am glad you feel that way, because I want you to know I am deeply in love."

He gasped. He had not expected her to broach the topic with such forthrightness. Had she tired of waiting for him to propose? She had given him enough openings, but then closed them as if she did not want him to ask her to be his wife.

His face must have betrayed the astonishment because Gwendolyn asked, "Why don't you stop regarding me like a gaping fool and say something?"

"I am not sure what to say." How could he tell her that he yearned to give his heart to another woman? Taking a deep breath, he said, "I am pleased, because it will make a marriage between us much more pleasant."

"Marriage? Between *us*? Did you think I was talking about being in love with you, silly boy?" She laughed as she used the name she had called him when she wanted to tease him. She pretended to scowl. "You need not look relieved to hear that."

"I am not relieved," he said; then needing to be honest, he added, "Perhaps a bit, but even more I am happy for you."

"And admit it. You are happy for yourself. How could you consider marrying me when it is obvious you are in love with your Miss Oliver?"

"Gwendolyn, I never said—"

She wagged a finger at him as if he were no older

than Bertie. "Don't try to dissemble with me, Arthur. I have known you most of my life, and I have never seen your eyes twinkle and you smile as broadly as you do each time you speak her name. She has turned on the light in you that dimmed in recent years. Have you told her that you are in love with her?"

With Gwendolyn, he had always been honest, so he found it easy to say, "No."

"Because of a silly scheme our fathers concocted?" She shook her head as she reached across the space between them and squeezed his hand. "You silly, silly boy. If I had known, I would have included a message to you in one of our communications, to let you know I had accepted Otis's offer to become his wife."

"Otis?"

"Otis Miller." Her face grew dreamy as she spoke her beloved's name.

Gwendolyn was going to marry their host's son? Arthur had met the young man a few times and would never have considered him a match for her. Otis Miller's quiet ways paled before her vivacity. With such a garrulous father, he probably seldom had a chance to air his vocabulary. However, Miller was an educated man, which would appeal to Gwendolyn. She was well-read, and if she had been a man, her intelligence would have made her a favored student at Oxford or Cambridge.

"Does he know?" Arthur lowered his voice as he leaned closer to her. "About your activities?"

"Yes. I would not be dishonest with him about such an important matter. He was, I must say, shocked. Yet, when he had a chance to consider the situation, his consternation became interest in helping me." She drew in a deep breath and let it out slowly. "I am happy to have his assistance. He collects the information when it comes ashore, and I don't have to worry about being out on lonely coastal roads after dark."

"You should have asked me to take that task."

"I was about to when I realized I needed to be honest with Otis." A soft laugh burst from her lips. "And your household suddenly increased in size."

Arthur chuckled, unable to restrain his happiness for her and for himself. He could not be certain Maris would welcome him courting her, but her kiss had been fervent and eager. That must mean something.

"How long have you been in love with him, Gwendolyn?"

"Six months."

"But the request from your father came a month ago."

Shaking her head, she said ruefully, "Father thinks Otis is too much like his father."

"Eager to get ahead and make a place for himself amongst the Polite World?"

"Yes, but Otis would not care if I were a queen or a scullery maid. He loves *me*, and he loves my children. As important, they adore him. Winnie does not remember her own father, of course, because she was young when he died. Tim is Otis's shadow when he calls, which delights both of them."

"I know." He thought of how Bertie wanted to be with him and copy what he did. To have the little boy become his son, and know Bertie would be in his life for good was a heady thought, so Arthur could guess how much Gwendolyn's son's adoration meant to Miller. "And I am glad you are not going down to the coast on your own to collect the information coming ashore."

"Otis has been wonderful to take over that task, and I

have been trying to teach him how to handle the correspondence with the couriers. He is learning more slowly than you did, but he is trying. In fact, you saw the results of an early attempt he made."

"The note that made no sense? Miller wrote it?"

She rolled her eyes and nodded. "Oh, Arthur, I never meant for that message to leave the house. Imagine my dismay when I realized I had sent you the wrong page. You must have thought I had taken leave of my senses."

"It did cross my mind."

"Arthur," she said, smiling, "I *have* missed talking with you. No one I have ever met is as droll as you are."

"Did he send the most recent note, as well?"

"The one without the message to transfer on to your next courier? No, that was my fault." Her cheeks reddened. "I was distracted by knowing Otis was about to call, and I thought of nothing but finishing my task so I could enjoy our time together. I am sorry, Arthur, to cause you extra work by my lapse."

"There is no need to apologize." Coming to his feet, he bent and kissed her cheek again. "I wish you every happiness." *And I hope I soon can tell you good tidings of my own.*

"Thank you." She took his hand and brought him to sit beside her on settee. "From you, that means everything. You are my first and dearest friend, Arthur. When Papa asked me to accept your proposal, I was distraught."

"I understand. You were distraught because you love Miller."

"Yes, but also because I love you. I love you as my friend, as the brother I never had, as the person I have always been able to trust. I want you to know the love

God created between a man and a woman. I want you, Arthur, to have the love of the woman who makes you glow." She gave him a sly smile. "Like Miss Oliver."

"That may be, but I am not sure the affection is returned." *Or at least not now*, he amended.

"You will never know unless you try."

He chuckled. "I have heard you say those words before. Just before I jumped from the stable's loft, I believe."

"That is likely." Gwendolyn relaxed, and he realized how stiffly she had been sitting. "You are not a man to give up, Arthur. Don't give up on your Miss Oliver."

"You are right. I don't give up."

Her happy expression fell from her face so fast he was startled. "But you must give up what you are doing, Arthur. Please stop."

"Stop what?"

"Searching for the man who caused Mr. Cranford's death."

"*Mr.* Cranford?" He stared at her in shock. Some husbands and wife were formal, even after years of marriage, but Gwendolyn and Cranny had never been.

She grasped his hand. Her fingers trembled against his. "I know how you idolized him. You believed him to be a good and honorable man."

"I did."

Her brows rose in a silent request for him to continue.

"I have learned I may not have known Cranny as well as I once believed."

"Nor did I when I wed him. I thought he was a wonderful man, and he was wonderful. Then. Everything changed after we exchanged our vows. The first time he raised his hand to me was during our honeymoon."

"He struck you?" His stomach rolled in disgust.

"His temper was frightful, Arthur. It could flare at any moment, and anyone could be its focus. A stranger, a servant, the children. Most often, its target was me."

"I had no idea." His mouth tightened so he had to spit out each word. How could he have been blind to the truth? He recalled seeing her with bruises she had tried to hide with lace and heavy powder. The one time he asked her, she had assured him that dealing with an active baby had caused the bruise on her arm.

Why, God, did I accept her lie? Was it because I did not want to believe a man I once respected could be evil? Or was I so intent on doing my duty for Cothaire that I put that ahead of everything and everyone in my life?

He had become focused on his tasks until Maris opened his eyes to the aspects of life he had forgotten. Laughter, music, an easy stroll, sailing a toy boat, flying a kite, the delight in the taste of a cake shared with children. While she introduced the little ones to many new experiences, she had reintroduced him to life.

"If I had known," he said quietly, "I would have insisted he stop, and if he had not, I would have made him wish he had never seen you."

"I know you would have, Arthur, which is why I never wanted you to know. Mr. Cranford would not have accepted criticism even from you. I feared what he might do if the truth became known beyond our household walls."

"But you worked with him as a courier."

"My hopes for Britain's victory over Napoleon had nothing to do with my private little war at home." She wiped her hands together as if dismissing her past. "I

am looking forward, and you must, too. Tell me you
will come to my wedding, Arthur."

"I would not miss it for the world."

"And promise me one thing."

"Ask what you will."

"Introduce me to your Miss Oliver before you return
to Cothaire. I want to give her a hug to thank her for
bringing you back to life."

"Me, too."

When Gwendolyn laughed at his words, he did as
well, though they had come directly from his heart.
The heart he was free to offer Maris, but would she
accept it?

The house was even busier than when Maris had arrived. She had settled the boys in the nursery with the
children of Mr. Miller's other guests. They were hungry,
so she left them with one of the other nurses and went in
search of something to replace the tea they had missed.

She was astonished that a justice of the peace possessed such a grand house. Everything within the walls
was new. There was no sense of tradition and perma-
nence as at Cothaire. Maybe in two hundred years this
house would have gained that aura of time.

Twice, she had to ask a footman for directions to
the kitchen. And she was still lost. She was sure she
was going in the right direction, but entered a room at
the end of the house that did not open into the kitchen.
Stopping another footman, she hoped he was not one
she had spoken to before, because they were all tall,
dark-haired and good-looking, like a set of tin soldiers
taken from the same box.

He pointed her in yet a different direction, and she

began to wonder if, once she found the kitchen, she could return on her own to the nursery with the food for the boys. She needed to hurry.

With her head down, Maris rushed along the corridor. Voices were coming from the opposite direction.

Familiar voices.

She looked up and stared. She had never thought she would see Belinda and her father again. Lord Bellemore was talking with a man Maris did not recognize. He was as handsome as Mr. Miller's footmen, but not as tall, and his brown hair matched his bushy mustache.

Maris sought a way to escape. She slipped into an intersecting corridor, pressing against the shadowed wall. The trio walking past paid her no mind. Or so she thought, until Belinda glanced in her direction. Her friend's eyes widened before Belinda looked away. She replied to something the attractive man by her side had said, acting as if she had not seen anything out of the ordinary. She did not look back as they continued along the corridor and disappeared into a room.

Resting her head against the wall, Maris blinked as she tried to keep tears from sliding down her cheeks. She never had imagined, even when Belinda did not come to her aid after the attack, and stood in silence while Lord Bellemore cast her out of Bellemore Court, that her friend would cut her direct.

She put her fingers to her lips to silence a broken gasp. Would Belinda tell Arthur that Maris was accused of seducing a young lord and then crying foul? She wrapped her arms around herself, but could not hold in the shivers racking her. What if Arthur believed Belinda, as Belinda and her father had Lord Litchfield? Once Arthur knew about Maris's lies, he would have no reason to believe anything she said. Even if she was foolish enough to admit she loved him.

And if he knew the truth of her falsehoods, how could she return to Cothaire? Nobody wanted to have a liar among the household staff. She closed her eyes and saw him in her mind's eye. Shocked, hurt, as betrayed as she had felt at Bellemore Court as he put her out of his life.

"Don't go," she wanted to cry out. *"Won't you listen to me? No one else did. Not even God. I don't want to be alone any longer. Stay with me."*

How addled her dreams were! She had been foolish to think a nurse, one who had written her own recommendation for the position, could win the love of an earl's heir. He treasured the truth and despised liars. Liars like her. Even if he had not yet asked Lady Gwendolyn to marry him, there could be no future for Maris and Arthur.

Lord Trelawney.

She must never think of him in any other way until he assumed his father's title as the Earl of Launceston. Marrying was his most important duty as the heir to the ancient title. He needed to marry a woman of impeccable birth who could give him a son to follow as earl after him. Not a woman who had lied about her past in order to become the nurse at Cothaire.

Somehow, Maris found the kitchen and food for the boys. Somehow, she traced her steps back to the nursery without getting lost. Somehow, she smiled as she gave the food to the boys and then asked another nurse to watch them while Maris did something about her roiling stomach.

Nobody else was in the attic room when she rushed

to where the visiting servants would sleep. She reeled as far as her simple bed beside a dormer window; then sank to her knees beside it. Dropping her head, she let the thin wool blanket absorb her tears and the sound of her sobs.

Lord, I feel alone.

The prayer burst from her heart before she was even aware she was sending it up.

Our lesson today is from Hebrews 13. The parson's voice from Sunday's sermon whispered softly in her mind. *I will never leave thee, nor forsake thee.*

So that we may boldly say, The Lord is my helper, and I will not fear what man shall do unto me.

"I need Your help," she whispered. The four words opened a floodgate long closed in her heart. *Father, You know how sorry I am I have had to lie. Now the lie weighs on my shoulders like a yoke. I cannot carry this burden any longer by myself. I thought it was my way to free myself of the past. I never thought it would threaten my future. Help me, God. Please!*

She pressed her forehead to her clasped hands. With her next breath, a calm settled over her. The heaviness faded from her. She raised her eyes toward the stars glittering between the clouds. From inside her came a knowing that was neither a voice nor a feeling, simply an awareness that she was not alone.

"You have always been there for me," she whispered, too in awe of the truth to speak more loudly. "Even at my darkest hour, You were there with me, leading me away from the pain. Nothing, even the worst my enemies and my friends could do to me, could change that. You have never forsaken me and kept hope alive in my heart. I cannot see Your path for me clearly, but I know

I want to walk it, because that is where You will be. I never want to forsake You."

She bowed her head again, awed by the power of the love that had always been all around her. When more tears fell, they were tears of healing and joy.

Chapter Fifteen

Maris hoped any signs of her tears had washed away when she returned to the nursery. Bertie and Gil clung to her, and she knew they were exhausted. She drew out a book to read them a story, but was interrupted by a call from Lady Caroline.

"I will be right back," she assured the boys.

"Read story?" asked Gil.

"Yes."

"Arthur come." Bertie had suffered as much as she had when Arthur—no, Lord Trelawney was how she must think of him—had stopped visiting them. Guilt tightened her throat. The viscount *had* given them a look-in in the nursery, but either she and the boys had been "helping" Mrs. Ford in the kitchen or the children were napping and she had been elsewhere.

"I am sure he will come to see you one of these days," she said, hoping for Bernie's sake she was right. "I will be back as soon as I can."

Maris hurried to Lady Caroline's rooms. The lady must want her to watch Joy while Mr. Miller's guests went in to dinner. Jubilation at rediscovering her faith made Maris's feet as light as the kite dancing on the wind. She felt as if everything in her life had been set to rights.

Almost everything, she realized when she entered Lady Caroline's sitting room and found the lady was not alone. The viscount stood beside her. Both of them were dressed exquisitely for dinner. The lady wore a bright purple gown with a string of gold beads woven through her black hair. Lord Trelawney—oh, how it stabbed at her to think of him formally—had never looked more handsome than he did in his black coat worn over a white waistcoat and breeches. His shoes shone with Goodwin's polishing. Brother and sister were talking intently, their voices low and sharp. Were they arguing?

Maris wished she had knocked instead of walking through the half-open doorway. She considered clearing her throat or speaking Lady Caroline's name, but interrupting would be rude.

A sharp cry from Joy saved her. The lady glanced toward the baby, noticing Maris as she did.

"Just in time," Lady Caroline said with forced serenity. "Joy needs to be readied for bed, then tucked in."

"I will see to her, my lady." She moved to lift the baby off the bed, where she was surrounded with pillows. "Enjoy your evening." She dipped in a curtsy. "Good evening, my lady. My lord."

As she turned to leave, Arthur said, "Maris, a moment please."

Lady Caroline swallowed a soft gasp as her brother addressed her by her given name. Maris looked hastily away from the questions in the lady's eyes.

Neither woman moved as Lord Trelawney came to stand beside Maris. He raised his fingers, but lowered them before he touched her arm. She looked at him and saw strong emotions clashing in his eyes.

"Arthur, we need to go," Lady Caroline said. "We do not want to delay the beginning of dinner."

He kept looking at Maris as he said, "Tomorrow after we ride to the hunt, I want to take the boys for an outing."

"I will have them ready for you, my lord." Many questions filled Maris's mind. *Did you ask Lady Gwendolyn to marry you? What answer did she give you? When I tell you the truth about my lies, will you dismiss me? How will I go on without ever seeing you and the children again?* She could not speak a single one.

"Will you join us, Maris?"

Again she heard Lady Caroline's quick intake of breath. Aware of Lord Trelawney's sister listening to every word, Maris said, "If my duties allow it, my lord."

"Good." His terse answer told her he felt as constrained as she did with his sister beside them. "I will send for you and the boys when I am ready."

Maris rushed out of the room, holding on to Joy. Even though she dreaded hearing that Lady Gwendolyn had agreed to his proposal and was unsure how he would react when she revealed her deception, she wanted to put the uncertainty and the dishonesty behind her.

She took Joy to the wet nurse staying in a small room not far from the kitchen. When the woman said she would bring the baby to the nursery after her feeding, Maris thanked her and headed toward the nearest set of stairs. She passed a door leading outside and shivered when the night air surged in, cold and damp and warning that winter was not far away.

As she went up the lower flight of stairs, a motion caught her eyes. She smiled when she saw a small shadow moving along the uppermost gallery. Bertie! The little boy had scanty patience, and it had run out. Grabbing the banister, she waved to him as she rushed up the stairs. He waved back.

She was almost to the top of the staircase when a man stepped out of the shadows. He blocked her way.

Lord Litchfield!

Panic swelled in her, but the quiet knowing of God's presence with her urged her not to give in to it. She was not alone, as she had believed she was the last time she encountered him.

"It is you!" he snarled. "I thought I saw you rushing through the house earlier."

"Good evening, Lord Litchfield." She tried to move past him, but he refused to let her go around him. "If you will excuse me, I will not delay you from joining the others for dinner."

He paid her words no attention. "What are you doing here?" His face was distorted with rage and, she realized with shock, fear. "Are you here to destroy my betrothal to Lady Eve?"

"I have no idea who Lady Eve is. If you will step aside, my lord…"

He came down one stair, then another. She had no choice but to back down, because he refused to stop. She would not let him knock her to the bottom.

"Don't even speak her name! To have it sullied by the likes of you…" He spat a curse that made her gasp. "If you think you are going to run to her with your lies and destroy my chance to marry a marquess's daughter, you are sadly mistaken."

"I have no interest in destroying anything or anyone." She met his eyes steadily as she reached the ground floor again. "Unlike you."

He swore again and drew back his hand.

It took every ounce of her strength not to cringe, but she continued to regard him with the cool hauteur she copied from Lady Caroline.

Slowly he lowered his hand. "I don't believe you. You are a proven liar."

He kept backing her down the stairs as she said, "Lord Litchfield, I did not lie. You know that as well as I do." She raised her chin. "But I have no interest in ruining you as you tried to ruin me. I believe vengeance belongs to God."

Seizing her chin, he ordered, "Tell me why you are here."

Maris faltered. If she admitted she had taken a position in the household of the Earl of Launceston, he would go to the Trelawneys to spread his poison. He would say she had wrongly accused him. With Belinda and her father to confirm his lies, who would heed a woman who had been hiding the truth since she fled from Bellemore Court?

When she did not answer, he said, "You need to leave."

"Gladly." She was astonished by her own audacity.

He was, too, because he stared at her long enough so she could turn on her heel and walk away.

She went two paces before he seized her arm. Spinning her to face him, he roared, "Where do you think you are going?"

"I am leaving." She tried to shake his hand off her arm, but he tightened his grip until she winced. "Release me, my lord, so I might do as you requested."

A motion on the stairs drew her gaze past him, and she almost moaned. Bertie! He was coming down. No, she did not want him to see how despicable Lord Litchfield could be. Panic curled around her throat, tightening until she could hardly breathe. Would the baron hurt a child?

"Like I said," Lord Litchfield snapped, and she guessed he had not noticed her looking beyond him, "you need to leave."

"I was trying to."

"Not from this corridor or from this house. You need to leave England."

She stared at him, sure she had misheard him. When a slow, cruel smile tilted his lips, she tried again to yank her arm from his grasp. It was futile. He was stronger than she was. He pulled her through the exterior door and out into the darkness. When she saw a carriage waiting there, she realized he had planned this from the moment he had seen her. She opened her mouth to scream. His hand clamped over her lips, pressing them into her teeth.

She tried to drive her fists into him. A few of her blows landed, because he groaned, then compressed his arm around her until she could not draw in a breath. When she thought she would swoon from a lack of air, he released her with a merciless laugh. She gasped as he snapped his fingers. A man stepped forward to open the door edged with bright crimson, as pretentious as Lord Litchfield himself.

He made another motion, and his servant picked her up roughly. As he swung her around, she saw a short silhouette in the doorway. Bertie had followed them.

"Let me go! I cannot *bear* the sight of you." Raising her voice, she shouted, "I cannot *bear* it! I cannot *BEAR* it!"

"Be quiet, woman!" When his man had tossed her into the carriage, Lord Litchfield followed, then shouted to the coachee to whip up the horses to their top speed.

She pulled herself up onto the seat facing him, but looked out the window. He reached past her and yanked down the leather curtain. He did the same at the other windows.

"Where are we going?" she asked.

"You will know when we arrive there. Be quiet, or I shall make you sorry you opened your mouth."

Maris obeyed, because screaming for help while the carriage careened along deserted roads would be worthless.

Her lone hope was that Bertie had understood her cryptic message. Had he caught how she emphasized *bear*? Would he connect the word with the need to alert Arthur? Had he even understood she was in danger?

She pressed her face into her palms. Her sole chance to escape Lord Litchfield's plans for her depended on a toddler.

Dear Lord, please help Bertie know I need help. Put wings on his feet and guide him to Arthur in that big, unfamiliar house. Open Arthur's ears to Bertie. I know You are with me in my darkest hours, even if my faith wavers. This time, I will take comfort in knowing that, no matter what happens, I am always in Your hands.

As she finished the prayer, her heart called out a single additional word.

Arthur!

Arthur strode out the terrace door and looked to his left, then his right, ignoring the lovely pool of water glittering in the moonlight in the center of the garden in front of him. He saw the light of a cheroot to his right. From the voices and the clink of glasses, he guessed Joel Ellington was not alone.

He continued across the terrace, his focus steadfast. Three men gathered in the shadows were talking about the horses they planned to ride for the hunt in the morning. Their voices faded away as one, then another turned to face Arthur.

"Ellington, we need to talk." He used the arrogant tone he despised in other peers who considered the rest of the world beneath them in every way.

The two men standing on either side of Ellington mumbled something, then took off as if they had to check their horses at once.

Ellington, a tall man with the florid face of someone who drank too much, hissed in a deep breath, before he said, "I see."

"You don't look surprised."

"Actually I am relieved, if you must know the truth, Trelawney." He ran his hand through his thinning, dark hair and glanced up at the moon. "And it would seem you do."

"At last." Arthur fought to keep his voice even. Like Cranny, Ellington was reputed to have a quick temper. If so, it was even more important Arthur restrain his. "I have been searching for the truth for months. Otis Miller revealed his suspicions to me tonight over dinner."

Ellington nodded, then sighed as he dropped the cigar and ground it beneath the heel of his boot. "I know you have been trying to discover what happened the night Cranford died."

"If you knew, why are you here, when I was also invited to the hunt?"

"Ask me something I know the answer to. Maybe I simply am tired of carrying around this burden."

"Is Miller right? Did you kill Louis Cranford?"

"Yes, I believe I did."

Arthur was shocked speechless. He had expected Ellington to try to baffle him with lies. He had been prepared to find their host and swear out a complaint against Cranny's murderer, so the truth could come out during a trial.

Something was not right. Why would Ellington say he *believed* he killed Cranny? Didn't the man know one way or the other? Otis Miller was sure whispers of Ellington's part in Gwendolyn's husband's murder were true.

"Answer one question for me, Ellington. Why would you kill Louis Cranford? You were his friend."

Ellington shook his head as he stepped forward into the light spilling from the ballroom, where the orchestra was beginning to play. His face was contorted with rage that was, Arthur realized, not aimed at him. "I was not Cranford's friend. Maybe once, but not for a long time. He had no friends."

"I was his friend." But Arthur would not have remained Cranny's friend after learning how he had abused Gwendolyn.

Lord, in how many other ways have I walked through life without seeing? Or seeing, but not comprehending what is before my eyes. Not being there for those who need me because I failed to recognize their need. Not holding up those whom I love. How many have I hurt or allowed to be hurt while I went on the path I thought

You chose for me? How can I learn how to tell them how important they are to me?

From the deepest recesses of his heart, he heard *Maris knows how.*

He glanced toward the ballroom. She would not be there. Instead, she would be in the nursery, close to the children who adored her and whom she adored. She never was stinting with her love, showing it freely. When he had drawn her into his arms and kissed her, love was on her lips. Why had he questioned it?

"If you were his friend," Ellington said, "you were his last friend, Trelawney. He liked keeping you in the dark about his true nature. I am not sure why, but I think it amused him." He swallowed roughly. "He joked about how you were as gullible as a child, and he could make you believe anything he wanted. As he had his wife until…" He looked away as he muttered, "No gentleman should act as he did with any woman, most especially his wife."

"I agree, now that I know the truth."

Ellington stood straighter. "I wondered why you did nothing about that, but I assumed you had your reasons."

"Ignorance is the only reason I had." Arthur rubbed his eyes with his thumb and forefinger. "Tell me about the duel you fought with him. The night he died."

"It began when he challenged me."

"You could have walked away."

"I tried, but he threatened to fire a ball into my coachee. I could not allow that to happen. Cummings has served my family long and loyally." Ellington's hands fisted at his sides before he crossed his arms in front of him. "I know what you are thinking. I could have fired in the air and let honor be settled."

"But Cranny would not have returned the favor."

"No."

"Go on."

Ellington did. "We fired at the same time. I was struck in the arm and knocked from my feet. I lost my senses. When I awoke later in my own bed, I was told my shot had found its mark. Apparently Cranford tried to flee, but was found dead among the trees." Tears rose in his eyes. "I am left with the burden of knowing I took another man's life."

"Are you certain it is your burden?"

Ellington's gaze searched his face like a man seeking water in the desert. "What do you mean?"

"You didn't see your shot take him down."

"But it must have. Who else could have slain him?"

Arthur sighed. "You know, as I do, the list of suspects would be very, very long. It could have been someone who took advantage of the situation or someone loyal to you."

"Not Cummings! He had no weapon."

"I am not accusing him. I have no doubts he, as a longtime servant to your family, was focused on your welfare. He must have been so busy tending to you that he would not have noticed anything else."

"And he is half-deaf." Ellington's expression relaxed from lines of fear and self-hatred. "If he had his back to the other side of the field, he would not have heard a pistol fired."

"It looks as if we will never know the truth." Arthur sighed, knowing Gwendolyn was right. He needed to put aside the past he could not change and look toward the future. "Thank you, Ellington, for being honest with me."

"I am glad I could finally tell the truth. I…" He looked past Arthur.

"Excuse me." A woman's voice came from the shadows. "Are you Lord Trelawney?"

He turned to discover a young woman emerging from the darkness. He could not see much of her face. "Yes, I am Arthur Trelawney."

"I am Belinda Bell. Lady Belinda Bell." She dampened her lips, then said, "Maris Oliver is…or I should say, she was my friend until I betrayed her."

"I am sorry. I don't understand." He noted the fine fabric of Lady Belinda's gown and recalled her father was a well-respected member of the peerage. Why would she call Maris her friend?

For the same reason you wish to give Maris your heart. Because she is a wonderful woman with a heart big enough to welcome everyone into it, no matter if they are of the ton *or a waif cast upon the sands of Porthlowen Cove.* Did she have a place for him there? He prayed he had not made such a complete muddle of everything that she had closed her heart to him.

"From a young age, we were friends," Lady Belinda said. "Her family's home was close to my father's estate. Both her mother and father hoped she would meet someone with a higher rank than gentry, so they were delighted with our friendship. My own father was mourning my mother's death, and he was glad for anything and anyone who kept me busy so he could be alone with his grief. When I asked, he even agreed to allow Maris to take lessons with me, both in the schoolroom and in deportment and dancing and other skills a lady needs to know."

"I see." That explained one aspect of Maris that always puzzled him. She curtsied as beautifully as a young miss about to be presented at court before embarking upon her first London Season.

"But then I betrayed her."

"You said that before. Would you please explain?"

Whatever Lady Belinda might have said went unspoken as his name was shouted in a childish voice.

Bertie!

Seeing the little boy poking his head past the open door, Arthur rushed to him. He knelt in front of the child, who stared at him wide-eyed.

"What are you doing here, Bertie?"

"Be a bear!"

Baffled, he asked, "A bear?"

"Arthur is a bear. Be a bear. Bite hard. Run hard. Go fast."

Arthur put his hand on Bertie's shoulder. The little boy shivered as if caught in a north wind. Something had scared him. What?

"I am sorry, Bertie," he said. "I don't understand."

From behind him, Lady Belinda murmured, "They get such odd ideas at that age. Do not let him unsettle you, my lord. I need to explain everything to you, so you can explain to Maris why I did not speak to her earlier."

"Maris!" Bertie exclaimed. He tugged on Arthur's sleeve as if afraid Lady Belinda had his full attention. "Maris!"

Gently Arthur drew the little boy's fingers away. Holding Bertie's elbows, he bowed his head so his eyes were even with the child's. "Maris is not here, Bertie."

"I know. Maris not here."

"Shall we look for her together?"

Lady Belinda cried, "But, my lord, I need to speak to you!"

"I am sorry, my lady, but it must wait." He never took his gaze from Bertie's face as he stood and held out his hand. "Shall we go? Maris may be looking for *you* because you are not in bed."

"No, Maris! Maris gone!"

Arthur froze at the child's panicked words.

"Oh, no!" Lady Belinda swayed on her feet. "My warning is too late. He has found her."

"He?"

"Lord Litchfield!"

"What are you talking about?" Arthur clamped his mouth closed when Lady Belinda swooned, dropping toward the terrace. He caught her before she could strike her head on the stones. Looking from her limp form to the little boy waiting impatiently in the doorway, he promised he would express his apologies to the lady later. For now…

He shoved Lady Belinda into Ellington's arms. "See that she is taken somewhere to lie down while she recovers."

"But, Trelawney—"

He did not wait to hear what else the man had to say. Scooping up the little boy, he pelted him with questions. With every word the boy spoke, Arthur's fear grew, until it crashed over him like storm waves upon the shore.

A man shouting at Maris and dragging her to a door.

A carriage waiting just outside.

Another man flinging her into it.

"Pray for Maris?" Bertie asked, pressing his cheek to Arthur's.

"Yes, Bertie. Pray Maris will be here soon."

And uninjured, he added silently.

Taking time to leave the boy with Carrie, along with a hasty explanation that left her as pale as Lady Belinda, Arthur ran to the stable. He called for a horse, urging the stable boy to move at top speed. While he waited, he talked to the servants there, asking if they had seen Litchfield's carriage and where it had gone.

South across the moor. There was only one road wide enough for a carriage in that direction.

Getting a description of the vehicle, which was distinctive with the red edging on its doors and windows, he swung into the saddle and turned the horse toward the gate. Litchfield had a head start, but a horse was faster than a carriage. If it did not turn off the road, he had a chance to catch it.

God, please help me get there before something more happens to her.

Chapter Sixteen

Pain crashed through Maris's head, and a moan slipped from her lips. Lord Litchfield had smiled as he struck her as they neared a city along the south coast of Cornwall. She had already guessed it was Penzance, so there was no need for him to knock her unconscious.

The floor beneath her shifted, but she did not hear the horses' hooves on the road. So why was the carriage still moving?

"Ye wakin' up, dearie?" asked a scratchy voice that sounded as if the speaker had not had anything to drink in too long.

"Who...?" The single word sent another cacophony of pain along her skull.

"Slowly, dearie. Make haste slowly."

It was good advice, and Maris heeded it. Talking was too much. Could she open her eyes? She tried and failed. She waited while she counted to twenty, then attempted again what should be easy.

Her eyelids rose, but it did not make any difference. The air was ebony, without a hint of light. Was she blind?

Did she ask that question aloud? Because the scratchy voice—a woman's, she realized now—said, "Even if ye had a cat's eyes to look through the dark down here, there be nothin' t'see except us poor souls."

Soft sobs came from the darkness.

"Who…?" She refused to give in to the pain. "Who else is here?"

"All of us who have been sent here t'be sent away."

Maris tried to unscramble the bizarre answer, which made no sense to her. Had Lord Litchfield's blow unsettled her mind?

She had to sit up. The motion beneath her was sending water through her clothes. Where was she? When she put her hand up to find a wall to steady herself, she recognized the horizontal curve of the boards beside her. She had touched similar ones during her tour with the children of Captain Nesbitt's ship.

What was she doing aboard a ship?

Before she could ask, a woman cried out, "My daughter! My daughter! My dearest child!"

"What happened to your child?" Maris asked. As her eyes adjusted to the darkness, she saw at least a dozen women in the hold.

One crawled to where Maris sat and pushed her face close. Her hair was a matted tangle, and her clothes were tattered and smelled like an open sewer.

"They took her from me," the woman cried. "I had her with me, and they took her and sent her back to Lord Warrick's minin' village."

Maris could not hide her astonishment as she asked, "A little girl? Taken from the mining village?"

The distraught woman pressed her filthy apron to

her face. Through the thin fabric, she wailed, "She be all I got left. My poor baby!"

Such a simple explanation for a mystery that had unsettled everyone at Cothaire, as well as Lord Warrick. As soon as she found her way out of this horrid place, Maris would return to Mr. Miller's house and share the truth with Arthur.

"I am sorry," Maris said. "I have children I care for deeply, too."

"I wanted to bring my child with me. How could I leave her behind forever?"

"Forever?" she asked, suddenly fearful of the direction of her own thoughts. A ship. Filthy women. A child left behind forever. That added up to…the nightmare that had haunted her after Lord Bellemore's threats. Being sent far from England to a penal colony on the other side of the world.

"There be no comin' back from bein' transported," the woman with the scratchy voice said. "Ye may be sentenced for seven years, but how will ye pay t'get back here? Once gone, always gone."

A chorus of agreement came from the cramped hold, and a woman who had not spoken before said, "It may be better than what we are leavin' here. I plan t'find me a fine young man who will treat me better than my husband did when he left me t'take the blame for his sellin' stolen stuff for his mates. Fourteen years I am banished from England, but they be fourteen years I don't have t'see his ugly face. I escaped a certain death, and I will take any chance for life." She leaned forward, her foul breath puffing into Maris's face. "How many years did ye get?"

"None!" Panic made her voice squeak. She took a steadying breath. "I am not guilty of a crime."

Laughter rang through the hold. Even the woman who lamented about her lost child laughed.

"Ye are not standin' in front of the justice, dearie. Ye can tell us the truth. No sense pretendin' t'be innocent now."

"But I am telling the truth!" She pushed herself to her feet, taking care not to hit her head on the low rafters. "I was never arrested. I never was brought before the justice of the peace. I was never convicted of a crime, because I never committed one! I should not be here. I need to get off this ship."

Jeers and hisses were aimed at her until a voice at the far end of the hold spoke.

"Heed her," the woman said. "She could be speakin' the truth. Listen t'her. Talks like a fine lady."

"Bah," argued the woman with the scratchy voice. "We got caught and convicted. Life isn't fair, but no sense pleadin' innocent now. And fine ladies do crimes, too."

The other woman said, "Shut yer chops, ye old crone! Ye know ye don't need t'be a criminal t'be sent off on this ship to the end of the earth. Captain Evans be willin' t'transport anyone for a price. Ye are not the first, m'girl, and ye will not be the last."

"But how is that possible?" Maris sank to the floor, ignoring the water that soaked her gown. "How can people just disappear?"

"Others know, but why would they admit they have paid the captain t'take care of their problem of gettin' rid of an unwanted wife, or a daughter who is just another mouth to feed?"

She put her hands over her face. Lord Litchfield had told her he wanted her gone from England so she had no chance to tell his betrothed what type of man he truly was. She had thought he was lying, as he had often, but for once he had told the truth.

"Where are we bound?" she asked in little more than a whisper.

"Van Diemen's Land."

She surrendered to tears. Her nightmare was coming true. Van Diemen's Land was in the distant reaches of the southern Pacific. If she survived the journey—and she knew many did not—she would be condemned to hard labor and horrible conditions that killed many more. That did not seem as horrible as knowing she would never see Arthur again, never be able to tell him of her lies and ask for his forgiveness, as she had asked God's. She would never again sing with the children and lead them in a jubilant dance.

From overhead, she heard running footsteps and shouted orders. The crew was getting ready to cast off. Once they did, she would never be able to return to the ones she loved.

Lord Litchfield had tried to destroy her life once before. This time, it seemed he had succeeded.

Feeling his horse straining beneath him, Arthur rode along the darkened street. He saw St. Michael's Mount in the bay, its great house at the top of the island's steep hill. He looked up every alley he passed and down onto the piers where ships waited to catch the tide.

He had not once seen Litchfield's carriage ahead of him, but he kept going. There were no signs of it turning off the main road on the nearly nine miles across the breadth of Cornwall. Following the curve of the bay, he slowed when he saw an elegant carriage near a pier where a ship was getting ready to sail.

The carriage looked as out of place as a saddle on a sow. As the ship beside it rocked, lights on the deck flashed over it, revealing the red stripes on its doors.

Arthur swung down from his horse and scanned the area. Seeing some men lounging, half-asleep, against some barrels, he walked to them. A quick question, and a few coins from his hands to theirs, and they were ready to answer his queries and follow his orders. He sent one boy running for the harbormaster, and another was directed to watch over his horse.

To the others, burly men he was glad could be bought to be on his side, Arthur said, "Keep that carriage from leaving!"

He did not wait to see how the dock rats managed that. He knew they would, because he had promised them a very generous additional payment if they did as he requested.

Instead, he charged along the pier to where a plank granted access to the ship the men had pointed out to him. As he thought of what they had witnessed, he raced up the plank. Shouts came from behind him, and he saw the coachee stepping out of the box as the dock rats blocked the carriage's departure.

A burly sailor stepped from the shadows as soon as Arthur reached the top of the plank.

Arthur did not give him a chance to speak. Instead, he demanded, "Where is your captain?"

"He is busy."

Again borrowing the self-important tone he despised

in other aristocrats, he said, "Tell him that Lord Trelawney is busy, too. Get him now."

"Y-y-yes, my lord." The man touched his forelock, bowed his head, and scurried away like a young boy caught stealing a pie.

Even more quickly than Arthur expected, a silhouette he surmised was the master of the ship came across the deck, pulling on his salt-stained jacket. He was of average height, but his cool gaze sizing up Arthur warned he was of more than average intelligence. A man to be reckoned with.

Lord, I ask You to put the right words on my lips as I stand here before a man who has no reason to help me. Help me save Maris from whatever is happening here.

"I am Captain Evans, my lord," the man said. "How may I assist you in the short time before we must sail?"

Arthur did his best to hide his distaste with how Evans managed to mix obsequiousness and arrogance in the same sentence. Now was not the time to start a quarrel.

"Do you have passengers on this ship?" He allowed condescension to seep into his voice, suggesting he considered it a poor excuse for a vessel.

"Not exactly paying passengers, but we do have people aboard."

"Send one of your men to find Miss Maris Oliver, whom I believe is among them."

Evans looked everywhere but at him. Arthur doubted he had ever seen a guiltier face, but he waited for the man to speak. "Miss Maris Oliver?" The captain scratched his chin. "I don't recall such a name, my lord, among my passengers."

"Try harder."

"My lord, I must ask you to go ashore. We will be sailing—"

"Are you certain of that?"

Evans's eyes narrowed, but whatever he had been about to snarl at Arthur went unsaid as shouts came from the dock. The captain looked past him. His face paled, but he gamely retorted, "What happens among those on shore has nothing to do with us. We will be sailing—"

"After *he* allows it." Arthur hooked a thumb over his shoulder as the harbormaster strode toward the ship. "I understand he has received word all may not be as stated on your customs forms. The government frowns on improperly filled out forms, especially in a time of war, when it has many expenses."

The captain gulped, and the sailors who had gathered around to listen shifted nervously. "An inspection could take days."

"While you must feed your passengers and lose time on your voyage." Arthur folded his arms in front of him. "Think hard, Captain, before you answer my next question. Do you have Miss Maris Oliver aboard this ship?"

A lock rattled, and Maris looked to the right. A small light seemed as bright as the sun. The glow seemed to explode through the hold as the door opened and a man carrying a lantern entered.

She raised her arm to protect her eyes, but dropped it when she heard a voice call, "Maris! Are you here?"

Jumping to her feet, she cried, "Arthur!" She blinked, desperate to see him through the glare.

Hands stretched out to grasp her by the waist. Instant recognition raced through her. Arthur's hands! She let them bring her to where he stood with two men. Leaning on his strength, she let him guide her out of the hold. He pulled her to him. Not caring that many eyes were on them, she returned his kiss with all the love in her heart. She prayed everything she found difficult to say was conveyed in that kiss.

His fingers framed her face as he raised his head. A soft smile curved his lips.

"You came," she breathed as she drank in the sight of him, windblown and filthy from the ride across Cornwall.

"Bertie got your message and brought it to me."

"God bless that child."

"Yes, God bless him, as Bertie has blessed us tonight."

At his words, Maris turned to look into the hold. She called to the woman who had had her own child abducted. "What is your daughter's name?"

"Fawna," she shouted. "Because she is my little dear."

"I promise I will make sure she is taken care of and never forgets how her mother loves her."

"Thank you, miss." The woman's sobs burst through the shadows again.

The door closed, locking the women inside until the ship was too far out at sea for them to escape. As Arthur hurried Maris up from the bowels of the ship, she heard voices behind other locked doors and realized there were scores of people being transported. She thought about the woman who was grateful for another chance at life, and she prayed the journey to Van Diemen's Land would be easy.

Her steps were unsteady even after they reached the

deck. When she stumbled as her toe caught on a warped board, Arthur lifted her into his arms. She rested her head on his strong shoulder, thrilled to be this near to him. Closing her eyes, she breathed in his scent, masculine and intoxicating.

The sound of vile curses opened Maris's eyes. She stared, speechless, at Lord Litchfield on his belly on the dock, a ragged man's boot against his spine. Other rough-looking men encircled the two.

Arthur set her on her feet and asked if she could stand. She nodded, unable to utter a single word. He walked to a man who wore a shirt half falling out of his breeches, after being routed from bed. In amazement, she listened to Arthur ask the harbormaster to take Lord Litchfield into custody.

"But he is a peer, my lord," argued the man, glancing at Lord Litchfield.

"I will alert the necessary authorities, and they will come to retrieve him so he can be brought before the House of Lords on charges of kidnapping and whatever else is deemed appropriate." When the harbormaster began to protest again, Arthur said, "Miss Oliver has endured a terrible trauma. I could not *bear* it if she has to be in her abductor's company any longer." He flashed her a smile.

Maris's lips twitched in return. She had doubted she would ever smile again, but Arthur's gentle teasing eased the pain of her invisible wounds. The bruises that ached along her skull and ribs would heal more slowly.

When the harbormaster agreed at last, Arthur ordered the men surrounding Lord Litchfield to take him to where he could be locked up. Lord Litchfield cursed as he was jerked to his feet.

Arthur walked over to him, and in a quiet voice chilling in its intensity, said, "Be grateful, Litchfield, that I am a forgiving man. Don't think I was not tempted to have you take Maris's place on that ship. It is better your crimes are made public so you cannot try something diabolical again."

"She lies!" Lord Litchfield screamed. "Don't believe a word she says. She was kicked out of Bellemore's house because of her lies."

"Why should I believe *you*?"

"Because it is the truth. Go ahead, Trelawney. Ask her! Ask her how she was sent away in disgrace."

Maris clasped her hands over her mouth to silence her moan.

Arthur turned to her. "He is lying, isn't he?"

Her tears blurred Arthur's beloved face and the triumph on Lord Litchfield's, but she said, "Not about that, he isn't. Lord Bellemore did send me away. I will not be false about that any longer. Nor will I be silent about Lord Litchfield's attempt to rape me and then blame me for the crime. He persuaded Lord Bellemore to believe his lies, which drove me away from the only home I had. For a while, even I began to believe it was my fault he attacked me."

Arthur stepped slowly toward her as Lord Litchfield was dragged away. "You know you are not at fault, don't you? If someone treated my sisters so coarsely, I would never rest until justice was done. But you were alone, weren't you?"

"I thought I was, but then I heard your brother's lesson. 'I will never leave thee, nor forsake thee. So that we may boldly say, The Lord is my helper, and I will

not fear what man shall do unto me.' I was never alone."
She took a deep breath to go on.

He spoke first. "Before you say anything else, you
should know Lady Belinda came to me tonight to ask
my help in persuading you to accept her apology for the
wrongs she has done you. Her regret seemed sincere."

"She did?" The tears refused to remain in her eyes
any longer. If she returned to Mr. Miller's house, she
would find Belinda and let her know she wanted to
offer the forgiveness she had denied both of them. "I
know you despise liars, Arthur, and I have been one."

"None of us is perfect. Everyone tells a fib now and
then."

"Not a fib. A lie." She glanced toward the ornate carriage, which must have cost Lord Litchfield dear. "I am
not who I claimed to be."

"You are not Maris Oliver?" In the lantern light, surprise raised his brows.

"My name is Maris Oliver, but I am not an experi-
enced nurse. The recommendation I brought to Cothaire
was a fake. I wrote it myself."

"Because you had nowhere else to go?"

"Yes. I have always loved children, and I heard of
the need for a nurse at Cothaire. If you would like me
to leave, my lord, I will."

"Don't leave," he whispered as he brought her into
his arms, his mouth on hers. She gave herself to this
kiss that must be the final one they shared. The thought
severed her heart anew, and she pulled herself out of his
arms. She did not belong there. She averted her eyes.

He tipped her chin up with a single finger. "Maris,
one thing I have learned is you cannot hide your
thoughts, especially when you are upset. Let me put you

at ease on one matter. Gwendolyn is marrying some-one else."

"Someone else? But I thought… The letters you wrote and the promise you made to your father. What of those?"

"I will explain about the letters when there are fewer people present, but trust me when I say they were never love letters. Father will understand, because how could Gwendolyn marry me when she loves someone else?"

"I don't know." She tried to look away.

He turned her face to him. "If you don't know that answer, maybe you will know this one. How can I marry her when I love someone else? Someone my father will approve of because, even though she is not of the *ton*, she has every quality and skill to be a future earl's wife. More important, my dearest Maris, I hope you love me as I love you."

Sure her mouth was gaping like a fish washed upon the sand, she whispered, "You love me? You really do?"

Chuckling, he said, "Maybe I should answer that question as you asked it. Saying 'I do' would be good practice. For both you and me."

She smiled as she realized what he was saying with his teasing.

"Gwendolyn and I," he went on, serious again, "know we would be doing our families and each other a great disservice if we wed. We share the affinity of childhood companions. Nothing more. She has asked me to attend her wedding. I would like her to attend ours, if you are comfortable with that."

"Of course." Happiness that eclipsed any she had ever known welled up in her as she put her arms around him. "I love you, too, Arthur. With every inch of my being."

The kiss he gave her was an invitation to even more joy. Leaning his forehead against hers, he asked, "Will you marry me, Maris?"

"Yes!"

He swung her around as he shouted in delight. Her head spun as he set her on her feet. Offering his hand, he laced his fingers with hers and said, "It is time to return to Miller's house and share the glorious tidings. I know one little boy who will be especially happy with the news."

"Let's go," she said and followed him off the dock and toward the life they would have together.

Epilogue

"What are you doing here?" Maris heard Arthur's question from behind her.

Before she turned from the bed, Maris pulled up the covers Bertie had kicked off. She put her finger to her lips and gave Arthur a feigned frown. When he put his hands up in a pose of surrender, she had to bite her lip to keep from laughing as she went with him down the stairs to the empty day nursery.

When they stepped into the light from the lone lamp, she watched him shrug off his soaked greatcoat. He tossed it on the window bench.

"Did the delivery go well?" she asked. Since Arthur had told her about his secret life as a government courier and how the letters from the new Mrs. Otis Miller were instructions, Maris had tried not to worry about the danger he faced each time he took a message to where the next courier could retrieve it.

"Excellent." He yawned. "But why are you up here?"

"Irene needs my help. She is learning quickly, but seems overwhelmed by the boys at times."

"She is on her own after tomorrow."

With a laugh, Maris gave a playful shove on his chest. "It is nearly midnight. The groom should not see his bride on their wedding day before they meet at the altar."

He gave her the boyish grin that always reminded her of Bertie's before he got into trouble. She wanted to sink into Arthur's arms and praise God for the blessings He had brought both of them.

Her uncertainty about how Arthur's family would feel about him marrying the woman who had served as Cothaire's nurse had faded as one Trelawney after another welcomed her into the family. The earl was especially effusive, and when she saw his twinkling eyes, she wondered if he had known before she had that his son was falling in love with her. Or it might be, as Arthur told her, that his father was thrilled with a wedding before Christmas and the chance of his heir's heir bouncing on his knee by next Christmas. Either way, the earl and the rest of his family were making her transition from nurse to the heir's wife easy.

"Give me a kiss then, sweetheart," Arthur said, "and I will be gone like Cinderella before the clock strikes twelve."

With a laugh, she slipped into his arms. The place, at last, where she truly belonged.

* * * * *

Dear Reader,

Thanks for coming back to spend some time in Cornwall. The village of Porthlowen is a hybrid of St. Ives, a charming resort village with sandy beaches (remember the nursery rhyme about the man with seven wives?), and Boscastle with its astounding cliffs that protect the village from the sea. I couldn't resist letting the characters pay a call to Penzance on its southern bay with views of the medieval monastery St. Michael's Mount, which later became a country estate. Creating a story in such a splendid setting with a delightful history was fun. I hope you had just as much fun reading about the adventures shared by Arthur and Maris and the children. And I hope you will look for *Her Longed-For Family*, the next book in the Matchmaking Babies miniseries, which will be out in December. The answers to why six babies were put in a boat and who put them there will be answered.

As always, feel free to contact me by stopping in at www.joannbrownbooks.com.

Wishing you many blessings,

Jo Ann Brown

COMING NEXT MONTH FROM
Love Inspired® Historical

Available November 3, 2015

A BABY FOR CHRISTMAS
Christmas in Eden Valley • by Linda Ford

For widow Louise Porter, a temporary marriage to Nate Hawkins seems the only solution to protect her unborn child. But it could also give her a second chance at happiness—if she's willing to risk her wounded heart once more.

THE RANCHER'S CHRISTMAS PROPOSAL
Prairie Courtships • by Sherri Shackelford

Wanting a mother for his twins, Shane McCoy proposes a marriage of convenience to Tessa Spencer. However, will Shane realize that this wedding could be the start of a love for a lifetime?

THE BACHELOR'S HOMECOMING
Smoky Mountain Matches • by Karen Kirst

Jane O'Malley offered her heart to Tom Leighton, but he only had eyes for her sister. Now back in town after several years' absence and the guardian of his niece, Tom is beginning to see Jane in a whole new light.

THE MISTLETOE KISS
Boardinghouse Betrothals • by Janet Lee Barton

When fiercely independent Millicent Faircloud is assigned to photograph the skyscraper Matthew Sterling is building, can they set their differences aside to find joy—and love—this holiday season?

LOOK FOR THESE AND OTHER LOVE INSPIRED BOOKS WHEREVER BOOKS ARE SOLD, INCLUDING MOST BOOKSTORES, SUPERMARKETS, DISCOUNT STORES AND DRUGSTORES.

REQUEST YOUR FREE BOOKS!

2 FREE INSPIRATIONAL NOVELS
PLUS 2 *FREE* MYSTERY GIFTS

Love Inspired HISTORICAL

YES! Please send me 2 FREE Love Inspired® Historical novels and my 2 FREE mystery gifts (gifts are worth about $10). After receiving them, if I don't wish to receive any more books, I can return the shipping statement marked "cancel." If I don't cancel, I will receive 4 brand-new novels every month and be billed just $4.99 per book in the U.S. or $5.49 per book in Canada. That's a saving of at least 17% off the cover price. It's quite a bargain! Shipping and handling is just 50¢ per book in the U.S. and 75¢ per book in Canada.* I understand that accepting the 2 free books and gifts places me under no obligation to buy anything. I can always return a shipment and cancel at any time. Even if I never buy another book, the two free books and gifts are mine to keep forever.

102/302 IDN GH6Z

Name	(PLEASE PRINT)	
Address		Apt. #
City	State/Prov.	Zip/Postal Code

Signature (if under 18, a parent or guardian must sign)

Mail to the **Reader Service:**
IN U.S.A.: P.O. Box 1867, Buffalo, NY 14240-1867
IN CANADA: P.O. Box 609, Fort Erie, Ontario L2A 5X3

Want to try two free books from another series?
Call 1-800-873-8635 or visit www.ReaderService.com.

* Terms and prices subject to change without notice. Prices do not include applicable taxes. Sales tax applicable in N.Y. Canadian residents will be charged applicable taxes. Offer not valid in Quebec. This offer is limited to one order per household. Not valid for current subscribers to Love Inspired Historical books. All orders subject to credit approval. Credit or debit balances in a customer's account(s) may be offset by any other outstanding balance owed by or to the customer. Please allow 4 to 6 weeks for delivery. Offer available while quantities last.

Your Privacy—The Reader Service is committed to protecting your privacy. Our Privacy Policy is available online at www.ReaderService.com or upon request from the Reader Service.

We make a portion of our mailing list available to reputable third parties that offer products we believe may interest you. If you prefer that we not exchange your name with third parties, or if you wish to clarify or modify your communication preferences, please visit us at www.ReaderService.com/consumerschoice or write to us at Reader Service Preference Service, P.O. Box 9062, Buffalo, NY 14240-9062. Include your complete name and address.

LIHI5

SPECIAL EXCERPT FROM

Love Inspired HISTORICAL

A marriage of convenience to rancher Shane McCoy is the only solution to Tessa Spencer's predicament. He needs a mother for his twins, and she needs a fresh start.

Can two pint-size matchmakers help them open their guarded hearts in time for Christmas?

Read on for a sneak preview of
THE RANCHER'S CHRISTMAS PROPOSAL
by **Sherri Shackelford**,
available in November 2015 from Love Inspired Historical!

"We could make a list." Tessa's voice quivered. "Of all the reasons for and against the marriage."

She had the look of a wide-eyed doe, softly innocent, ready to flee at the least disturbance. She'd been strong and brave since the moment he'd met her, and he'd never considered how much energy that courage cost her. For a woman on her own, harassment from men like Dead Eye Dan Fulton must be all too familiar. He felt her desperation as though her plea had taken on a physical presence. If he refused, if he turned her away, where would she turn to next?

A fierce need to shelter her from harm welled up inside him, and he stalled for time. "It's not a bad idea. Unexpected, sure. But not crazy."

These past days without the children had been a nightmare. Being together again was right and good, the way things were supposed to be. He hadn't felt this at peace since he'd held Alyce and Owen in his arms that first time nearly two years ago.

"We don't need a list." Her hesitant uncertainty spurred him into action. "After thinking things through, getting married is the best solution."

"Are you certain?" Tessa asked softly, a heartbreaking note of doubt in her voice.

"I'd ask you the same. It's a hard life. Be sure you know the bargain you're making. I don't want you making a mistake you can't take back."

"You're not a mistake, Mr. McCoy."

"Shane," he said, his throat working. "Call me Shane."

The last time he'd plunged into a marriage, he'd been confident that friendship would turn into love. Never again. He'd go about things differently this time. With this marriage, he'd keep his distance, treat the relationship as a partnership in the business. He'd give her space instead of stifling her.

She was more than he deserved. Her affection for the children had obviously instigated her precipitous suggestion. Though he lauded her compassion, someday Owen and Alyce would be grown and gone, and there'd be only the two of them. What then? Would they have enough in common after the years to survive the loss of what had brought them together in the first place?

"You're certain?" he asked.

Her chin came up a notch. "There's one thing you should know about me. Once I make up my mind, I don't change it. I'll feel the same in a day, a week, a month and a year. There's no reason to wait."

Don't miss
THE RANCHER'S CHRISTMAS PROPOSAL
by Sherri Shackelford,
available November 2015 wherever
Love Inspired® Historical books and ebooks are sold.

SPECIAL EXCERPT FROM

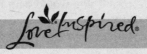

When an Amish bachelor suddenly must care for a baby,
will his beautiful next-door neighbor rush to his aid?

Read on for a sneak preview of
THE AMISH MIDWIFE,
the final book in the brand-new trilogy
LANCASTER COURTSHIPS

"I know I can't raise a baby. I can't! You know what to do.
You take her! You raise her." Joseph thrust Leah toward
Anne. The baby started crying.

"Don't say that. She is your niece, your blood. You
will find the strength you need to care for her."

"She needs more than my strength. She needs a
mother's love. I can't give her that."

Joseph had no idea what a precious gift he was trying
to give away. He didn't understand the grief he would feel
when his panic subsided. She had to make him see that.

Anne stared into his eyes. "I can help you, Joseph,
but I can't raise Leah for you. Your sister Fannie has
wounded you deeply, but she must have enormous faith
in you. Think about it. She could have given her child
away. She didn't. She wanted Leah to be raised by you,
in our Amish ways. Don't you see that?"

He rubbed a hand over his face. "I don't know what
to think."

"You haven't had much sleep in the past four days.
If you truly feel you can't raise Leah, you must go to
Bishop Andy. He will know what to do."

LIEXP1015

"He will tell me it is my duty to raise her. Did you mean it when you said you would help me?" His voice held a desperate edge.

"Of course. Before you make any rash decisions, let's see if we can get this fussy child to eat something. Nothing wears on the nerves faster than a crying *bubbel* that can't be consoled."

She took the baby from him.

He raked his hands through his thick blond hair again. "I must milk my goats and get them fed."

"That's fine, Joseph. Go and do what you must. Leah can stay with me until you're done."

"*Danki*, Anne Stoltzfus. You have proven you are a good neighbor. Something I have not been to you." He went out the door with hunched shoulders, as if he carried the weight of the world upon them.

Anne looked down at little Leah with a smile. "He'd better come back for you. I know where he lives."

Don't miss
THE AMISH MIDWIFE
by USA TODAY *bestselling author Patricia Davids.*
Available November 2015 wherever
Love Inspired® books and ebooks are sold.